"I was hoping you'd be up for a little game of nine-ball."

Nikki took a sip from her beer and raised her brow in question. Nine-ball was the hustler's game. It was short and quick, and without all the rules of straight pool.

He nodded his head toward the tables in the back. "I heard you played."

"Then you heard wrong." She took another sip, eying him the whole time. "I've given it up for Lent."

The corner of his mouth hinted at a smile. "Found God, have you?"

"Among other things."

Jett glanced to the tables, then back to her. "One game. No money."

Nikki shook her head. "I don't play for fun. No thrill in it."

He swallowed, and she could see his jaw work. "Then we'll play for a favor. A debt. You up for a little more red in your ledger?"

She didn't want to ask, not really, but gambling was too deep in her blood not to hear the stakes. "What's the favor?"

He smiled. Not the golden boy smile she'd come to know, but instead one that lacked any charm at all. "Well, Texas, that's the thrill part. You don't know until the end. Anything goes. No boundaries."

Also by KC Klein

Texas Wide Open

HUSTLIN' TEXAS

KC Klein

Kella,

Happy Reading.

Thanks for stopping by

KC Klein

KENSINGTON
KENSINGTON PUBLISHING CORP.
www.kensingtonbooks.com

First Electronic Edition: December 2013
eISBN-13: 978-1-60183-149-1
eISBN-10: 1-60183-149-8

First Print Edition: December 2013
ISBN-13: 978-1-60183-150-7
ISBN-10: 1-60183-150-1

Printed in the United States of America

This book is dedicated to my Charli Bear, who never shied away from telling me when I was spending too much time on the computer.

No book comes together by itself and this book was no different. I need to thank my wonderful editor, Alicia Condon, whose great sense of story has saved me much heartache and time. To Nancy Yost and Sarah Younger who took me on and have already started treating me like family. I have to thank my crit partner Erin Kellison, and my BFF and plot partner, Pamela Denton (I can't wait for you to write a book of your own). To my trainer, Julie Ripley, for helping me keep my backside smaller than my desk chair. To my lovely and supportive LaLas—thanks for cheering me on and listening to me when everyone else has had enough. Last but not least, to my family. Without their love and support, I would be lost.

Chapter 1

Nikki loosened her grip on the steering wheel and lifted her sunglasses to wipe the sweat from under her eyes. It was hot. And not just middle-of-the-summer-sticky-hot, but driving-across-the-largest-state-in-the-union, with-no-AC, middle-of-a-heat-wave hot.

At least her car stereo worked. Well, it had before the station faded out and the twangy sounds of Alan Jackson crackled in. She hated country music—too predictable. It reminded her of that bad joke: what does a country song sound like played backward? A man singing "I got my dog back, got my house back, got my wife back."

Nikki pressed the scan button, and then in disgust turned the whole thing off. Before she'd made the trip, she'd had the option to either tune-up her 130,000-mile Toyota or get a new stereo. She'd chosen the latter. At the time, driving over a thousand miles across the grand state of Texas, with nothing but the bugs on her windshield and the crazy thoughts in her head, were enough for her to put down the cold, hard cash for a radio. Now, as she obsessively watched the gas gauge drop and the temperature gauge rise, she started to question her decision.

Not as if questioning herself was anything new. Her father used to tell her he'd never seen a person get stuck between a rock and a two-headed snake quicker than Nikki. Life had a way of beating her down. Life had a special way of treating a Logan.

She'd graduated from college; at least she had that going for her. That still didn't make what she had to do any less distasteful. She was going back to her hometown, Grove Oaks. The one place she'd never really belonged. The place she'd run away from, in the middle of the night, without saying goodbye. Nikki had done better in the bigger city, where no one had known her past, her family, or her reputation. Anonymity had been a good thing.

She'd burned a lot of bridges when she'd left Grove Oaks. Set them afire and then turned her back. In retrospect, not her best decision.

A Logan never owes.

Or at least that was what her brother Cole had always said. Worked his fingers to the bone on the ranch he'd inherited when their parents died, to make sure that was true. But Nikki wasn't like Cole. She'd never been that noble. Hence, Nikki owed. And this debt she couldn't dismiss, couldn't walk away from. There was red in her ledger, and it was time to go into the black.

So back she went to the town with narrow streets and even narrower minds, with nothing more than a red hatchback full of dirty clothes and a freshly printed diploma certifying she was competent enough to be someone's accountant.

Nikki checked the passing mile marker and guessed at how much farther her tank of gas would get her. With less than twelve dollars in her wallet and enough change rolling around in her cup holder to buy a drive-thru taco, she had cut this trip close.

Twenty miles to next exit.

Yeah, maybe a bit too close. The next miles were only populated by jackrabbits and cactus. Her only contact with civilization was the mobile phone lying on the seat next to her. Of course, said phone was dead, courtesy of the phone company wanting over three months back payment before restoring service. But 911 was still free, right?

Nikki smoothed her now wet hair off her forehead, and plucked at her white tank top. The toothpick-like gauge on her dashboard rose a bit and hovered just below the red zone. Nikki sighed, then threw the heater on full blast to prevent the car from overheating. Sweat dripped down the hollow space between her breasts like an abandoned Popsicle in the sun. Nikki blew hot breath down her shirt as her car continued to eat up the double white lines that stretched across the pavement. It seemed as if she'd been chasing those parallel lines and snaking blacktop for so long, only to come back to the place she'd started—home.

Home was the wide-open spaces of south Texas. The same open spaces she'd felt closing in on her when she'd left.

Nikki watched the car ornament hanging from her rearview mirror spray colorful prisms of light across her dashboard as if on some high-speed chase.

When will you be done chasing rainbows, Nikki darling?

Her mother had always had a way with words.

I'm done, Momma. No more rainbows for me.

Yep, she was done, especially since the only rainbows left in her life were the ones that came from a dull, dusty crystal swinging from her rearview mirror.

Chapter 2

Jett opened the door to the diner and breathed in deep at the rush of AC, the coolness a sweet reprieve from the thick humidity that sucked at the lungs and drained a person's desire to even roll out of bed in the morning. Of course, some people wouldn't consider one o'clock in the afternoon to still be morning. But it was hard to dredge up desire to see the eastern sunrise when he'd only made it home at half past two the previous night.

He took off his hat and hooked his sunglasses to his already dampened shirt. His eyes adjusted to the dimmer light inside and made out the regulars who considered Hal's Eats their place for breakfast or lunch, depending on who was asking. Not that Hal even owned the place—hadn't since he'd been a kid—but that was the way it was in Grove Oaks—nothing changed.

"Hey, Jett," called an older man, whose dark-rimmed glasses stood out in contrast to the steel wool of his hair. He waved Jett over to his table. "Did you see that game last night?"

Jett threw up his hand to stop the conversation. "Nope, Jim, and don't you dare tell me. Didn't get to see the game, but I have the sports section right here." He patted the folded paper under his arm. "I'm going to read it over coffee and my omelet."

"Okay," Jim chuckled. "I won't ruin it for you."

With a smile and a handshake, Jett turned and made his way toward his booth in the back, stopping along the way to greet some of the other patrons, his brother-in-law, the school board president, and a long time neighbor. Jett hung his hat on the rack. Out of habit, he ran his hand across the polished table. Not that Greg, the current owner, didn't run a shipshape place, but Jett liked the reassurance. One could never be too careful.

"Hi-ya, sweet cakes," said Ginger in a sugar-laced Texas drawl.

Jett sat and threw his best smile of the day to the tightly teased, slightly blue haired waitress, whose smile pushed her skin into thin rows of wrinkles. "Ah, Ginger."

She sighed heavily. "You keep saying my name like that and I'm gonna start thinking you're serious about wanting me to throw over old Ted and run away with you." The creases in the corner of her eyes did nothing to detract from their sparkle as she threw him a saucy wink.

"Name the time and the day, Ginger, and I'm there." He threw her wink right back at her.

"You just like me because I make the best coffee."

"Fresh?" He nodded toward the coffee pot in her hands.

"For you always, sweet cakes," she said as she juggled his rolled silverware, cup and coffee pot with the ease only years of waitressing could bring.

Jett had grown up in Grove Oaks, never had any desire to live anywhere else. There was a reason he made his home away from the glitz and noise of the big city. He might schmooze with the movers and shakers of the political scene, all part of being a senator's son, but that didn't mean he had to sleep in the same town as they did. A man needed a place where he could enjoy the small things in life— a cool star-lit evening, a long slow kiss, a good cup of coffee the way it was supposed to be—no fufu cream and sugar— just black.

Ginger poured him a cup, and he took a sip. "Perfect as always."

She exhaled a loud humph, but smiled anyway. "Greg saw you come in and has your breakfast already started." She nodded toward the folded newspaper. "What a game, huh?"

"Ginger, hush that pretty mouth of yours. Don't be ruining it for me, now."

"Have it your way." Ginger arched her penciled-in eyebrow and sashayed away with that fast walk of hers, filling up two customers along the way.

Jett smoothed out the paper and scanned the headlines for last night's Rangers game.

"Just the man I was looking for," said a deep voice from over his head.

Was it really so hard for him to read his paper in peace? But Jett was careful to school his features before he looked up. Public opinion mattered, and as his dad always said, treat every year like it was election year.

"Mayor." Jett lifted his cup in greeting as the bigger man squeezed into the booth opposite him, causing the table to shift to accommodate a belly grown large on bacon, and Jett was sure, significant amounts of barley hops.

"I wasn't sure you'd be around this weekend. I've heard you've been flying to Vegas on your father's business."

The trips to Vegas hadn't been for his father, they'd been personal. But there comes a time when you have to cut your losses. Jett shook his head. "I'm not returning to Vegas anytime soon."

"Good. Good," the mayor said. "I've been hearing some real fine things about what you and your family are doing for this town. Stepping in and saving the Boys and Girls Club after the budget cuts was real good of you." The bigger man wiped at his flushed face, pushing his comb-over back in place.

Jett nodded and smiled. Jett's mother had wanted the donation to go to the town's Rotary Club, but Jett had a soft spot for lost kids. Besides, there was no way this conversation was about the Boys and Girls Club, but images had to be maintained and pleasantries kept up. Such was politics. "I'm glad you approved, Mayor. My family is all about doing the best for Grove Oaks."

"Good. Good. Glad to hear that." He bobbed his head in a brisk manner, causing the loose flesh around his face to jiggle. "Because I wanted to ask for a favor."

Don't they all. Jett caught Ginger's eye as she walked over with his breakfast. He raised a finger, indicating to hold off a moment. To her credit, the older waitress didn't bat an eye, but turned and placed his plate under the orange heat lamps.

Jett took a sip of coffee to hide his sigh. "I'm in no position to grant favors, Carl. That's what my father was elected to do."

His family might have been in politics for years, but for Jett the family left a sour taste in his mouth—too many late night deals and rich-man-handshakes for Jett to have kept his belief in the system. Politics were messy, and he liked to keep his life simple.

"I need access to the big charity event this weekend."

"Barking up the wrong tree, Mayor. I don't run those events. I just show up with a tux and a smile." There were only a few requirements to keeping his father, and Jett's trust fund, happy. The charming of senators and, more importantly their wives, at parties wasn't too high a price to pay for a life of luxury and leisure.

"But you usually show up with a pretty girl on your arm. Beth's been asking about you."

"Beth?" But Jett knew whom Carl was referring to. The mayor's daughter was a man-eater on two legs. She was smart, gorgeous, flawless, and blonde, with designer handbags that always matched her shoes. She would make the perfect socialite wife. The only thing was that she made Jett nervous. He had it on good authority she'd eat her young to step up to the next rung on the society latter.

Jett smiled, but only with his lips. "I'm sure Beth could get her own date to the event. Isn't she with, what's his name, that oilman?"

Jett knew exactly who Beth was dating—Senator Roberts, who was three times Beth's age and married, but if her father could forget that little detail, then Jett guessed he could also.

Carl smiled. And that was the thing about Carl. When he smiled, a person saw their brother, their best friend, the neighbor across the street. Carl had the "I'm a regular Joe" so down that Jett sometimes forgot he was talking to a politician.

Something he should never forget.

Jett had learned that to survive without the devil making claims on his soul, he had to live by a simple set of rules: Only date one woman at a time and leave the married ones alone, never mix whiskey and tequila, fishing on Sunday morning was the closest any man could get to God, and never, ever, make an enemy out of a person who'd one day make a very good ally.

It wouldn't be such a bad thing to have the mayor owe him a favor; one never knew when a mayor's kind word or sudden look in another direction would come in handy.

But hell if he'd walk into this agreement blindly. The big man wanted more than a date for his daughter, and Jett didn't give away favors that easy. "There's an unsaid *but* at the end of that sentence, Carl. Just not sure when you're gonna get around to saying it."

Carl nodded. It wasn't his fault he looked like a bull; he was just built that way. Jett knew he had a neck somewhere beneath the folds of his chin and width of his shoulders. He just wasn't sure anyone had ever seen it. "Old Harry has been bugging me for years to retire. I need to fill the sheriff's position and was hoping an Avery could help me out."

"Not sure my dad would give up a seat in the senate to become a sheriff."

Carl smiled. "I was thinking more along the lines of his son."

Jett suddenly lost interest in the conversation, his mind flashing on eggs growing cold and wheat toast going soggy. "I've no interest in running for office. Especially one that makes a man work so hard."

But there must've been something in the way Jett delivered his "no" that had Carl doubting him. "All I'm asking is that you take Beth to the event. Listen to what she has to say. I have a knack for backing the winning horse, and I have a good feeling about you. Didn't I say your daddy would win?"

Not waiting for an answer, the mayor slid himself off the bench as Jett lifted his coffee.

"This is gonna work out, you'll see. Beth makes a mean banana-nut bread. I'll tell her to drop some off at your place." Carl hitched the wide belt buckle back up around his waist.

Jett sighed, not as optimistic as Carl. But Beth, thank goodness, had the look of her mother, making Carl's strong-arming a bit easier to take.

With a pat on the back, Carl swaggered down the aisle and out of the diner.

Ginger hurried over with Jett's breakfast. "Sorry, sweet cakes, I would've gotten Greg to make you another, but we got caught in the lunch rush."

"Not a problem." Cold eggs he could handle. Carl he could handle. And he sure as hell could handle Beth. There was a rule to dating women like her—hands off. No sense getting saddled with a paternity suit and court-mandated DNA testing. He'd heard of women rummaging through the hotel trash for used condoms the morning after. At one time he never would've been so cynical, but not anymore. Everyone wanted something.

No, he'd just take her out, keep things non-committal, and eat her banana-nut bread. He'd heard it was good, just never had the pleasure.

He bit into his once perfect egg-white omelet, now a bit dried out. The front door chimed, and from years of assessing people across both party lines, he looked up.

His fork stilled mid-path to mouth.

Unfortunately, it took him a full moment to close his jaw, swallow, and reverse his fork back to the plate. No one noticed. Everyone else was staring at the door to the diner. Or more accurately, at the person who'd breezed through like she owned the place.

Nikki Logan. Or at least a devil who sure looked a lot like Nikki. Jet-black hair streaked with copper highlights, with bangs long enough for her to blow out of her face—which she did, making him remember another completely inappropriate gesture. White tank top damp across her skin, a shadow of a black bra beneath, jean cut-offs riding low around her waist, and strong tan legs that looked ready to run a mile or squeeze a man to death.

Of course, she had a reputation for both.

Nikki dropped a duffel bag by her feet and whipped some incredibly big Hollywood-like glasses off her face. He watched her scan the star-struck crowd. All over the diner, cups were stilled, forks with fluffy eggs were suspended mid-mouth, and not a single click of a plate or clatter of a cash register broke the lull.

White trash, immoral, loose, and sexy as hell—Jett had heard them all in regard to Nikki. And he was sure she was seeing those accusations all over again in the stares of the town's people. But to Nikki's credit, she unabashedly smiled and nodded to every pair of eyes as she looked around the room.

"My car broke down." She tossed her head in a perfected starlet move that he'd bet his father's elected position she'd practiced. "I was hoping for some help."

The silence continued. Jett considered himself a southern gentleman to the core, but even he didn't immediately jump to her rescue as he would've for any other female. And he should've. She was his best friend's sister; he owed Cole at least that much.

But things were never clear-cut when it came to Nikki, and there was a part of him that believed revenge was best served cold. Even if it had taken him over two years to see the fruition. His life was clean. His life was neat. And even if he agreed with the term "car-stopper" in regard to Nikki, he had no room in his life for a walking train wreck.

Yeah, maybe it wasn't such a bad thing that Nikki squirmed a bit, because he'd had first-hand experience with her and could add another adjective to the long list after her name.

Nikki, a bona fide, certifiable . . . heartbreaker.

Chapter 3

Jett knew exactly when Nikki caught sight of him because two things happened. A warm open smile eased her features, transforming her face into the young girl he'd known years back. And his gut tightened as if he'd just been given an invitation—a thought he spit out of his mind like he would gum that had lost its taste.

Nikki strutted down the aisle as if she was walking down a red carpet lined with paparazzi. Dang, she looked like a wet dream. Not his wet dream of course—he appreciated his women a bit more put together and a lot more grown up—but he was sure she'd be gracing someone's fantasies tonight.

Nikki slid onto the bench opposite his without bothering to ask—like she ever had.

"Hi there," she said, without a trace of Texas accent. He wondered how long that would last.

"Hi there." His greeting was edged with a challenge.

And there they sat like they had a dozen times before—like there was no past between them. Like they hadn't had one night of extremely hot sex, and he hadn't practically begged her to give them a chance. But now, with her greenish-blue eyes smudged with black eyeliner and the f-you attitude she wore like a superhero's cape, he had to wonder if she even remembered.

Then her impish eyes softened, and her naked lips slipped into a sexy smile only Nikki could pull off.

Jett felt his jaw muscle twitch.

Every man had his thing, and if Jett was out drinking with the guys, he'd label himself a "boob man." Saying he was a "lip man" didn't quite cut it. But there was something about bare lips, unadorned with color or sticky gloss, ready for kissing, which made him want to nibble.

"Miss me?" Nikki pulled his cup closer to her and added cream and sugar. She took his knife and stirred. He watched his black coffee turn the color of mud.

"Like stomach cancer."

She made a soft *tsking* sound. "Ah then, you thought of me often."

Jett pressed his teeth together, not appreciating how close to the truth she'd come. He caught her eye and made sure she watched as his gaze traveled down her shirt—Christ, she really was wearing a black bra—then back up to her face. "All class, Nik."

She didn't blink, just picked up his newspaper and scanned the front page. "Ouch, Rangers lost in extra innings. Hope you didn't have money on that game."

He grabbed the paper and quickly found the headline: "Rangers Win in Blow Out," then threw the paper back on the table, pissed he'd been taken in so easily.

She laughed.

Jett knew that laugh. It was the same laugh that had suckered him into thinking there was more heart to Nikki than she'd let on. He knew better now.

"Why are you here, Nik?"

"That's a fine welcome, Jett." She scooted down in the booth as if she hadn't a care, but Jett knew better. She placed the heel of those damn platform shoes on his seat—right between his legs.

He almost smiled—almost. Who did she think she was playing with? One of her college boys? He shook his head instead. "Well then, let me try that again. When are you leaving, Nik? Seems to me, you got the running away part down better than the coming home part."

Like shutters snapping shut on windows, she blinked and her

eyes lost that smoldering look. She sat up and reached for his toast, gooped purple jelly on it, and then took a bite. "I'll be leaving soon. Won't be here long."

"Just long enough to get into trouble?"

Her eyes narrowed, and he surprised himself by missing the playfulness of the moment before.

"Long enough to clear my ledger."

His gut tightened, but he refused to let his pasted-on smile slip. "You always had a knack for owing the wrong people."

"And who are the right people, Jett? The Averys? Not much of a difference between politicians and criminals."

"That difference, of course, being the law. But that's all subjective, right, Nik?"

She laughed and plucked some scrambled egg off his plate with her fingers.

Jett had to look away when she licked her lips.

Ginger walked over and set a glass of ice water before Nikki. "Here you go, sugar. Looks like you need this. Don't worry, you rest up a bit, and Jett will get you on home."

Thanks, Ginger. Why did everyone insist on putting Nikki in his lap? She wasn't his responsibility.

Nikki looked up at the older woman and showed one of her more genuine smiles. "Thanks, Ginger. You're the best."

Jett couldn't remember the last time Nikki had flashed one of those his way. Not that he cared. It just annoyed him that he couldn't pinpoint the last time. Or maybe he did, and he just didn't want to remember.

Jett watched as Nikki's gaze zeroed in on the table across from them. Mrs. Burns's pinched face and spiteful glare was tough to ignore, but with her husband's gaping mouth and glazed-over look, his lecherous stare was even harder.

A shadow of something flickered across Nikki's face. On another person he would've named it hurt, but on Nikki one could never be sure. Then it was gone, her chin came up, and her eyes took on an expression that never boded well for man or devil.

Nikki cast a hooded glance at the old woman, turned to Mr. Burns and blew him a moist, sexy kiss that would've done Marilyn Monroe proud.

The sound that came from Mrs. Burns could've made dogs howl on a moonless night. She was up and dragging Mr. Burns out by the arm, not even stopping to pay their bill.

Jett looked at the empty table and the half-eaten breakfasts. He calculated the extra he'd put in his tip to cover the couple's bill. It wasn't Ginger's fault Nikki had the manners of an alley cat.

He took his time turning back to Nikki, already knowing what he'd see. "Really?"

She lifted a careless shoulder. "Not my fault her old man's a perv," she said around a bite of toast.

"Never is, Nik. Do me a favor: Don't talk. No, better yet, don't make eye contact with anyone else while you're in town."

"Sure thing, boss." She dusted her hands free of crumbs, signaling she was finished eating.

Jett looked at his plate and put down his fork. The remains of his breakfast had been drowned in ketchup, de-crusted, and his coffee turned into chocolate milk.

He glanced at the empty table across from them, and then back at the half-girl, half-woman in front of him. And he couldn't help wondering how the hell he'd gotten back into the business of cleaning up after Nikki Logan.

Chapter 4

Nikki hefted herself up on the passenger seat of Jett's truck, and looked around. The truck was immaculate, typical Jett. Not a layer of dust or an orphaned penny in the cup holder, just the smell of wax and leather. Nikki tugged at her T-shirt, doing a quick courtesy sniff-check, suddenly very aware of how long ago her deodorant had given up the fight.

Jett, on the other hand, cool and calm in his cream Stetson, looked as if a heat wave was too mundane a matter to be bothered with. She'd bet her last twenty dollars—if she had twenty dollars—that he even ironed his T-shirts. Sure, some girls in town, okay—most, went a little crazy over his all-American good looks. And even though Jett was a bit too high-maintenance, and a bit too glossy GQ for her, he sure could make a person appreciate the beauty of the male species.

Jett pulled out of the parking lot, one arm casual-like on the wheel while the other fiddled with his phone. "I'll get Bo to tow your car to the garage." His gaze did a quick once-over of her. "I don't suppose you've got enough money to pay for the repairs?"

And there it was. His voice held a perfect blend of condescension and arrogance that was all Jett, along with a bit of judgment thrown in to seal the deal. Like he was one to judge—what did he know? He was the town's "golden boy" whose childhood resembled an old fifties sit-com. Yeah, he had the whole package—living parents, good education, looks, and brains. It was sure hard for people like her when the whole town would simply lie down and put out for a sexy wink or a sugar-coated line that tumbled from his lips like others spit tobacco.

"Nope." She pronounced the "p" with a loud pop, loving how annoying she was. She opened his glove compartment and rummaged through, finding the emergency pack of gum he always kept on hand in case he was on a date. "I figured I'd just offer a blow job and consider it even."

She had a piece of gum unwrapped and ready to place in her mouth when his hand reached over and snagged it. He threw her piece and the whole pack behind her, causing the truck to swerve and bump up over a curb.

Well, she'd wanted a reaction . . .

"Cut the crap, Nik. We both know you're full of it."

Nikki hitched her thumb toward the back seat. "So, um . . . no gum then?"

"Buy your own damn gum." Jett stared straight ahead.

Nikki crossed her arms and waited. She didn't have to wait long.

"You're a piece of work," Jett said, talking to the windshield. "You know that? What's with you and the crap you pulled back there at the diner? Was all that really necessary?"

Nikki didn't respond since he already knew the answer. It hadn't been.

She'd meant to do things differently, but when she walked into that diner and saw most of the town there, it was as if she'd never left. There, concentrated in that one place, were all the opinions, judgments . . . censure she'd run away from two years ago. Then, as if slipping on a comfy pair of jeans, she simply fell back into old patterns. Fell back into how she'd learned to cope as a mostly parentless adolescent on the loose.

What she really wanted was for things to go back to normal between her and Jett. To have this tension between them over and done with. Sure, they always drove each other crazy, got on each other's nerves, but now there was an underlying current that made her uneasy. There'd been a time when she considered him her best friend. Too bad she'd gone ahead and ruined it by sleeping with him. Well, sleeping with him and then leaving town in the middle of the night without saying goodbye. At the time she'd thought it was a good idea—hadn't been able to deal with what Jett wanted from her—but now, not so much.

Nikki blew her hair out of her face with a heavy sigh. Her life always seemed to run toward the complicated.

They drove the rest of the way in silence. It wasn't long until they were pulling up to her childhood home. The dirt drive led to a one-story ranch house with a gray, sloped roof that didn't keep the water out during the hard rains and kept the heat in during the summer. The only new addition to the house in years had been the white wrap-around porch that seemed sturdier than the dwelling it was attached to. Not many tornados in Texas, but if she needed shelter, she could always hide under the porch. Better than taking her chances with the leaning pile of timber that was her family home.

Nikki turned her head, not wanting to deal with what she'd come back to. Her gaze drifted over the flat brown land with hardy tufts of green pasture that had been in her family for generations and came to rest on the stables.

And of course, the stables were new. Newly redone, freshly painted, and she was sure, outfitted with an all-weather roof that didn't leak. But why was she surprised? It all came back to Katie, her sister-in-law, and Katie loved those horses. And what Katie loved, Cole poured his blood and sweat into. It had always been that way. As long as Nikki could remember, it had been Katie and Cole against the world and to hell with the rest of them.

Nikki couldn't believe they were married and with a baby already—nothing like holding back or anything. She guessed they'd been sniffing around each other long enough, but even after two years, she wondered if her brother knew what he was doing.

"You okay?" Jett asked, all traces of anger gone. And that was what she loved about Jett. He rarely lost his temper, and if he did, it wasn't for long. She smiled as she remembered the nickname Cole had given him years ago: "Cool man." Being even-tempered around the Logans was a much sought-after talent. Probably why Jett had stuck around as long as he had.

It took a moment for her to realize he was waiting for her to get out. She reached behind to the back seat and grabbed some gum, hoping to cover her procrastination. She got out and pulled her duffel bag along with her. Jett came around the other side to help.

"I got it," she said.

"I know." But he took her bag anyway.

Nikki arched a brow in question.

"What? I'm a nice guy, Nik."

"So you say." But she softened her words with her eyes. He smiled back, and just like that, there was a glimmer of hope that they could be what they had started out as—friends.

Jett headed toward the house. "It's been empty for a while, but Cole has kept the electricity on. I think the phone is off, so keep your cell handy."

Nikki nodded. She was enough of a loser already without adding the phone confession to his opinion of her.

She fumbled with her key in the lock, suddenly nervous. This was the closest she'd been to coming home since she'd walked down the front steps two years ago. It could be worse. She could be coming home to live with her brother, but Cole had moved out, which left Nikki their parents' home—the place she'd dreamed about running away from ever since her mother took sick.

But that was then and this was now. *All roads lead back home.* Was that something she read on a fortune cookie or was it from another lame country song?

She hadn't known she'd been hesitating until Jett's hand covered hers, surprising her with the warmth of his skin on her icy fingers, and pushed the door open. He always had a knack for knowing what she needed.

Everything looked the same, as if the walls of peeling paint and faded wallpaper could freeze time and keep ghosts. There was the brown shag carpet, linoleum floor, and horns from an elk that neither her father nor Cole had killed, which hung in a place of honor above the worn couch. The only difference was a darker rectangular spot on the carpet where Cole's old recliner had been parked.

Nikki smiled. "Did Katie really let Cole take his La-Z-Boy?"

"That was Cole's one demand, but I've heard it only made it as far as the back porch." Humor laced his words, but Katie thought she heard something else . . . longing?

Nikki shook her head. Then she laughed, really laughed, and it felt good. She had built up coming home in her mind for way too long. But it was just a house. She was fine. Nothing here could hurt her.

She turned to Jett, suddenly relieved. "I'm good. Thanks for the lift."

His brown eyes had her remembering how she liked her coffee—light and sweet. With only two small flaws of a slightly crooked nose and a star-shaped scar that kissed the corner of his right eye, he was a beautiful man.

Without questioning why, she reached up, and with a light touch ran her finger down the bump on his nose, courtesy of Cole's fist. "Ouch. Did I ever say I was sorry?"

He pulled away. "A broken nose should be last on your list of what you need to be sorry for."

She'd meant it as a joke, but he didn't sound nearly as light-hearted as she had. Her hand fluttered to her collarbone, seeking the necklace her mother had given her when she was sixteen. "What's higher? That I ruined your modeling career?"

"I was told I had potential," he said with a twinkle in his eye, once again giving her hope they could find their way back to being friends.

"I saved you." She hadn't meant to say that, the phrase a little too close to home. Instead she pulled back to keep the conversation from going *there*. "From your modeling career that is; guys shouldn't be too beautiful."

Whatever flashed in his eyes previously died a quick death. "Jealous?"

"Maybe." She threw up her shoulder in a shrug. "We all know you're pretty, Jett. No contest there."

"But do *you* think I'm pretty?"

"I only date the pretty ones."

"So we dated?"

"If that's what you want to call it."

"That's not what I want to call it."

She stepped back, no longer wanting to finish the conversation. She wasn't quite sure she was ready to define what had happened between them. Over the last two years she'd convinced herself all they'd had was a one-night stand. From the look Jett was giving her, he didn't agree.

Her leaving had been for the best. Things between them would've ended nowhere but in a fiery, hot mess. "Jett, I don't . . . I don't know what you want me to say."

There was a slight twitch of his eye, the only indicator that he was annoyed. "You know what, Texas?"

She swallowed hard, not trusting where this was going.

"I was wrong. I'm not a nice guy." He tossed the duffel bag to her—hard. Then turned and walked out the door.

Chapter 5

Nikki was running hard and fast. Uphill. Heat radiated from the pavement, burning the soles of her feet through her shoes. The sun was hot on her neck. A sharp stitch knifed in her side, preventing her from catching her breath. Her legs were heavy as if moving through water, and then, all of a sudden, she was. Water foamed and crashed in on angry white-caps, wetting her shoes, her shorts. Her clothes entrapped her like wet nets, her shoes like anchors chained to her feet. Murky water stretched out as far as the eye could see, meeting the distant horizon in a blend of blue-gray. Then she looked up.

The wide-open sky hardened and turned cold—a slab of concrete above her. The sky lowered until she could brace her palms against the wet barrier. Water lapped at her chest, neck, and then her chin. And kept rising. She tried to scream, but white foam filled her mouth. She spit as she took tiny sips of air from the small gap between the rising sea level and lowering ceiling. One breath, another, then she was in over her head. No air. No space. She was drowning.

Bang. Bang.

She pounded on the ceiling with her fists.

Bang. Bang.

She wasn't ready to die yet. Not like this.

"Nikki!"

She startled awake, gasping for air, and for one horrible second she was home, and her mom was calling from her sick bed. Nikki sat straight up on the couch, desperate to remember where she'd put her mother's medicine.

Help me, Nikki.

I'm coming, Momma!

Then the world righted itself, and Nikki remembered. She was home, but her mother wasn't.

Another pounding came from outside the front door, then a soft swear. "Nikki, open the damn door," Cole yelled. "I forgot my key."

Nikki took a moment to slick back her hair and calm her racing heart. Her legs were still unsteady as she stumbled to the door, flipped the latch, and then turned and threw herself back down on the couch. Cole entered, armed with a folded newspaper and a travel mug, not caring that sunlight and the smell of horse followed in his wake.

Nikki turned her face into her pillow and groaned.

"Glad to see you're alive, Sunshine. Could've told someone you were here."

Nikki ignored his sarcasm. It was too early. "Who told you?" she murmured into her pillow.

"I heard it from Al down at the post office that you'd come into town. Guess you made quite an impression. He asked if he could have your phone number."

Nikki's head snapped up. "Ugh, what is it with this town? Al's like forty years old. Bunch of perverts."

Cole's mouth turned into what some people deemed a smile. "Men are the same everywhere, Sunshine. You should know that by now." He walked into the kitchen, then called out from behind the corner. "What's up with you sleeping on the couch?"

"Nothing." She didn't want to tell him that sleeping in her bedroom meant that she lived here, but if she slept on the couch, she was just a guest. "Oh, and thanks for leaving the TV, by the way." She glanced at the faded spot on the opposite wall. What did he expect her to do, play shadow puppets in the dark?

Nikki grabbed the blanket and wrapped it around her, letting the excess drag on the floor. She made her way to the kitchen table, knowing Cole was here for a reason and wouldn't leave until he'd seen it through.

"Consider it a favor," Cole said, his voice more grating than usual. "You won't have much time for television after you see my surprise."

"Does it contain caffeine and come in that silver mug of yours?" She plopped herself into the chair, hugging one knee to her chest.

"No, coffee's from Katie." He set the mug down in front of her, then stepped back and leaned against the counter, propping his elbows behind him.

Nikki resisted the urge to grit her teeth, but barely. She knew that stance. Her brother was a man of few words, and Nikki could count on one hand the conversations between them that had lasted more than ten minutes. But Cole's posture told her he was settling in, getting ready to talk. Or in her world, getting ready to lecture.

"So, are you going to tell me what's going on?"

"What's going on about what?" She knew exactly what Cole was asking about, but it was way too early to start in on that conversation. Maybe he'd get the point. Besides, she hadn't even had time to drink her breakfast. She took a sip. Ugh! Black. She had to force herself to swallow the coffee. "No cream or sugar? Really?"

Cole shrugged. "Katie thought you liked your coffee sweet, but I told her you liked it like mine—black and strong. But if you don't want it . . . "

He reached over to take back the silver mug, but she kept it out of his reach. "Get your own damn coffee," she grumbled.

"I will as soon as you tell me if you're home for good? Did you graduate? What are your plans for the rest of your life?"

Nikki resisted the urge to throw her blanket up over her head and pretend she hadn't heard him, but that wouldn't deter Cole. Never had. "I'm home . . . for now. I already told you I graduated. And as far as the rest of my life . . . Lord, Cole, I don't even have the rest of this day figured out."

He crossed his arms over his chest and peered down at her with those steel-blue eyes that had a way of making her feel cold. She snuggled deeper into her blanket and warmed her hands with the heat from the travel mug.

"Are we going to have this conversation or not, Nikki?"

Well, given a choice . . . "I'm all for not."

"How did you get the money for college? We both know your

scholarship story is bull. Was it gambling at pool? Are you hustling again?"

"What? No, I told you. I've stopped playing for money. Haven't done that since . . ." She let her voice trail off. She hadn't hustled at pool since the night she'd gotten arrested, and Jett had to come bail her out of jail.

"Then what is it?" Cole pulled out the kitchen chair next to her, turned it, and then straddled the ripped plastic cushion. "Are you in some kind of trouble, Nikki? Did you take money from people you shouldn't have? I need to know that you're okay."

His eyes had warmed and the tiny lines in the corners had deepened over the last two years. She wasn't surprised. With a wife, horse ranch, sick father-in-law and now a new baby, Nikki was sure the stress had started to wear on him.

She reached over and lightly rested her hand on his arm. "I'm fine, Cole. Really. And you don't have to worry about me. I'm okay."

He smiled, but it was only half there. "That's my job. I worry."

Nikki removed her hand as she shook her head. "Not anymore. I've gotten a degree in accounting. I can support myself."

He leaned back, eyebrows arching in surprise. "I always knew you were good with numbers, but I never figured you to be an accountant."

She hadn't either, but that was the promise she'd made Mike when he'd paid her way through college. But how she was going to explain that she owed a debt to a man who wasn't even family had been beyond her for the last two years.

Cole seemed thinner than she remembered. His arms were more defined. Cheekbones more pronounced. "There've been rumors, Nikki."

She let her hand cover her heart and arched her brows. "What! People are talking about the Logans? Say it isn't so."

This was why she hadn't wanted to come back home. A girl could leave town, but a bad reputation stayed forever. "Let me guess: I made out with some guy behind the Tasty Freeze. I cheated on my SATs because we all know that a Logan couldn't score that high. Or I flirted with the pastor during Sunday service."

"That one was true!" he laughed. "And to think you did it in front of the whole congregation."

Nikki rolled her eyes. "He deserved it. He'd been hitting on me for years. I just finally called him on it."

Cole groaned. "It was worse than that. What did you say again? It was so horrible I must have blocked it out."

"I only said that if he ogled my breasts one more time, he'd better be willing to put his money where his eyes had been."

"Christ, it was as bad as I thought. I can't believe I didn't throttle you after that comment."

"You would've if you'd been sober." She brushed her hair out of her eyes. "Let's not pretend the Logans earned this reputation solely by my account."

Cole dropped his head in his hands. "What a mess we were—you angry and pissed off at the world. And me, well, me angry and pissed off also."

She reached across the worn, polished table and touched the back of his hand. This time she lingered. "It's not like that anymore. What I mean is, you're not like that anymore. You're not the same man. You're different. Better."

He arched a brow. "This is me happy."

"I never thought I'd see the day." She smiled, but was only half-joking.

"Well, I can't wait to say the same about you."

She moved her hand back, not liking where this conversation was going. She was happy. Well, not happy back here at home, but she would be as soon as she worked off her debt to Mike. "You don't have to worry, Cole. I'm fine."

"But I do. Besides, this time is different. It's got me scared, Sunshine. People are saying you've borrowed money from the wrong people. That you owe the wrong people. And the hell of it is I can't defend you because I really don't know how you got the thirty grand to pay for a degree at a university."

Nikki looked away. Took a sip of coffee. Not caring now that it was black and strong.

"You left in the middle of the night. Not a word, not a phone call. I thought something terrible had happened to you."

Nikki chipped at the last of her black nail polish, suddenly unable to look him in the eye. Cole hadn't deserved that. She'd handled the whole thing badly. At the time she hadn't cared since she'd still been reeling from her arrest, Cole and Katie's surprise wedding, and Cole's ending the ceremony with a fist to Jett's face. She opened her mouth to tell Cole her excuses, but stopped herself. When had she started lying to herself? She had to have some standards. No, the truth was, she'd left because of what happened the day after. "I did call. When I got off the road. I called to let you know I was okay."

Cole shook his head as if not hearing her. "You should've seen Jett. He went crazy. I thought he'd call in the FBI to come and track you down."

Nikki stood, signaling the end of the conversation. "I don't want to talk about Jett."

Jett's comment yesterday still stung. It bothered her that he was hurt. She hadn't realized how much his opinion of her mattered—funny since there wasn't anyone else in town she cared two figs about. She had harbored a hope of patching things up with Jett. Nothing romantic—she'd set that bridge aflame—but friends at least.

Cole stood also. "Regardless, I'm glad that you're home. Really glad. Just a thought—the ranch could use a real accountant. Lord knows, we could use an objective third party. Katie seems to want to spend every penny we make, and I can't help but want to live on the frayed shoestring budget I was used to growing up."

Nikki crossed her arms. "I can get my own job."

She loved her brother and she liked Katie. Okay, she didn't *not* like Katie. Maybe there was still some childish resentment over Katie having more advantages growing up than Nikki. Or maybe it was that Katie still had her father when Nikki had lost both parents? Or . . . Nikki groaned. Maybe the truth was that Cole had been Nikki's whole life when she was young, but it wasn't Nikki who made Cole's face light up when she walked into the room; it was Katie. And when Cole watched Katie, there was happiness in his eyes. When he watched Nikki, there was resentment and duty. After all these years, Nikki couldn't help but want her older brother's approval, even though she'd never stoop so low as to ask for it. Besides, it wouldn't be long before there'd be way more than resentment and duty in his eyes—there'd be shame.

Cole readjusted his hat, and then peered down at her with those steel-blue eyes. "I heard Mrs. Lewis has an opening for a tax advisor. Maybe you should check it out."

Nikki answered with a shrug.

"Just trying to help, Sunshine. But you want to go it alone. Just like always."

Nikki sighed, but in the end Cole was the last of her family, and regardless of their past differences, she didn't want to end this conversation on a bad note. "I'll come over this afternoon. I can't wait to meet Jimmy."

The grin that split his face lightened her heart. Cole didn't smile, not like *that* he didn't. Cole had had a hard life, but he'd never run from responsibility. Parents dying, raising his only sister, a destitute horse ranch—Cole had shouldered his responsibility like he always had, with grace and honor.

He would never run. Not like her.

Nikki sat in the kitchen chair and stared out the window long after her brother had left. The pane was slightly warped with age and dirty after years of neglect. With a fist full of blanket, she wiped a spot clean. There was no need to look at the want ads her brother had left for her. She knew where she'd be working.

She just had to figure out how she would tell her brother. Tell Cole—the one who had washed her Sunday dress in the sink when the washing machine busted so she'd be presentable at church. The one who'd made her do her homework since education was the only thing that beat out abject poverty. The one who'd worked two, sometimes three jobs, so she could finish high school. He had tried so hard just so Nikki would never have to set foot in the one place she owed the biggest debt to.

Cole was going to be so hurt when he found out she was working where dreams went to die and men went to take advantage. The town's one and only strip joint—The Pitt.

Chapter 6

Cole had been right about one thing—Nikki needed a job. With her car in the shop, and no food in the fridge, she needed to drive over to The Pitt and see what arrangement Mike and she could work out. Nikki showered and dressed quickly, glad to be leaving the house for a while. How many years had this house felt like a prison and her mother the warden? And of course, there was always the question—how bad did that make her, to be resentful of her dying mother?

Nikki shook off the painful memories as she walked to Katie's place and tried to keep past sins in their place—behind her. The path was a straight shot from Nikki's front door, past the stables and arena, over a small hill, and smack onto the Harris's porch. Or was it Cole's and Katie's house now? No matter, it would always be the Logans and the Harrises. There was more than simple distance separating their homes.

Nikki slipped her hands into her back pockets and watched her favorite combat boots slice through the native grass that grew like wildfire between the properties. Though Nikki avoided any real, live animals, she couldn't avoid the evidence they left behind. Yeah, this ranch was built on thirteen years of horsesh—manure.

Nikki shook her head. Even after all these years, her mother's words were still ingrained in her brain. She could see her mom, sitting at the polished kitchen table, sipping sweet, iced tea, and looking at Nikki with that sad, disappointed expression. *Nikki, just because we're poor as dirt doesn't mean we have to act like it.* Even after all these years, after all this time.

It's time to grow up, Nikki.

Except she'd grown up way too fast. She'd spent years taking care of her mother. Instead of dating or picking out colleges, she'd been counting out chemo meds and scheduling doctor appointments.

Gritting her teeth, she kicked at a dandelion weed. She didn't want to think about what her mother would say to see her daughter, broke, unhappy, and drifting through life with a ruined reputation.

I am so disappointed. I raised you better than that.

She scrubbed her hands over her face to clear her thoughts. She'd had this conversation with herself before, and always, it was pointless. Her mother was dead. And no amount of resentment, anger, or pleading could change what her mother had thought of her.

Nikki climbed the steps of the Harris's front porch, stomping her boots a few times, leaving a trail of dark Texas earth behind. She raised her hand to knock before she spotted her brother sitting straight up on the two-seater swing, fast asleep. For one moment, with the stress of life eased from Cole's face, he looked like the brother she had once thought hung the moon. The tight constriction she had in her belly since driving into town loosened a bit.

She walked over and softly patted his knee, surprised she felt guilty about disturbing him.

Cole startled awake, eyes wide as if assuring himself he'd never been asleep in the first place. "Hey, what's going on?"

Nikki smiled. Fatherhood must be hell on a new marriage, but that didn't mean she'd pass up the chance for a dig.

"Trouble in paradise already?"

"Huh?" Cole rubbed at the bridge of his nose.

"Sleeping on the front porch? What's next, the doghouse?"

It took no more than a second for Cole to resettle his hat, and then he was fully present. "What do you want, Nikki?" His tone was hard.

She regretted her comment, or maybe she didn't. It was easier dealing with Cole like this. She knew where she stood.

"A ride. Can I borrow your truck?"

"Yeah, keys are inside on the hook. But be quiet, everyone's asleep."

"Even Mr. Harris?" Nikki knew Katie's father was living with them and had since he'd gotten sick a few years past, but it must be worse than she'd thought if he was in bed during the day.

"No." Cole shook his head. "Dad went into town for supplies. He'll be back later."

Her gut flinched. *Cole called Mr. Harris Dad?*

What did she care what Cole called his father-in-law? Cole had married Katie. He was family. It's not like she ever wanted Mr. Harris as her father, not really. Well, not since she'd been a kid. She'd been ten when her father had died, and yeah, there had been fantasies about Mr. Harris asking if she would call him Dad, picking her up, tousling her hair, but he'd always seemed more into Cole and the horse ranch.

She shrugged. It didn't matter, not now anyway. She wasn't that pathetic little kid anymore—needy, always running after Cole and Jett, begging them to spend time with her. But it just made her wonder . . . if Cole and Katie were a family now, what did that make her?

Cole must've interpreted her shrug the wrong way. His gaze narrowed at her. "I'm serious, Nikki. If you wake that son of mine, I'll kill you both."

Nikki did a mock two-finger salute. "Quiet like a burglar."

"A *successful* burglar."

Nikki opened the front door with care. Inside, every drape was pulled tight against the sun, and the quiet swish of the ceiling fans cooled the air. As Nikki walked past what used to be a formal dining room, she could tell the house had been invaded. A baby swing, a bouncy thing, and a playpen littered the room. And of course, the pervasive scent of baby—formula, lavender, and something that had her thinking of wet wipes and moist diapers.

And Cole wondered why it had taken her so long to meet her new nephew. It wasn't like her idea of a good time had anything to do with a chubby, bald, and drooling male. But Nikki knew the real reason she wasn't up to spending all her time with Cole and his new family. She was happy for Cole, she really was, but that still didn't mean she was up to watching Cole gaze at his new family with love and affection, when for years all Nikki had seen was disappointment.

She found the hook, and was in and out of the house in record time. She walked down the steps toward Cole's truck, fumbling with the keys, trying to find the remote button.

"Ah no, Sunshine," Cole called from the porch, "not that truck. The one you're driving is parked by the barn."

Nikki turned, already regretting that she hadn't kicked her brother when she'd had the chance. Hidden behind weeds that grew up past the driver-side window was a pickup, once red, now the color of rusted primer.

"Really? Does it even run?"

"Old Bertha runs like new."

Nikki leveled him with a look.

"Okay, runs more like she's been around the block a couple of times. But if you don't push her over forty-five, you'll be fine."

Nikki stomped toward the truck. She needed to settle things with Mike, needed to get paid, and then needed to get her own car.

"You drive a stick, right?" Cole said with a smirk in his voice she would've been able to hear from any distance.

No. Who would've taught her? Dad had died before she was of driving age, and Cole had always been working. But she'd bite her tongue in half before admitting as much. It was bad enough she had to ask Cole for a truck. She wasn't about to ask for a driving lesson—something Cole should've taught her at sixteen—to add to her humiliation.

Chapter 7

Cockiness got her a whole four feet, or as far as the truck coasted after the first stall. Nikki gritted her teeth and restarted the engine. Would it be too much to hope that Cole would go back into the house? She checked the rearview mirror—apparently it was. Over the roar of the engine she couldn't actually hear Cole's laughter, but got the visual. His arms were wrapped around his stomach, folded almost in half as if he couldn't breathe.

She hoped he choked on it.

The driver's seat was stuck and refused to move forward. She might've been tall, but she couldn't measure up to Cole's six-foot-plus frame. On the edge of the seat, she pushed the clutch in as far as it would go. She knew there were gears and a stick shift. She figured the logical progression was to start with one, but Cole's yelled advice to get the truck out of neutral was of no help. How she ever got the truck out of the driveway, she never knew. Well, maybe it had something to do with refusing to touch the gearshift again.

Nikki cruised along the deserted dirt road at a Mach speed of five miles per hour. The engine whirled into a high-pitch whine, and one gauge bordered a red zone. Nikki checked the road behind her—all clear—then switched gears. A screech that sounded like Godzilla tearing through the Empire State building came from under the hood. Scared, she popped the clutch, pressed on the gas—and stalled again.

Banging her head against the steering wheel, she let the truck coast. She rolled down the window and counted the blades of grass as they went by. It was truly a toss-up. Should she continue to try to drive or would it be faster to get out and push?

Nikki sighed. Apparently "running like new" to Cole meant the AC blew like a tepid old maid and the shifting of gears sounded like gravel in a blender. Figured. This meeting with Mike already had her on edge and showing up soaked with sweat was exactly the strong, confident image she wanted to convey. She turned the key again. Two dozen attempts later, and with a vital car part left behind in the road, Nikki turned into the parking lot of Mike's place.

In the light of day The Pitt lived up to its name. Apparently, cheap beer and fried food didn't call for much curb appeal. Of course, the promise of a view of pretty titties made up for quite a lot.

At the center of a make-do parking lot was a windowless, black building, which proudly sported its one ornamental flare—a neon sign. During the day a person could read all the red letters, but at night the "P" had long ago burned out, thus the name the locals had christened the bar—"The itt."

Nikki reapplied some lip gloss and gave herself a sniff check. The last time she'd seen Mike, she'd been a mess—broken-hearted, running scared. This time she wanted to at least give the impression that Mike hadn't wasted his money. Having no idea what was appropriate for that kind of meeting, she'd decided to go with something she felt comfortable in—her favorite jean shorts and combat boots.

The door jingled as she walked in, her only greeting other than the smell of sour beer and old grease. One glance and it was easy to guess that nighttime could only improve things. A few tables were scattered here and there, a bar lined the back wall, and off to the right was a room that used to hold the pool table. In the middle was a stage, a stripper pole proudly in the center. Nikki hoped they Lysoled that thing between shows. She stopped short. What if that was one of her duties as she worked off her debt to Mike? She rolled her eyes—here was rock-bottom. The only surprise was it took her twenty-four years to find it.

"Put the deliveries on the bar, and come on back for a signature," Mike said in a grizzly voice from behind the office door.

Nikki followed the voice and walked back to Mike's office. Bald and with a long white beard, Mike leaned back in an over-sized office chair. Even sitting down, Nikki could tell he'd put on weight. He was dressed in a faded, gray Ozzy Osbourne T-shirt and holey jeans. Suddenly Nikki felt better about her outfit.

Mike looked up from his desk, and Nikki could see right away the cloudiness in his eyes—cataracts maybe?—or maybe it was simply the years claiming their due. He covered one eye and squinted with the other. "Oh hell, it's you. Go away."

He looked down, and with a wave of his hand, dismissed her the way one would shoo a fly.

Nikki arched her brows and put on her best "you got to be kidding look," but it was wasted since Mike wasn't looking, and no one else was around.

Nikki stepped forward. "Mike, I'm here. That was the deal. Go to school, get a degree, come back, and help you out with The Pitt."

"There's no way you coulda gotten your degree in two years." He scratched at the beard on his upper lip. "I may be old, but don't be thinking me stupid. Many a dead man has made that mistake."

Nikki rolled her eyes, but again the expression was wasted. "I got my degree, Mike. I took double classes and some over the summer. It was accounting, not brain surgery. It wasn't too hard."

That got Mike's attention. His one unclouded eye zeroed in on her. "Are you telling me you got your degree in half the usual time, and it was easy for you?"

Nikki shrugged. "Yes."

He shook his head, disgusted. "You overachiever, you. Too bad you couldn't apply some of those smarts to your real life."

She smiled. People had been underestimating her for years; too bad her new boss wasn't one of them. "Hey, what do you expect from a Logan? We weren't created to rule the world."

"No, just cause hell in it."

That comment, so true, wasn't even worth remarking on. "So, when do I start?"

Mike did a quick and dirty glance up and down—good eye squinting hard. "Is this how you dress for a job interview?"

Nikki didn't even try to suppress her sigh. Maybe she should've changed out of yesterday's shorts and put on a nicer top, but this was Mike, and she'd made her first impression years ago. "Is that what they're calling indentured servitude these days?"

"Is that what giving someone thirty grand without doing a day's work is called?"

Nikki raised her hands in the air in surrender. "I'm here, aren't I? Besides, it looks like you need the help if you're actually still keeping your books with legal ledgers." Nikki reached across to grab the hard-bound, two-holed, punched binder. "I didn't know they still made these. I saw them in a history book once."

He snatched the ledger out of her hand and quickly put it behind him, out of reach. "I told you, I don't want you working here."

Nikki stepped back, shocked and more than a little hurt. Did Mike not trust her? She would expect that from anyone else in town, but not from Mike. Mike had known her since she was a kid, had known both her parents. Mike had been one of the few people who'd believed in her.

Nikki adjusted her bra strap and shuffled her feet. Whatever, she didn't care, but she was a Logan and a Logan never owed. "Fine, but I won't leave until you get me a job. That was the deal. I'm here to stay."

"I don't have any openings."

Something was up, but Nikki had no idea what. But just because she didn't know what he was hiding didn't mean she couldn't call his bluff. She hadn't been a successful hustler for years without picking up some skills. She shrugged. "A dancer then. I know you're always looking for fresh talent."

His face went chalk white, and Nikki was glad at that moment he was half blind—since he couldn't see the smirk she allowed through. Checkmate.

"I don't need another dancer."

"You always need another dancer."

Mike blinked. "You remind me of him, you know . . . your father. He was wily, calculating. That's what made him a good pool player. If he'd worked on his ranch as hard as he did hustling men for money, he might've not died broke."

There'd been no love lost between her father and Mike. The ancient history was they both had dated the same woman—her mother. Apparently, Mike still held a grudge. But she'd learned long ago to keep her mouth shut when it came to her family—a product of growing up in a small town.

"The position of bartender is open. You do know how to pour a draft and make a whiskey neat, right?"

She nodded.

"And you do know how to handle a gun and ain't afraid to use one if you have to?"

"Like a pro."

Mike shook his head. "God, let's hope not or else my thirty grand was a waste."

Mike covered one eye and watched as Nikki walked out the door of his office. He waited for the door's tell-tale jingle to make sure she'd left before he breathed a sigh of relief. That Nikki Logan was too smart by half. Christ, an accounting degree in less than two years. There was no way he'd be able to cover his tracks in time. He hadn't expected her back so soon. He'd thought by the time she returned, he'd be in the clear. He'd have everything covered and be ready to retire. 'Course, now death seemed more likely than retirement. He still couldn't believe that his whole savings were gone. Gone in one swipe of a bad economy.

He wasn't stupid. He'd invested in secure stocks. Things his advisor said were safe and low risk. Except no one had foreseen how far the market would crash. Mike had lost everything, and it was shameful to admit, but he'd panicked. His eyesight was going, and the doctor told him that his ticker was wearing out. His worst fear of ending up in some crappy nursing home that smelled like urine and smashed peas was staring him right in the face. He'd crumbled.

He'd never been a gambling man, but he looked around at where playing it safe had gotten him—alone, broke, and desperate. So he'd borrowed some money—a lot of money from people a smart man should never get involved with. Mike still couldn't believe he'd done it, but his advisor had said this stock was a sure thing.

Mike should know at his age there was no such thing.

He'd lost it all. And now the people who a smart man should never get involved with wanted their money back, and Mike didn't have it. If it was just him, he'd be fine. He'd sell The Pitt, go hide out in some cabin deep in the woods. But he had employees. Employees who worked The Pitt as their last stop before the streets.

Mike scrubbed his hands over his face and stood. The numbers in the ledger wouldn't change no matter how long he looked at them. He walked to the back door, reaching for the lighter in his front pocket. He'd quit smoking years before, but just recently gave up the fight. Hell, lung cancer had to be an easier way to go than a baseball bat to the kneecaps.

Mike lit his cigarette and took a long draw, savoring how the smoke felt deep in his lungs. Funny how the small things in life started to become more pleasant when your days were numbered.

The little girl sitting on top of the overturned milk crate surprised him. He didn't like children hanging around The Pitt. He knew most of his employees had kids, but he had a strict policy about bringing them to their place of work.

He jutted his head in her direction. "What're you doing?"

He sounded harsh, but a lot worse could happen to a kid hanging around here than getting a little scared. Besides, he'd had his fill of charity cases and lost souls.

The girl's long, straggly hair looked like it hadn't been brushed in days, and the long arms wrapped around her boney knees could've used a little meat on them. A strong wind or light push and this kid was done for. To make it in this world a person needed a little backbone, and this gal had as much as a plastic bag in a rain storm.

"Waiting for my mom," she said.

Well, no kid would be hanging out in the back of his place for the fun of it. "What's your name?"

Then the gal did something that changed his opinion. She stood and unfolded her gangly limbs, brushed the dirt off her palms on the back of her shorts, and held out her hand for an introduction. "My name is Frankie. Frankie Johnson. You must be Mr. Pitt."

Mike smiled. No one had called him Mr. Pitt in years. He took her hand. "That's right, but you can call me Mike."

Frankie's mouth widened, showing a nice size gap between her front teeth.

"How old are you?"

"Thirteen. I'll be turning fourteen in a few weeks."

Mike nodded. Now that she stood up, he could see she was much taller than he'd first realized. He wouldn't have put her at thirteen. Still too thin. But there was a depth in her eyes that hinted at

maturity beyond her years. With such nondescript hair and blah col-
oring, he would've expected brown eyes, but they were green—
moss green. And there was an intelligence there that had him
guessing she was sizing him up as much as he was her right now.

"Who's your momma?" For some reason he couldn't place her
with any of his girls. Most of the women in this line of work bred
the same type of kid—desperate, lonely, and hopeless. But not this
one. Some woman had got herself a gem, because this one
shrugged off desperation like the sun shrugged off the night.

"Stella."

She said the name, and his heart sank. He had good women working for him. He didn't take the losers or users. Most were okay moms,
some were darn right good, but Stella . . . Stella was a problem.

But Stella knew how to dance. Knew how to work a crowd.
Stella was good for business, and right now he needed all the "good
for business" he could get.

"It's too early for your mom to be working. She doesn't get on
until late."

Frankie shrugged, her one shoulder reminding him of a chicken
wing. "She didn't come home last night. Sometimes I know she's
too tired to drive home and so she stays here. I thought maybe she
was sleeping in the back."

Mike took another long pull on his cigarette to give him a moment. He knew that Stella sometimes slept in the back room, but it
was never because she was too tired. But she wasn't there now, and
her whereabouts were anyone's guess.

"You lookin' for her tips?" Mike knew the routine. Living hand
to mouth was never pretty.

Frankie looked down at her feet. Her toes were dark with dirt,
her flip-flops two sizes too big. "I just thought maybe . . . maybe
she'd have a couple dollars on her, and I could go down and get
some milk from the store."

Mike nodded, understanding things all too well. He stubbed out
his smoke on the bottom of his shoe and threw the butt into the
dumpster. "Let me ask you, Frankie, are you a good girl? You responsible?"

Frankie looked up at him, her green eyes wide in her plain face.
She nodded.

"I got her paycheck. How about you and I work out a deal? I'll tell Stella I'm giving her check to you, and she can keep the tips, but you gotta promise to use it on rent, food, and things you need."

She nodded.

"You also gotta promise to stay in school. If I hear of you, even for one day, ditching and hanging out at the park or that shopping dump they call a mall, our deal is off. I'll give you my number, and you'll have to check in at least once a week. Got that?"

She nodded again, and he could tell she understood exactly what he was saying and all the things he wasn't.

"I understand, Mr. Pitt. I'll take care of her. I have since . . . forever."

The cold lump of coal he had instead of a heart cracked a little. Then without overthinking things, he threw the pack of cigarettes in the dumpster after the butt. "I bet you have."

What had he been thinking? Just been feeling sorry for himself, that was all. He'd been in worse financial places before and pulled through. What was one more lost soul? And not like he'd have to do it alone. It wasn't as if that Avery boy had a full-time job, or anything. The Pitt had never been about him. Not really. He'd forgotten for a moment the most important life lesson—when you quit putting yourself first, all your other priorities have a tendency to line up.

"Come on, kid. Her check is inside."

Then Frankie smiled that thirteen-year-old smile at him, and he promised himself he'd never forget again.

Chapter 8

Wet and cold was about the only thing Jett could say about the beer in his mug, but with the humidity clinging to around ninety percent, and not a cloud in the sky, that was the only thing a beer needed to be considered good. It was late afternoon, evening really, and yet the sun lazed in the sky like an old arthritic dog on the front porch.

He ran his hand through his damp hair, grateful that O'Brian's Bar & Grill had great AC and served beer in frosted mugs. He was supposed to be across the street at city hall, sitting in on the town council meeting. He was supposed to be helping his community, making good use of the family money, getting his political career on track, but to do that he had to at least attend one of the meetings.

Grove Oaks was a small town—quiet, simple. He preferred this town over the bigger, more affluent one his parents had moved to when he'd been in high school. Here in Grove Oaks there was a sense of connection, of family. And sure, he might care about the people here in Grove Oaks, but that didn't mean he wanted to hear about how Mr. Sanchez's dog barked all night long, keeping Mrs. Crabfield up. Or how the four-way stop sign had been vandalized, and Mrs. Bates was sure the Johnsons or Rodríguezes were to blame. But that was high-minded philosophy compared to the most classic and enduring complaint—The Pitt and how its mere presence stained such an upstanding and God-fearing municipality. Of course, no one wanted to mention how The Pitt seemed to be doing quite well just over the county line from this upstanding and God-fearing town.

The thought of spending a perfectly good afternoon cooped up in a cramped room with only an ancient ceiling fan squeaking under protest had been too much. So, instead of doing his duty, he'd spent the better part of the afternoon cooped up with the much more esteemed group of daytime drinkers and hardened bar flies. One had to pick one's poison.

Jett glanced out the window and watched the steady stream of Ford trucks and Dodge Rams go up and down Main Street. He was just about to take another swig of beer when he stilled mid-motion, then just as carefully, and just as deliberately, lowered the mug, turned and focused on the TV playing ESPN in the corner.

Nope. He shook his head. No, he was not going to get involved. He was going to play like he hadn't watched a 1970 Chevy truck, once cherry-red, now long faded into dull orange, roll through a solid red light, almost taking Mrs. Smith and her golf cart out in the process. He was going to forget that he knew that truck. Pretend he hadn't jump-started it, hadn't worked on it alongside Cole, and hadn't pulled the POS out of a ditch once. And he would conveniently not remember he had any idea who was behind the wheel because he knew what admitting to all that meant—another Nikki-sized mess to clean up.

A muscle in his shoulder started to tighten. He rubbed his neck. Probably stress from the job. Of course, drinking fine wine and shaking hands with politicians had never stressed him out before, but there was always a first. Regardless, whatever was going on outside was not his problem. Not his concern.

Out of the corner of his eye a blue-and-red light flashed—a police car? Jett watched a white and black car pull over the 1970 Chevy. The officer walked to the truck, leaned over the driver-side window, and then with a gesture indicated for Nikki to step out of the vehicle.

Jett tried to identify the officer. Was it Bert? Bert was a total dick. He hoped it was Smith. Smith he could deal with. Jett caught himself. This was not his mess to deal with. He snapped his focus forward. The twitch from his shoulder started to travel upward.

Why did golf have to be on ESPN? Anything else would've kept his attention. He was sure geriatric shuffleboard was mesmerizing.

Someone was yelling.

Of course, there was yelling. Why wouldn't there be yelling? He ignored the muscle in his cheek that started to convulse, and traced the condensation pattern the beer mug had left instead.

"Geez, Jett, what's wrong with your eye?" Jenny's expression was somewhere between concern and horror as she brought him another beer.

Jett liked Jenny. She was a bit on the plump side, but it worked for her. Her face was round and soft and made almost pretty with kind eyes. She worked the second shift so her husband could stay home with their six-month-old, but right now he didn't want to talk to her. Didn't want her concern. Or her horror. Just wanted her to go away. He grabbed the beer before she could set it on the table. "Nothing."

"No, something is wrong." She bent closer to examine his face. "It's all twitchy."

He slapped a hand over his eye. "Perfectly fine, Jenny."

She snorted, then her brow furrowed as she leaned closer to peer out the window. Jett couldn't blame her. It was hard not to watch a train-wreck in progress.

Another well-modulated snort. "Well, it seems like a waste of time, really."

"Exactly." Jett sighed. Finally someone who understood. "A complete waste of time."

Jenny's eyebrows arched, disappearing under her uneven schoolgirl bangs.

Finding a sympathetic ear, Jett unloaded. "I know. It's crazy. I never remember signing up for the Logan babysitting job. Not my problem, right?"

"Oh." She shrugged a shoulder, causing her bra strap to slip from underneath her dark tank top. "I meant, it's a waste for you to just sit here. Seems to me it would take a heck of a lot longer to bail Nikki out when you're called down to the police station."

The twitch in his eye sped up double time.

"Might be easier to talk to Smith now. Save you the trouble and a couple of bucks later."

He gave Jenny a look, then cursed. He downed his beer in thirty seconds, and then just so there'd be no misunderstanding where he stood on the matter, cursed long and loud again. He threw a few bills on the table, grabbed his hat, and made for the door.

Christ. Of course, Nikki would call him. Or more than likely, Suzy from the police station—to post bail. Nikki hadn't been the only Logan he'd gone and pulled out of a holding cell. Cole had had a rough couple of years. That seemed to be the protocol. Arrest a Logan, call an Avery.

The air blew hard and humid as soon as he stepped outside. He barely had time to put on his sunglasses before he watched Nikki being turned, handcuffed, then bent over the squad car as Deputy Smith started to frisk her.

Jett couldn't help himself. He smiled. The view was almost worth getting up from the table.

It was a standard frisk. Sure, it was a little hard to keep one's hands off the best looking cut-off jean shorts Jett had ever seen, but Deputy Smith was nothing if not a professional.

Jett had every intention of going over and talking to Deputy Smith, using the Avery charm, possibly his father's influence, to make the whole thing go away. Except, when he got an eyeful of Nikki leaning over the hood of the police car, short shorts riding really high, sexy tan legs slightly spread and propped up high on those damn ugly boots, he got a whole other idea.

Deputy Smith was happily married, or at least that's what he told Jett and the guys every Tuesday poker night. Smith was a good cop, but a lousy card player. He owed Jett more than his paycheck, which Jett had never had the heart to call him on.

Until now.

Smith, hearing Jett coming up from behind him, turned. Jett placed his finger to his lips, indicating silence. Then with palms pressed in a prayer gesture and a mouthed "please," he practically begged Smith to step aside.

Smith threw him a "you're crazy" look and shook his head.

But to Jett the answer *No* was simply a jumping off point for negotiation. He mouthed, "You owe me," and then put another please on top, just to seal the deal. It never hurt to be polite when bribing authorities.

Jett could see the options warring in Smith's eyes. What was it gonna be? Honorable or debt-free? Jett flashed his most charming smile, and that's when he knew he had Smith. Because really, who could say no to an Avery?

Smith stepped aside and mouthed that this made them even.

Fine with Jett. He had money, but opportunities to rile Nikki only came along as often as a politician with an honest heart.

Jett took Smith's place behind Nikki. One hand he placed on her neck, the other on the small of her back. With his boots he kicked her feet wider apart.

"Spread 'em," Jett said, in a gruff voice. Luckily, Smith's a-pack-a-day-voice was easy to mimic.

"What the hell, Smith?" Nikki balked at the rough treatment. "Are you not getting laid often enough? It's only a few unpaid parking tickets. Not like I'm swindling blue-haired ladies out of their social security checks or anything."

Jett bit the inside of his cheek, a bit annoyed. Nikki was nothing if not ballsy, but it would go a long way to making him happy if she was just a little more scared than she let on.

"You owe the state a lot of money. Not sure a Logan like you is good for it."

"Screw you, Smith."

This was where Jett should turn Nikki around. If he were really Cole's friend, he would let her in on his little joke. If he were really over Nikki, then he'd let her punch him on the arm, take her guff, then deposit her safely on Cole's front doorstep. But it hadn't been that long ago when Jett had been the one on her front doorstep, Nikki crying in his arms, him begging her to give them a chance. And damn it if there wasn't a small part of him that was still irritated she could walk away so easily. A part of him that wanted to watch her sweat. Or heaven forbid, beg just a little? What was it about Nikki that brought out the worst in him?

"Now that's a thought." He whispered the words as a rough caress across the spot on her neck, the one he knew from experience drove her crazy. "One quick trip to the backseat of my squad car, and this whole thing could go away."

Jett glanced back toward Smith, who'd turned beet red and was shaking his head. If Jett felt a twinge of guilt, he ignored it. He'd make it up to Smith later.

Jett watched as Nikki's skin tightened with chills, and he felt her move against him as her breath came in and out with an audible hiss.

He remembered another time she'd breathed hot and heavy against him. Another time when she would've welcomed his kiss. And as hard as he tried, maybe he wasn't as over her as he'd like, since he was hovering behind her, and soliciting sexual favors from his best friend's little sister.

Her body trembled slightly beneath his hands. Was she frightened? Nikki, scared? Nah. But maybe it was time to let her go. He was sure he'd crossed a line somewhere. Funny how he didn't feel the least bit guilty. 'Course, it was hard keeping in touch with his conscience when his body was remembering how it felt to have Nikki under him.

Still he needed to let her go. And he would . . . just as soon as he was done frisking her. One more hand pat on her backside, and then a slow slide down her outer thigh and that was it. Except his hand slipped . . . sorta, and traveled even slower on the way up, but this time on the soft inside of her leg.

She stiffened. The muscles in her back flexing.

He swallowed a groan, no use letting her know how uncomfortable he'd suddenly become. Judging from his body's reaction, he'd possibly gone a bit too far. He loosened his hold on her, ready to step back and apologize. Or at least let her vent her anger at him.

In retrospect, he should've seen it coming. He knew Nikki better than to underestimate her.

Her head reared up and connected with his face. A sharp poker of fire shot up his nose. His hands went to his face as he stepped back, hunching over the pain. Bright flashes of red and white exploded behind his closed eyes, and for a second he thought he'd black out.

"Oh my God, Jett?" Nikki screamed.

He dropped to the ground.

"What the hell, Jett?" Her voice sounded far away, and yet she was shrieking right next to his ear.

Maybe if he got his head between his knees he wouldn't throw up.

"Oh my God, are you okay? What the hell were you thinking?"

Smith crouched down beside him, hand resting on his back in a show of support. "You okay, bro?"

"She brotf my fuky nosse."

"What? What did he say, Smith?"

Jett stood. The world spun. "I saith youvf froke my fuky NOSE."

Yelling hurt, but damn, she'd been here less than twenty-four hours and already his face was regretting it.

Very carefully he pulled his shirt over his head and used the cloth to staunch the blood dripping down his lip. "Damn Nik, I was just playin'."

"Some stupid joke. And I don't feel bad. I don't." Though she looked like she did. "You shouldn't scare me like that."

"You were hardly scared," he shot back. "Not with that head butt in your arsenal." Jett groaned, then stopped. The sound seemed to vibrate through his nasal cavity. What had he been thinking? Nothing about the Logans was easy. "Just uncuff her, Smith. Let her get back into the truck and get the hell out of here."

Smith spun a set of handcuff keys around one finger, looking a bit too smug for an officer who'd just taken a bribe. "That's the thing. I can't let her drive back home. That's why she got pulled over in the first place."

Jett looked over at Nikki.

She looked down at the ground and rubbed the toes of her boots together. "I can't drive stick. I didn't want to stop for the light. I was afraid I wouldn't get Old Bertha started again."

Jett closed his eyes and groaned. "Fine. Take my car and I'll follow you home."

Nikki's mouth twitched from side to side. "I let my auto insurance expire."

There went Jett's eye again. "Cole's insurance on the truck should cover you."

"And . . . " At least she had the sense to look ashamed. "My license got suspended."

Both he and Smith stared at her. Really, what was there to say?

"Campus parking was a real bear."

What a freaking mess. What the hell was wrong with him? He'd been sitting in a comfortable air-conditioned bar, sipping an ice-cold beer and now . . . He grabbed the keys from Smith. He uncuffed her one handed, the other still trying to stop his nosebleed. "Let's go." He threw the keys back to Smith and stalked to the truck. "I'm driving you home."

"I can call Cole," she panted, running to keep up with him. "Or better yet, I'll walk. I haven't gotten around to telling Cole about the parking tickets."

He didn't want a discussion. It was too much effort. "Get in the truck."

For once she listened to him and got into the passenger seat. If only everything with Nikki could be as easy.

Jett started the truck and pointed the AC vents in his direction. When nothing but tepid air blew, he turned toward Nikki. "You kidding me?"

She shook her head, her cat-like eyes wide, contrasting with the dark mass of hair stuck to her cheeks.

He must really look bad for her to still be feeling guilty. He lowered his shirt and checked himself in the rearview mirror. *Unfreaking-believable.*

He took his ruined shirt and threw it in Nikki's lap. "You owe me two hundred dollars. That shirt was brand new."

She picked up the blood-stained rag with two fingers and tossed it behind the seats. "Sorry, I don't reimburse for stupid. Only you would spend an entire month's worth of groceries on a single shirt."

"I guess that means you won't be reimbursing me for the doctor bill, either?"

Nikki didn't laugh, but he caught that turquoise twinkle in her eye. "Oh, for Pete's sake, you are such a baby. You're still a good-looking man. Nothing a little ice and a good night's sleep won't fix."

He threw her a look. Why was it with Nikki he could never leave well enough alone? His heart raced, eye twitched, nose throbbed, his whole life went to utter crap, and yet, here he was driving her back home to Cole. "Do you realize the only time I've ever gotten into a fistfight has been over a Logan? Both times I've gotten my nose broken have been because of you."

"I do like to keep things interesting."

"You like to keep things crazy."

"Crazy is a family trait." She leaned closer to him and flashed one of her more stellar smiles. "Ah, come on, Jett, it's funny. Or at least it will be in a year or two. And if it helps any, I think this break will fix the bump—you know, from before."

He shot her a glance. "It doesn't."

The sooner Nikki was dropped off at Cole's doorstep, the sooner he could relinquish any and all responsibility. What pissed him off even more was why he was even bothering. Hadn't he said he was done cleaning up the mess that was her life? And yet, here he was, coming to her rescue like some freaking knight with a lance.

"Look." Her hand went up to fiddle with the necklace she always wore. For some reason that gesture rubbed him the wrong way. Maybe because the charm was the cheapest of diamonds. Maybe because it was her tell when she was scared. And maybe because she seemed to be doing that gesture around him a lot lately. "I'm sorry."

They were driving along the dirt road, the high whining of the truck making the journey even slower. He rolled down the window to try and catch a bit of breeze. Even without his shirt, he was sweating way more than a man of his age should. "Sorry about the nose? Great. Your apology's noted."

"No, you totally deserved to get your nose broken. Well, at least this time you did." She smiled, then fidgeted in her seat, plucked her shirt out and blew down the front. After that, Jett stopped watching. Like placing a steak dinner just out of reach of a starving man—pure torture.

"I'm a . . . I'm sorry about leaving."

He shot her a look.

She bit her lip. Her gaze fluttered all over the cab, never resting on any one spot, especially not on him.

"Not even a goodbye, Nik. Not even a damn phone call. I thought something terrible had happened to you."

She buried her head in her hands, then raked her fingers through her damp hair. "I know, Jett, and I'm sorry about that most of all. I should've called at least. You deserved better than that."

He sighed. He still didn't get it. She felt bad, but so what? What kind of person would just up and leave after what they'd shared? "What happened, Nik? What changed from the afternoon when you said you'd be willing to give us a try, to the next day when you left? What changed?"

How many times had he kicked himself for leaving her that day? He should've insisted she come back to his house. He'd known she was scared. He'd known she was terrified of losing someone else she loved.

Nikki turned, her full attention focused on him. Her breath came in short gasps. If panic was a scent, then she wore it like perfume. She swallowed a few times. Her hands fluttered around her throat as if she was having trouble breathing.

In years past, Jett might've felt sorry for her. Might've remembered all the crap she'd been through, and how hard it had been growing up without any parents. In years past, he would've given a flying rat's ass. But now, today, he just wanted some answers.

"Jett, don't you know? Don't you understand? I saved you. This . . . " she made a gesture toward herself. "This is a mess. This is not what you want on your arm during a Senate ball. This is not what will help you. This," she pointed to herself again, "will only make your life miserable."

Her confession turned his stomach. He knew everything Nikki had just said was exactly what she believed. But he'd been down this road before. He'd comforted Nikki, had gotten involved, and then had gotten his heart broken as she ran away. He was no match for her self-hate.

He meant what he'd said earlier. He was too old for this crap. Maybe it was time to let Nikki go. So instead of doing what his heart told him, for once he listened to his head. He stared straight ahead, watching the truck eat up the dirt road. "So when are you leaving?"

There was silence, but he couldn't afford to look at her. So her feelings were hurt. Welcome to his world.

"I'm here for a while."

"What's a while?"

"I have a debt to pay. So until I'm even. A while."

"A debt or a bet?" He couldn't resist mentioning her pool-hustling days. There'd been more than a few times Nikki had called asking him to help her out of situations that had gotten a little crazy.

"I'm not hustling pool anymore, Jett. I made a promise to Mike."

"Mike? As in Mike Pitt?"

She nodded.

The throb in his nose pulsed a little harder. At least the twitch in his eye had gone away. "So you're telling me you've made a promise to the owner of the town's one and only strip club to stop hustlin' pool when your brother and I have begged you repeatedly, only to be ignored?"

At least she had the decency to look abashed. "It's different."

"How's it different?"

"It just is. God, Jett, what do you want from me?" Her voice broke and vulnerability flashed across her face. Then she shook her head, and the moment was gone. "A lifetime commitment to stay in this town?"

That would've been nice, but he'd have scooped his tongue out with a spoon before admitting as much.

"I'm here. I'm trying to set things straight. I've made some mistakes that I regret. But I've also made some promises I can't break."

What about the promises she'd made to him? Was he the mistake she regretted? He'd rather get his nose broken a third time before asking those questions.

Nikki fiddled with her gold chain again. There'd been a time when he thought about surprising her with a new necklace. Something special. Something that would've made her believe she was worth it.

"I burned a lot of bridges before I left." Nikki paused as if trying hard to find the words. "And if there's a chance of getting my life back together, I'm gonna need every friend I can get."

If Jett was the religious type, he would've asked God what past sin he'd committed to get pulled back into Nikki Logan's orbit. He shook his head. No. Nope, he would not . . . he caught sight of the liquid greenish-blue of her eyes and the way the sprinkle of freckles popped off her now pale face. He hung his head. Who was he kidding? He'd never been able to say no to Nikki. For better or worse, he was addicted.

He pulled the truck over with a sharp yank to the wheel. He might be willing to help Nikki out, but it didn't mean he had to be nice about it. "Get out!"

"What?"

"Get out of the truck," he said, before walking around to the front. In his mood, he'd pull her out by the arm if need be. It wasn't necessary; she met him head on.

They stood toe to toe. Jett liked petite women—the ones who were blonde and fit perfectly under the embrace of his arm. Nikki, of course, was tall and it took only a slight bow of his head to look her in the eye.

Nikki tilted her chin up. Turquoise eyes snapping. If there'd been a moment when Nikki was vulnerable, it had long passed. "So what?" She arched her brows. "It's payback time. Is that it? Your turn to leave me here in the middle of nowhere?"

And there it was. Under that foul mouth and rather large shoulder-chip was the one thing Nikki feared the most—being alone.

He laughed. Really? She'd said that to him? "In your whole life, Nik, have I ever left you? Ever? No, Nik, let's get one thing straight. You're the one who leaves. And I'm the one that stays and cleans up the messes."

Her silent gaze met his, but he saw the hurt clear enough. He took a deep breath, pissed off at himself for still being here. For still trying.

"But I'm your friend. And as my first official friend duty, I'm gonna do you a favor and teach you how to drive a stick. So get in the driver side, Texas, before I wise up and change my mind."

By the time they had pulled up to Cole's house, Jett was glad Nikki's driving had smoothed out to passable—he'd almost started to feel sick. Jett got out and waited for Nikki. They climbed the front steps to where Cole was sitting on his porch swing, his new baby bundled and propped up against his shoulder.

Cole's gaze went from Jett to Nikki, then back to Jett. He cocked an eyebrow north.

Jett was sure he looked a mess. And really, there was only one explanation. "What can I say? One afternoon in the presence of your sister, and she's already asked for the shirt off my back."

Nikki smiled up at him, her hands slipping into her back pockets. She would be mortified to realize how that stance made her breasts pop out. Or maybe she knew, and that was the whole point. "Oh Jett, you love us. We bring excitement to your otherwise privileged whitebread world."

"You say excitement. I say crazy."

"You, Jett Avery, looovve crazy." With that, she turned and strutted down the well-worn path from Cole's house back to Nikki's childhood home.

"No! No, I don't," he shouted to her retreating back. "I hate crazy."

He turned toward Cole, looking for support.

"Bro, you're half naked, blood smeared across your lip, hair sticking straight up. I'd say you fell into some crazy."

Jett walked up and sagged into the porch swing next to Cole, but then made himself drop his head into his hands because he couldn't stop watching a pair of jean shorts—denim never looked so good—sashay their way back home.

He stifled a groan, not sure which got to him more—Nikki or the thought of having to ask Cole for a ride back to his car.

"Don't be causing any trouble," Cole grumbled from beside him.

"What? Me?" Jett lifted his head. "I'm the innocent bystander here. In case you didn't pick up the subtle nuances, she's the one who head-butted me."

"I'm sure you deserved it. Deserved it the first time also. I don't want you and Nikki sniffin' around each other. The first time cost me over two years of her life."

"Oh yeah, real easy to blame all that on me," he said, gently palpating his nose, remembering how long it had taken to heal the first time. Cole had done that honor after finding Nikki at his house, clothed in nothing more than his shirt and his scent. "You had nothing to do with it, right?"

Cole nodded. "Fine, but all I'm saying is that she doesn't need to be distracted right now. I want her to stay around this time."

The baby whined, and Cole's booted foot pushed off the floor, getting the swing in motion again. "Nikki needs to be home. She needs to be surrounded by people who love her. I don't want her running off again."

Jett looked down from the slight hill, carpeted with wild grass and yellow dandelions, separating Cole's old house from his new one. Cole had somehow managed to bridge the distance from drunken white trash to respectable husband and father.

Nikki, on the other hand, didn't have a chance.

Cole saw what he wanted to see—his baby sister who'd lost her way, but would find it if given some tough love and direction. He didn't see the chip Nikki wore on her shoulder like some kind of freaking medal. But Jett knew, and he knew Nikki.

She'd been here a total of two days, and the whole time he'd been waiting for her to run away. The way his heart slammed into his chest at the words "I'm staying" was humbling.

He'd been a fool the last time. He knew that now. He'd been hung over, bleeding on his kitchen floor from a broken nose, and yet, he'd still made out the panic in Nikki's eyes. But he'd pushed anyway, hoping he'd read the signs wrong. Hoping she was ready. He'd told her, right then and there, at the worst possible time, that he loved her. He could still remember her expression—eyes widened with fear, face leached of all color.

And how she had rubbed her throat as if she couldn't breathe and bitten her lips red—his only warning she'd be gone by morning.

He'd been fixing Nikki's messes and watching her run away her whole life. But Cole's comment brought up a good point. He knew what it took to her get to run. That was easy. The question he should be asking was, Did he have what it took to get her to stay?

Chapter 9

What the hell had that been about? Nikki could still feel the effect of Jett's gaze, boring into her back as she'd walked away. No wonder she was pissed. Jett and she rarely argued. Well, they hadn't before they'd slept together, but after that things changed. Jett had changed. She guessed she couldn't blame him. The whole thing had gotten way more complicated than she would've liked, but that didn't change the fact she had no idea what to do about it. Hadn't two years ago, didn't now.

It wasn't until Nikki had a cold shower, unpacked her stuff, and then made her way into the land of Formica countertops to watch the freezer-burned pizza squares rotate on the microwave turntable that she remembered why Jett had been her best friend for most of her life.

He made her forget. Or at the very least made her not remember in vivid Technicolor the images her mind loved to throw across the movie screen in her head.

How could she have forgotten being with Jett made the tomb of this house less strained? When she'd left for two years, being without Jett hadn't been so bad. There had always been distractions—coming and goings of roommates, music from some party, the low hum of the television. But now, as she watched the neon numbers count down and her dinner cook behind a mesh screen, the suffocating stillness came back to her louder than any rock concert.

The quiet here had a different rhythm than anyplace else. It was in the occasional clink of the icemaker, the whirl of a ceiling fan, the clunk of the old dishwasher. It was how the whole house seemed laced with trepidation as if everything was holding its breath—waiting for death.

The death-like silence was in the walls. All the tears she'd wanted to cry had seeped into the two-by-twos and chicken wire, making the paint bubble and fade, and cracks in the plaster widen and spider out from the corners. Making the ceiling grow low and heavy, as if waiting to close the casket lid.

Or maybe the death-silence had been because of the nights. They'd been the hardest. During the day she went to school, saw people, pretended to be alive. But when the sun set and darkness rolled in, things were different. Cole would leave for the graveyard shift. The sound of the door slamming behind him would echo like the dull clang of a prison gate. Nikki would watch out the window as he pulled away, the red of his rear taillights swallowed by an ocean of black. It didn't take much to believe she was the only one around for miles—maybe in the world.

During those years she'd tried to be a good daughter. Had never left her mother alone. No matter how much she wanted to run, she stayed.

All except that last night.

Cole had left for work, and her mother had spiked a fever Nikki couldn't bring down. After a while, she stopped trying. Her mother's hands had been so dry and hot that Nikki wrapped cool wet washcloths around them to soothe her feverish skin. Earlier the hospice nurse had come and gone, leaving only a sad look and a brown bottle of liquid morphine.

Nikki would never forget the nurse's instructions, not even if she lived to be hundred. *One dropper, once an hour.* Very simple, couldn't mess it up. And Nikki watched, counted the minutes even, and at seven after the hour she would go in and slip a dropper of liquid, one that slowed heartbeats and quieted breathing, between her mother's cracked lips.

Nikki had told herself it was for the fever, for the pain, to help her mother go peacefully in her sleep.

But really—it was for the sound. The hospice nurse had told Nikki what to expect, but nothing could have prepared her. The nurse had called it the death rattle. Nikki called it sucking mud through a straw underwater. Each breath a fight for life—a fight for air to find its way past the fluid slowly filling up her mother's lungs. With each of her mom's exhales, Nikki waited and held her own. And then waited again for her mom's next—or would it be her last?—labored breath.

All the days spent caring for her mother, Nikki had railed against the sheer stillness of the house. The place where time painfully crept forward and the hours were marked by different colored pills in brown, child-proof bottles.

But that last night had been different. That was the night she'd killed her mother.

As her mother's labored breath panted on, each breath a reminder of the coming end, Nikki would've given any price to bring back the quiet.

In the end she'd paid. And the price had been high.

She'd poured the entire contents of the morphine bottle down her mother's throat, then turned and ran into the yard.

In bare feet and cut-off sweats, she ran. Except, in the middle of the country, there was no place to go. There was just open land, black sky, and four-legged animals, not all of which were domesticated. She didn't even remember making her way to the barn, but in the end that was the only place she had left to go.

Tires crunched on the gravel drive outside the house, snapping her back to the present. She took a few ragged breaths to clear her head and rushed to the front door, desperate for the distraction. Even before she'd left town two years ago, the Logans rarely got visitors. Now only the postman ever had the need to pull up to the house. Nikki didn't care. It could be an ex-con straight from the penitentiary, and she'd still invite him in for dinner and a cozy chat.

Nikki opened the door and stood stock still. There in the middle of her gravel drive was a shiny, cherry-red Dodge Ram. Decked out with custom chrome wheels and an extended bed, the truck all but screamed confidence and entitlement. Of course, the long-legged, white Stetson, custom shirt-wearing cowboy leaning against the driver-side door only added to the image.

A smile flirted around her lips. Only an Avery could wear a five-hundred-dollar shirt as easy as another man would wear a ten-dollar one. And there'd only ever been one Avery who'd graced her doorstep.

There were a few rushed heartbeats of weakness, when all Nikki wanted to do was run across the porch and throw herself into Jett's embrace. Instead, she looped her arms around the porch post and held tight.

Jett didn't seem to have the same trouble. One designer-booted foot was propped on top of the other, arms folded over his chest. With a small tilt of his head, he raised his gaze, and let his smile spread like sweet honey over a hot biscuit.

Nikki didn't like the sudden rush of heat that prickled her skin. She hugged the post tighter, hoping to pull off the same nonchalant look, but really needing the support for her weak knees.

Jett shook his head knowingly as if he saw her every weakness. "Katie sent me over to check and make sure you had dinner. She didn't think you'd had time to go to the store yet."

She lifted one shoulder up, but had to swallow first to find her voice. "I'm fine. Enjoying the quiet evening, actually."

She had pulled off her tone perfectly, not too needy, very casual.

With one finger he pushed on the brim of his hat. His molasses eyes crinkled at the corners. "Having a hard night?"

Her stomach sucked in at those two words. It was hard to BS someone who knew you so well.

Jett took pity on her. He always did. "So I told Katie that I'd do one better and take you out to dinner."

"It's Saturday night. I'm surprised you don't already have a date." Desperate she might be, but she'd never tag along with him and whoever his flavor of the week was.

He shrugged. "She got sick."

So there was a God. "Sorry to hear that."

"Oh, I'm sure you are," he said.

Her breath quickened into the rhythm of want, and the song in her heart betrayed every vow she'd made to herself. The thought of turning around and spending the rest of the night in the house was too painful. *If she could forget just for one night . . .*

Nikki had always gone easy on Cole during those dark years when alcohol had gotten the better of him. She, better than most, understood the need for a crutch. Drinking had been Cole's, and Jett was hers. How many times had she run to Jett to make her feel better?

She knew that didn't make her a good person, but there it was, plain as day.

Coming home wasn't supposed to be this hard, and having dinner was just a small Jett-fix to help ease her into being back. She could be cautious. Could have things both ways—be with him, but just remain friends. She needed to set boundaries. "Only dinner?"

Jett laughed—a low rumble in his chest. "That's right, Nik, just two old friends having dinner. Nothing worth getting excited about."

She didn't trust him for a minute. Jett had sex appeal that could make a smart woman lose her higher powers of reasoning. She had to keep her wits about her. She had to remember the consequences of getting involved with an Avery. Jett wasn't known for his long-term relationships, and Logans weren't known for being easy to love.

"A girl doesn't like to be second choice."

"Oh well, then." He nodded, turned, and opened up the car door. "See you around."

Jett started the engine and actually began pulling out of the driveway.

"Wait!" she yelled, annoyed as hell that she had to run after him.

Jett stopped and looked back, a mock "yes, dear" question on his face. "I'm sorry, did you say something?"

Nikki sighed. "Can you wait a minute?"

"I'll give you five."

She turned and completely ruined her nonchalant attitude by sprinting up the stairs and into the house. Her clothes were all over. She hadn't really unpacked, just spread out. She grabbed a clean shirt, red with a low V-neck. Threw on some make-up, heavy on the eyes, light on the lips. After a tease and a spray for her hair, she was ready. She searched for her combat boots, and then remembered she'd left them outside, too covered in mud and horse offerings to do her any good. Other than a pair of sneakers and a few high heels, Nikki's shoe collection was the bare minimum. Then she remembered.

She headed down the hall to her old bedroom. She didn't look at the hand-stitched quilt that was spread out over her bed, or the oak vanity that her father had made her when she was just a baby. She didn't need to; she knew it was all there.

Instead, she dived into the back of her closet, found what she needed, and then sprinted toward the front door.

"Nice boots," Jett said as she slid into the truck. His earlier mock surprise was replaced by genuine pleasure.

Nikki didn't glance down at the tan leather boots with lace embroidery—the ones that Jett had off-handedly given her upon graduation. "One more word and I'll put on my other boots, horse smell and all."

The corner of his mouth lifted. "Careful, Nik, you might find there are some things you actually like about Texas."

Nikki rummaged around until she found Jett's pack of gum and popped a piece in her mouth. "Never gonna happen."

Chapter 10

Okay, so there were some things about Texas that Nikki did miss. Well, at least one thing. Texas prime rib. And no one in Texas made prime rib like The Smoke House.

The Smoke House was the closest thing the town had to a monument. A reminder of what Texas life was all about. With the smell of charcoal and sawdust, the smoky atmosphere still persisted, even though smoking indoors had been banned for years. The dance floor was intimate and dark, and the local four-piece band played all the country favorites.

Nikki ate her whole dinner, finished off Jett's baked potato, and only then felt the need to start slowing. She pushed her plate back, and rested her head against the back of the vinyl seat, inching her waistband underneath her belly. "As God is my witness . . . I'll never be hungry again."

Jett had long since leaned back and seemed to enjoy watching Nikki polish off both dinners. He took a sip from the beer he nursed. "Okay, Scarlett, that reference was too easy, it's actually an insult to my intelligence."

It was a shame he was so cute. That boyish smile got him into a lot of trouble. And had gotten him out of most of it.

She stretched a bit, loving the feel of food in her belly and a beer in her blood. "I'm sorry. I didn't realize we were playing."

His boyish smile widened distracting her from the slight bruising under each eye, courtesy of his broken nose. "We're always playing, Nik. But because I'm a gentleman, I'll let you go again."

Nikki made a *tsk* sound, but she closed her eyes to think of a movie line that would stump him. They both shared a passion for all things cinema. Television had been her babysitter growing up. And he had lived at the drive-ins as a way to get girls alone in his truck.

"Okay, I got one." Nikki shook her hair around her face, channeling her inner actress. "You're not too smart, are you?" she said, doing her best deep-throated, sexy voice. "I like that in a man."

His gaze seemed to linger on her mouth, and she watched him swallow hard. "Good impression—but child's play. Kathleen Turner, *Body Heat*. My turn." He paused, then got a twinkle in his eye that made Nikki nervous. "There are two kinds of women: high maintenance and low maintenance . . . .You're the worst kind. You're high maintenance, but you think you're low maintenance."

Nikki laughed. "Are you trying to tell me something?"

"Just a game, Texas."

"In that case, too easy. *When Harry Met Sally*." Nikki took a long sip of beer. "All right, here's one." Nikki placed her cool hands on her cheeks to keep from smiling and screwed her face up in anger. "No wire hangers. No wire hangers, EVER!" She pounded on the table at her last word.

Other patrons turned to look at who was making such a racket. Jett almost choked on his beer as one lady loudly shushed her. "Okay. *Mommie Dearest*. And I do have to say, it's a little scary how easily you slip into insane."

"Crazy keeps things interesting."

"Crazy is exhausting."

"And you know this from experience?"

Jett leaned forward. She watched the collar of his crisp white shirt pull down, revealing a strong, corded neck. His brown eyes snapped, and his mouth held just a hint of a smile. "I know this from spending my time with you."

Nikki didn't think she should take that as a compliment, so she turned herself in the booth to face the couples who were two-stepping across the dance floor. Soon an easy silence settled. That's how it was most times between Jett and her—easy. If it were always like this between them, then maybe she'd be willing to come home more often. But it was the other times, the complicated ones, that sent her screaming for the hills.

But now it was simple, and Nikki didn't even mind the soulful twang of the Johnny Cash song that the band played, or the obscenely large belt buckles the old cowboys wore. The waitress came with another round of beers and cleared their plates. There weren't places like this in the city. Or if there were, she hadn't found them. In her college town, every place catered to the younger crowd—loud music, thumping beat, anything to make hooking up at the end of the night seem like a good idea.

The Smoke House was different. On the dance floor the newly dating swayed right next to couples celebrating their twentieth anniversary. This place spoke of history, steadiness, of believing that time could stand still even if just for one night under the forgiving lights. Here a person could believe that love did exist, and not for just the lucky, but for everyone, even the broken and the scarred.

The thought made Nikki want to cry. She blinked and opened her eyes wide, hoping Jett wouldn't notice. She couldn't remember the last time she'd cried. There were times when she'd wanted the release, prayed for it even, but not here, not in public, and not in front of Jett.

A light brush on her hand had her looking down as Jett's finger encircled her own. She swallowed hard, not ready to look up.

"What's going on?" he asked.

Of course, Jett would notice. She threw him a quick smile meant to dazzle and shook her head. "Nothing."

He didn't buy it.

She shrugged. "I wasn't expecting to miss this place."

"Nothing wrong with missing home."

But there was. Nikki didn't miss home. She didn't *want* to miss home. "It took me by surprise, that's all."

"Welcome to my world."

Nikki shook her head. Whatever that meant. But she let their fingers remain touching, and then wondered why she hadn't pulled away yet.

"You still remember how?" he asked, with a nod of his head to the dance floor.

"It's like riding a bike, right?"

His lips twitched up. "Yeah, something like that."

He took her hand and led her to the center of the floor. Most of the sawdust had been brushed away, and the band played an old love song. Jett held her close, the way sweethearts and lovers do, with her hand tucked to his chest and his palm pressed low on her back. For a moment Nikki bristled, but just as quickly let go. With a good dinner and the buzz of alcohol still in her veins, Nikki relaxed. She didn't have anywhere to go. It had to be okay not to run, just for one night.

Her head rested against his shoulder, and her feet found a rhythm she'd known since Cole taught her to dance when she was ten years old. One song bled into another, and Jett didn't let her go. Even during the fast ones, he just held her and swayed to a beat that only lovers and fools heard. Nikki had to wonder which one described her.

Jett's fingers splayed even lower on her back. His thumb slipped under the edge of her shirt to touch right above the waist of her jeans. A secret chill ran up along her spine. Her heart caught on, did its own happy dance. And then, of course, there was the tingle. The one that made her blood run hot, and gave her the feeling of walking a tightrope with no net below.

Just for tonight. The morning is time enough to feel regret.

She shifted her body a bit closer, and in case that wasn't enough, lifted her head so he could read what was in her eyes. Her own desire was reflected back to her, and she wondered how she'd ever thought his eyes were brown. Even in the smoky light she could tell they were more coppery, reminding her of candy. Maybe it was the beer, maybe it was the night, or maybe all her old feelings for Jett had never really died.

Was she crazy? Here was a beautiful man, sexy, able to afford dinner, and if she read things right, more than willing to kiss her, and take her home. Nikki hated to admit it, but for all her worldliness she was still baffled by men. Before, when she'd been with Jett, she'd been young and naïve. She hadn't had much experience with boyfriends, hadn't known how to keep things from getting too complicated, too emotional. Maybe it had been the tequila she drank that night or maybe she didn't know how *not* to throw her entire heart into loving him. Either way, it wasn't a mistake she could bear to repeat.

This time could be different. She was young, unattached, nothing wrong with having a little fun. But caution flared up in her heart. The same feeling she had when a pool player shot under their skill or a mark was getting ready to run. The reality was, things were not that simple with Jett. There was too much history. Too much . . . of everything.

"Your mouth is pressed into a thin line. You're thinking too much."

Nikki sighed. "I'm not thinking enough. That's the problem."

"So you've missed Texas, you've missed home. You've missed me." He took her palm and brought the fleshy part of her thumb to his lips. "What's the problem with that?"

She couldn't think of one. And that in and of itself was a huge problem. Nikki extracted her hand and placed it in a fist over her stomach. "Give me a minute, will ya? Order another round, and I'll be right back."

Without waiting for an answer Nikki made her way to the Ladies'. She needed a quiet breath to still her heart and clear her thinking. Inside, she braced hands on the counter and studied her reflection. Serious blue eyes and flushed cheeks stared back at her. She was no longer a little girl, no longer the little sister who tagged after Cole and Jett. She could do this. She could have a fling with no strings attached. The whole town accused her of doing that anyway. Maybe it was time to reap the benefits of a bad reputation.

But even as she had the thought, she knew that just sex with Jett wasn't an option. Jett was her friend. Had told her he loved her once. She didn't believe that, not really, but whatever was between them was more than just a passing fling. Was she strong enough now to take the next step with Jett? She was a college graduate. Cole was a respected rancher. Maybe the Averys would accept her dating one of their own now?

She heard the bathroom door open and hurried into the closest stall. She'd only been in town for a few days. She wasn't ready to run the gamut of: Where have you been? What are you going to do now? And the one she sure didn't want to answer: What's up with you and Jett?

The click of boots on the floor and the thump of purses placed on the counter signaled that a group of women had invaded the small space.

"Oh my God, did you see her? The way she was throwing herself at him was pathetic. I mean, everyone knows he's just being nice," said a woman with a raspy voice.

There was a chorus of high-pitched laugher, followed by a few, *Oh, I know*s.

Nikki couldn't help having a small twinge of empathy for whatever girl had been caught in the crosshairs of this catty group. Small-town talk could be vicious and small-minded people even worse.

"He told me that he had to do a favor for his friend. That's why he had to cancel our date to the fundraiser tonight. But I know what really happened. He got roped into doing a pity-date as a favor to Cole. It's not like anyone in this town would really date her."

Now Nikki recognized the raspy voice that some men had described as sultry— Beth.

"Maybe not date, but the guys in town sure would sleep with her. I heard she screwed the entire football team," said another woman, whose voice was just one octave below painful.

"No way!"

"Yes, way. The way I heard, it happened right in the locker room. One after another." There was a rapid succession of finger snaps. "Just like that."

"What a slut," Beth said. "Like she'd ever have a chance with Jett."

There was a sound of running water and the crank of the paper towel handle. "Don't stress, Beth. You know all guys like to slum from time to time, but when they are ready to settle, the Logans of the world are never a consideration."

Nikki could only imagine the careless shrug and smug smile as the women assessed themselves in the mirror. There were a few more clicks of make-up compacts and lipstick tubes, and then only the low bass of the music in the otherwise quiet bathroom.

Nikki counted to ten to make sure she was alone before she

turned and lost the entire fifty bucks Jett had blown on dinner down the toilet.

Nikki composed herself in the bathroom mirror. Why she was even remotely surprised, she didn't know. Small town, small minds, same talk. But why she cared was the harder question. She'd had years to fireproof herself against this type of thing. It shouldn't hurt anymore, and it didn't. Not really. Maybe she could have believed that if she hadn't just lost her entire stomach contents in the bathroom toilet.

Nikki sighed, then washed her face. She rummaged through her purse and pulled out her travel toothbrush and lip gloss. She'd known coming home wouldn't be easy, but she was different now. An adult. Not some reeling teenager with the taste of wildness in her blood. She pushed her long, black bangs back behind her ear and took a deep breath. She couldn't afford to get distracted and get caught up in the town's drama. She was here for a reason. She had a debt to pay and screwing around with Jett, no matter how tempting, wasn't an option.

But cowering in the bathroom wasn't one either. The Logans might not have much, but they had pride in spades. Nikki squared her shoulders and went to find Jett, but her confidence was shaken. Was the whole town talking about them? Was everyone in the bar whispering behind her back? She'd been a fool, had almost believed that things had changed, and life in Grove Oaks wasn't the same as when she'd been a teenager and reeling from her mother's death. But she'd just had the best reminder. Now, with her mind readjusted, she'd be stronger than ever. "Let's go."

Jett looked up from the booth he'd been waiting in. His denim clad legs were in a sexy sprawl longways over the bench, arm draped over the back. She refused to get sucked into his butterscotch eyes and playboy smile. "I thought you wanted a drink. Kelly just brought another round."

He seemed so relaxed, confident, so in his element. He had no idea how it was to live without his family's name and protection. This was why they could never be together. This was what Jett never could understand. The town, his mother, her past would never let a relationship between an Avery and a Logan stand.

Nikki shook her head. She fingered her necklace and gently tugged on the chain. "No, I think I'm good."

Jett's eyes narrowed. "What happened?"

Nikki had been a pool player long enough to know what her tell was. *Stupid.* She slipped one hand in her back pocket, then picked up her bottle to give the other something to do. "Nothing. Just tired is all."

Jett nodded, then glanced around the crowded bar. When he turned his gaze back on her, a person would be hard pressed to describe his eyes as anything sweet or candy like. "I was hoping you'd be up for a little game of nine-ball."

Nikki took a sip from her beer and raised her brow in question. Nine-ball was the hustler's game. It was short and quick, without all the rules of straight pool.

He nodded his head toward the tables in the back. "I heard you played."

"Then you heard wrong." She took another sip, eying him the whole time. "I've given it up for Lent."

The corner of his mouth hinted at a smile. "Found God, have you?"

"Among other things."

Jett glanced to the tables, then back to her. "One game. No money."

Nikki shook her head. "I don't play for fun. No thrill in it."

He swallowed, and she could see his jaw work. "Then we'll play for a favor. A debt. You up for a little more red in your ledger?"

She didn't want to ask, not really, but gambling was too deep in her blood not to hear the stakes. "What's the favor?"

He smiled, not the golden boy smile she'd come to know, but instead one that lacked any charm at all. "Well, Texas, that's the thrill part. You don't know until the end. Anything goes. No boundaries."

Her heart did a funky jump-start in her chest at the possibilities, but her game face was ice-cold. "No limits?"

"None. Unless that's too much heat for you? We could place some ground rules if you want to play it safe."

Nikki knew what Jett was doing. It was so obvious, and yet, there was that achingly familiar thrill that zipped up her spine and buzzed in her blood. Some families were predisposed toward red hair or near-sightedness. The Logans were addicts. Throw a dart at the family tree and you'd hit a vice—drinking, smoking, shopping. You name it, and the Logans could turn anything into a compulsion. But really, under all the addictions, there was only one. One vice that was as indicative of a Logan as dark hair, brown skin, and blue eyes.

It was very basic, really. The Logans were gamblers.

There were stories as far back as her grandfather, if stories in the Logan family could be believed, who won his first car—a 1950 Cadillac—on the toss of a coin. Then there was her father, Dakota, who'd bet on every sports game invented, and even ones that hadn't, like golf without clubs. Her father had once bet a hundred dollars on his ability to throw a golf ball through the eighteen holes. Legend had it, he'd won that hundred, but lost the money in the same night in an "I can piss into a can from the second story" contest.

So Jett knew what he was doing. And Nikki was smart enough to know this was more than a simple favor and way more than a simple game of pool. She also knew something else. Jett was no match for her in this game.

She hid her smile with a sip of her drink. The thrill of a "sure thing" was headier than any shot of tequila, more exciting than a leather-jacketed man on a motorcycle.

"Oh, I can take the heat," she said.

"But can you handle *this* much heat?"

"Oh, I can handle it. Because we both know I can beat you with one hand tied behind my back and blindfolded."

His eyebrows arched. "Then you'd best start figuring out what your favor will be."

Nikki put down her bottle, no longer needing the buzz. "Already have." Her car fixed . . . for starters. "You really think you can beat me at pool?"

God, he was so cocky. It was almost tragic.

His eyes narrowed and there was absolutely no humor in his voice when he spoke. "Oh, I'm betting on it."

Chapter 11

It had been a while since Nikki played pool. When she first made her promise to Mike that she wouldn't play again, she thought that meant she wouldn't hustle pool players for money. What she hadn't realized was that pool and gambling went together like bars and beers. You couldn't have one without the other. Serious players were gamblers, and players who weren't serious were a waste of Nikki's time. The bigger the stakes, the more exciting the game. It was as simple as that.

As a kid, she'd always been searching for the angle. She'd worked on the twirl-a-ride when the fair came to town. She'd charged two dollars a ride, pocketing one for each paying customer. She was making a couple hundred dollars a night until she had to call in sick, and the owner realized the twirl-a-ride grossed double the night she was gone. As a teenager her damaged reputation hadn't all been lies from spiteful teenage girls. She *had* been caught in the boys' locker room, a wad of cash in her hand. The vice principal, never assuming a sophomore girl could run a successful football pool, assumed the worst, and Nikki hadn't disabused him.

It had taken Nikki one game of "just for fun" pool, with no money involved, to realize she'd have to forgo playing at all. But now, as she walked back toward the tables, she felt the familiar zing electrify her blood in the way only nine-ball could. The Smoke House was not known for being a place of "action" in the hustler community. Most of the money that crossed the table was low: ten, twenty, more than likely just for the next round of beers. Almost all of the players were casual—couples on first dates, buddies from work, but there were a few washed up wannabes that Nikki remembered from her golden days, who had nothing better to do than shoot a few balls and get drunk on The Smoke House's cheap beer.

Nikki recognized the two men playing on the corner table near the back. Ron, a scruffy faced man with a lumpy belly and a John Deere logo on his hat, was busy angling his shot. Ron was a decent player, had good aim, but was lousy at ball placement. Ron's partner in crime, Cocky, was waiting his turn, his lanky frame a mirror image of the pool stick he was propped on.

The name Cocky had been given at birth was Bob Brown, but most people knew him simply as Cocky. In general, people never knew or cared how a person got their nickname, but everyone in town knew how Bob had gotten his.

Cocky betted on everything and anything, and betting on the length of his manhood was only a matter of how many beers and how much money he was down. It was inevitable—mix gambling men with alcohol, shake rather than stir, and a guy's penis would come up in conversation. Cocky was no different. He claimed his cock was so big, it hung down below his knee. When anyone stupid enough or drunk enough would call him on it, Cocky would roll up his pant leg and show off his winning bet.

There, on his calf, was a tattoo of a rooster, hanging from a noose. Thus, he had a "cock" hanging below his knee. For a while he'd win a couple hundred dollars every time a new sucker would walk through the door. One time he won a broken nose. After that, word got around and no one took him up on his "my cock is bigger than your cock" bet. But his name stuck and so did his reputation.

Nikki walked over and slammed her palm down on the pool table's rail. "We're commandeering this table."

Ron looked up from the shot he was studying. "No way, Nik. I'm in the zone. I still have two more racks to go before I beat Cocky."

"I'll give you some side action—I'll run the first three racks without Jett getting off a shot in a race to seven if you let us take the table," Nikki said. She had no doubt she'd get them to agree. She knew these men, spoke their language. In the end, it was all about the bet, regardless of who was actually playing.

"What's the game?" Cocky asked.

Nikki looked up at Jett. "You sure?"

He shrugged.

She smiled. "Nine-ball it is."

Nine-ball could be quick and dirty or long and hard—either way it was all about the hustle. The rules were simple. Whoever was first to hit all their balls in order, and then pocket the yolk-colored nine-ball, won the rack. There were other games, one-pocket for instance, which was pool's answer to chess, requiring one player to sink eight balls into one pocket, but that needed extreme patience and a different mind-set. When given the choice, Nikki preferred the fast and easy.

As the men started to retrieve the pocketed balls, Jett walked over to her and whispered in her ear. "I thought you weren't betting on pool anymore?"

Nikki grabbed a house cue and started to chalk the end. She gave him a sidelong glance. "Oh, I'm not betting my money. I'm betting yours." She gestured with her hand. "Come on, give me a twenty."

Jett leaned against the wood of the table, his palms resting casually on either side. He had a way of making every space he occupied his—as if he belonged to the secret club of "cool for life." "So let me get this straight. If you win, I lose my money, but if I win, I still lose my money?"

Nikki smiled. "Oh, no need to worry your pretty head about what's gonna happen. You and I both know I'll take the game and," she winked, "the favor you're offering."

The copper in Jett's gaze warmed, and the star-shaped scar got lost in the crinkles around his eyes. He pulled out his wallet and threw a twenty on the rail. "So really, there's no way I can come out ahead on this."

She patted his cheek. "You're one smart cookie. Whoever said you were 'all beauty and no brains' was a liar."

Jett threw up his hand. "Really? And nothing about my shoulders? I've been working out. Picked up a few extra classes of Pilates, and—nothing?"

Nikki rolled her eyes and walked away. Sometimes Jett not taking anything seriously was annoying.

"Hey," Cocky yelled in Jett's direction. "What happened to your face?"

Jett glared at him. "None of your damn business."

"Okay." Cocky put his hands up in surrender. "Moving on. So are we playing here or gabbing?" He pulled up his baggy jeans, which immediately fell back below the waistband of his underwear.

Nikki took a deep breath and tuned everything else out. With Jett it was too easy to get distracted. She racked the balls tight and set up the cue ball for the break. Her fingers tingled where they gripped the pool stick. She loved the feel of the smooth wood as it slid through her fingers, the smell of chalk in the air, and the way her body rocked slightly, looking for the rhythm of her stroke. In one power thrust, she broke the balls apart.

Full colors and stripes burst across the table like artful buckshot on a green canvas. The explosion of balls was the same as the opening chord of a full string orchestra. Two stripes split off and pocketed in separate corners.

The room silenced. At least to Nikki it did. In her mind's eye, she mapped out her first shot, her second, her third. In her head the balls zigzagged across the table in a carefully choreographed dance as she played out the entire game before the third ball was even sunk.

There were some things a person just knew. Nikki knew the sun rose in the east and set every day behind the low, muted green meadows in the west. She knew the Texas summers were thick and sticky like melted cotton candy. And she knew she would win this game.

A prerequisite for being a hustler was learning to hide the truth. Some would say it was lying; Nikki approached it the same way an actor would a role. To be successful, a pool hustler had to hide their true skill, true intention, true emotions. Knowing the win was only twelve strokes away, she let her toes curl inside her boots. If this were a real hustle, she'd have let her exultation stop there, but since she was playing Jett, she didn't have to hide. She let the curl travel upward and settle on her lips.

She spared Jett a glance, then went to work on the table with the passion of an artist and the precision of a surgeon. When she'd been younger and the win was within reach, she'd rush through the shots, pocketing the balls with speed and spin. Not anymore. Now, each stripe was kissed by the cue and gently tucked into bed, dropping one by one into the table pockets.

She finished without breaking a sweat, but her heart was pumping like an oil drill hitting pay dirt. Nikki tucked a long strand of dark hair behind her ear and stood straight. "Again."

The balls were pulled and racked, and she found herself back on the business end of the pool stick. The sets opened up before her like a well-read book. It was as simple as knowing the angles on the table. Time lost all meaning. There was no need to eat, drink, or sleep. Her body fed off the high of the game. She could go for hours before noticing she was tired. Unfortunately, the owners of The Smoke House didn't agree. The lights flickered for "last call," and in that brief moment Nikki lost the zone.

It was during the break that the fifth rack didn't open as cleanly as she would've liked. The three ball went in nice and easy, but her only other shot, the solid four, got stuck behind the striped nine and five. The shot wasn't impossible, but highly improbable, especially coming from her angle. She licked her lips and fought the urge to reach for her necklace. Carefully, she angled the cue ball to play off the rail, but her speed was a touch too intense, and she snookered her shot.

Nikki straightened for the first time in an hour, feeling the strain in her lower back.

Jett chalked his stick and walked the table. "I'd forgotten how good you are."

Nikki stepped back. "Really? Not a good thing to forget."

By this time they'd collected a number of "rail birds," observers from among the other patrons. Nikki hadn't noticed earlier, but now wondered if she shouldn't have obliterated Jett in such a fashion. Men had a tendency to be prickly about losing to a woman.

Jett didn't take long. That was one thing she'd always admired about him. He was careful, but when he made a decision, nothing stood in his way. His run was going good for a while until the cue ball got stuck behind the eight and nine near the corner pocket. Jett stopped, took his time, studied the table. Nikki studied him. She knew exactly when he found his shot. He aimed down and center on the cue ball, jumping the white between the two balls and kicking the eight into the nine into the corner pocket, winning the game.

There was a low whistle from someone on the sideline. Cocky let out a whispered "shait," and Nikki felt a tightening in her gut that could only signal surprise.

Jett let his gaze travel to hers. She read the message clearly enough. *I've been practicing.* And he sure had.

Nikki fingered the necklace at the base of her throat and began to watch him through a whole new set of eyes. Instead of seeing Jett the friend, the lover, or her brother's best friend, she observed him for the first time through the eyes of a pool player. She'd played him in the past. Not often, but enough to know his style. Before he'd had power and speed that showed well, but in the end he had been unpredictable.

Things had changed. He'd acquired the sway of a pool player. His touch was gentle, as if each ball he pocketed went on invitation, not demand. He found the angles with the quiet assurance of an old man making love to the same woman for the last fifty years.

Jett had always been a player, with women, with the townspeople . . . with her. But now, across the slick green felt of the table, Jett had become an opponent.

Chapter 12

"New lovers are nervous and tender, but smash everything. For the heart is an organ of fire."

Jett looked at Nikki as she triumphantly rolled out another movie quote. They were driving home in his truck after the pool game. In the end, The Smoke House kicked them out shortly after Jett's break. Not that he minded. To his way of thinking, everything had gone according to plan, but it did rub a bit to have to pay out to Ron and Cocky.

The radio played softly in the background and the scent of leather and spearmint gum filled the cab as Nikki busily chomped away. Seeing her this way, her eyes sparkling, a flush to her skin, happy and relaxed, reminded him of how things used to be between them. "Ouch," he said. "You had to really dig deep for that movie quote. I think I see sweat on your brow."

"You're never gonna get it. There's no way." She almost danced in her seat at the thought of beating him. "When are you going to understand? I always win at this game."

He let out a disgusted sigh. "You never win at this."

"I win all the time."

"No," he laughed. "You can't just make up a new reality and call it the truth. You've never won."

Her wide smile brightened her face, making her look younger and carefree. "Right now, I just did."

He shook his head. "*The English Patient.*"

"No way!" She slammed her hand on the dashboard. "How could you possibly know that?" Nikki shook her head in disbelief. "No self-respecting, straight man should know that line."

"I saw it three times."

"What! That movie was like three hours long."

"Just over. Three hours and ten minutes of heaven in the cab of my truck. I knew if I hadn't reached second base by the time the plane crashed, there'd be no second date."

"You are so lying."

He laughed. "Okay, maybe I didn't see the movie from the back seat of my truck, but I did see it three times. I have sisters, remember, and a fatal love affair seemed to make all the girls in my household go nuts. But I watched and learned. And to this day I credit my first real kiss to *The Breakfast Club*. Reruns of old movies at the dollar theater over the summer were a godsend."

Nikki laughed. "Okay, now I have to know. Who was she?"

"Jealous? Never mind, she was an older woman who took an interest. I was the tender age of fifteen, and she was a worldly sixteen. I blew my whole allowance on tickets and popcorn, but it was so worth it. To this day, I associate buttery topping with French kissing."

"Leave it to a guy to combine food and sex," she said, throwing in an exaggerated eye-roll for good measure.

"Hey, don't knock it, *9½ Weeks* was revolutionary. I knew chocolate could be a turn on, but the cough syrup thing opened a whole new world." They both laughed. "So, fine. What was your first kiss?"

"Hmmm. My first kiss? Easy. Frankie Shumdt. He dared me to kiss him inside the tunnel slide in the third grade. To this day, I get claustrophobic around playground equipment."

There was no way he was going to let her get away with that lame story. "Cheater."

"What? How so? Sorry, not everyone can live up to your extra-butter popcorn kiss. But what can I say? Frankie was young."

"No, a peck on the playground doesn't count. I want your first *real* kiss."

Nikki quieted, all the laughter died out of her eyes, and he immediately wanted to put it back. She rubbed her arms like she was cold. "You already know that story," she said in a quiet voice.

"What? When?"

Then he remembered. Not that he'd ever really forgotten, but he hadn't known her first time had been *that* time. Nikki had been what—barely eighteen? Too old for her first kiss, but then she hadn't had the opportunity to date much during the years her mother was sick.

He remembered that night so clearly. The uneasiness he'd felt, the desperation that poured out of her along with her tears.

Cole had called him to go over and check on Nikki. He'd told him his mom hadn't been doing well, and he was afraid she didn't have much longer. Cole didn't wanted Nikki to be alone, and so asked Jett if he'd go over and sit with her.

When Jett pulled up to the house, the front door was wide open with only a few lights on. Any other time he'd come upon an open door to his best friend's house, he would have run in, certain there was trouble of some sort. But now he hesitated. He wanted nothing more than to turn around, go home, grab a beer, watch the game. Whatever was waiting for him in that house was way beyond anything he wanted to deal with.

The house was neat, homey, and always smelled of cinnamon and baked goods that Nikki would make to tempt her mother's appetite. Despite the effort Nikki put into keeping up their family home, Jett hadn't been comfortable there since their mom had gotten sick. It always seemed that everyone was holding their breath, waiting for the next pile of crap to hit the fan. Or maybe it was simply waiting for her to die.

Jett closed the door behind him and softly called out Nikki's name. He had no idea why he was whispering, except for the fact the house was so still, even his footsteps seemed clumsy and loud. He went through each room, Cole's, Nikki's, even the bathroom, until he had no choice but to peek inside Mrs. Logan's room.

He couldn't ever remember being inside that room. If he ever saw her, it was at the kitchen table sipping sweet tea and more than likely wrapped in a worn blue bathrobe. Even so, Jett saw Nikki's hand in everything inside her mother's room. It was as if Nikki fought against death lingering in the shadows, and had pushed back by trying to infuse her mother's room with life and energy. Numerous potted plants hung in the windows. Soft country music played from a small radio in the corner. There were bowls of dried leaves that covered up the smell of sickness with scents of lavender and vanilla. A romance novel lay open on the nightstand where Nikki must've sat and read aloud to her mother.

Jett took a deep breath and let his gaze travel to the bed. Under a white blanket tucked up around her neck was Mrs. Logan. He knew immediately she was dead. Her face looked as if gravity was sucking her into the mattress; her skin was taking on the blue tinge of death. Jett backed out. Scared, shaken, he had no idea what to do in this situation, except find Nikki.

He found her in the first place he looked, and the last place he thought she'd go. Nikki never had bought into the whole horse ranch thing and had become even less enchanted after her father died, but where else could she go? Jett stepped into the darkened stables and heard the choked sobs coming from the tack room. And there was Nikki, looking so young, curled in a ball in the corner, with her long dark hair tangled down her back.

He knew some men felt uncomfortable with female tears, but he'd grown up with too many sisters to be fazed. He walked toward her, slowly and carefully, so as not to startle her. She lifted her head, and his heart simply broke. Here was Nikki, the girl he'd known her whole life, the little sister of his best friend, who'd always tagged along and pestered them. Who'd thrown tantrums if they dared to try and leave her behind. Who cried so hard for weeks after her father died, that Cole had taken to sleeping in her room at night.

"Nik?" he asked, not quite sure what to do.

Her face was tracked with tears, eyes wet and shiny, nose red. And he didn't say anything more, didn't need to, just fell to his knees and took her in his arms.

Then she was in his embrace, face buried against his neck, her tears dampening his shirt. Her body shook violently against his as if a war raged inside. He just held her tight, desperate to keep her from flying into pieces. And right there he made a promise to her. He whispered it into her ear, not sure if she heard or would even remember later. But it didn't change a thing. "It's okay, Nik. I'm not going anywhere. I'll be here for as long as you need me. I won't leave. I'll keep you safe for as long as you let me."

He shifted to rest his back against the wall and eased his legs under her so she was sitting on his lap. It took a while. Seemed like hours that they sat there while he stroked her hair, and she fisted her hands in his shirt. Finally, the fierce sobs turned to soft shudders, and her breathing grew closer to normal.

Jett waited, knowing what was going to happen. Even as a little girl, Nikki didn't like to be hugged. Not that Cole or he were in the habit of trying to hug a pestering sister, but as they'd gotten older, Jett's feelings had begun to change. There'd been more than a few times when he suggested they go swimming on the off-chance that Nikki would come with them. He remembered that summer specifically because Nikki had to go to the second-hand store for a bathing suit, and the only one that fit her was a racy black bikini that was nowhere near age-appropriate for a girl of twelve. That was the summer Jett started believing in God.

He'd been so cool back then, thinking Nikki would be intrigued by an older guy. He'd told her as much, said something along the lines that he'd take pity on her by taking her to the movies with him. Nikki would have none of it. She told him in no uncertain terms to drop dead, then pushed him off the deck. After that it was over. He'd been in love ever since.

So he waited and would've bet his shiny new truck that Nikki would stand up, push him away, and then pretend the tenderness between them had never happened.

Of course, he should've realized he'd never figure Nikki out. She sat up and looked him straight in the eye. If he lived to be a hundred, he'd never forget the way her eyes reminded him of summer lakes and wet grass after a rain.

"Jett, will you do me a favor?"

Right, like he could refuse. He'd just been thinking of summers and afternoon rains; he was so screwed.

"Anything," he said. Did he just say *anything*? What he meant was, he was about to push her off his lap, get up, and call Cole. Because even though he'd always said Nikki was like a sister to him, he knew damn well she wasn't, not even close. It didn't help that, after patting her back for the last hour, he realized she wasn't wearing a bra, and her knit shorts hung dangerously low in the back.

Her fingers released his shirt and moved up to caress his face.

She was so close, he could feel her breath. His blood raced, and then just as quickly rushed to a very inappropriate area. His heart, a fool of an organ, leapt at what his mind hoped he saw in her eyes.

"Kiss me."

He had dated a fair share of the girls in town. Yep, probably taken out the entire eligible population at one time or another, and not one had ever said *kiss me*. Sure, they might've said it with their eyes or with the poutiness of their lips. Women's language was spoken with their bodies, and Jett considered himself to be a consummate linguist.

But God, to actually say the words.

He was so screwed and so ... .turned on! He shifted Nikki around. All of a sudden having her in his lap had become painful.

He drew in a ragged breath. He'd like nothing better than to take those moist lips in a kiss that would teach her a lesson—the lesson being, it was dangerous to say those things to a man. But this was his best friend's sister. She'd just lost her mom. She was broken and sitting on his lap, completely vulnerable and only a total dick would take advantage of the situation.

She must've seen the doubt in his eyes. "Please, Jett, just this once. This one time because I need to feel something, anything to feel alive. I need to know I'm still here and didn't get buried in that house. I've been sad for so long. I need to know one day, maybe when I'm old and gray, that one day I can be happy."

She didn't wait for a response, just pulled his head down to meet hers. As soon as her lips touched his, he knew it was too late. No, he wouldn't hurt her by breaking away. Instead, he made himself a promise that he'd keep the kiss sweet, tender, something for her to remember after she buried her mother. After she grieved. Something for her to look back on fondly. He'd keep it to just a touch of soft lips, a gentle kiss to the corners of her mouth, maybe a quick taste of the fullness of her bottom lip. Then he'd pull away, finish off with a kiss to her forehead, and take her back inside.

If Nikki saw his line in the sand, then she blew past it with the confidence of a woman who knew what she wanted. A few breaths later, a few heartbeats more, and she was there inside his mouth.

His first taste of Nikki was all contradictions. Salty from her tears, sweet from the tea she must've drunk. Naiveté from lack of experience, wanton from desperation. The kiss turned opened mouth, and her knees straddled his hips. He could taste her need. Feel it as it moistened her skin with sweat, burned his with desire. Hell, one taste of Nikki and he was thirteen years old again, and just figured out that his lower half had far more uses than pissing in the woods.

Her shorts were, well . . . short and loose and it took everything he had to keep his hands along her thighs and not go and find out what she was wearing underneath. But Jett knew himself. He wasn't applying for sainthood like Cole. Jett loved pleasure, and women had always been a pleasure to him. No, Jett wasn't in the habit of denying himself. And why not? When things came easy, it was a shame to say no.

And he wanted to give in. Especially when his vision went hazy after she un-tucked his shirt and ran the flat of her palms up his chest. But even then, he would've been fine, except with her mouth on his, she breathed one word—*yes.*

He didn't know if she was aware she'd spoken, but he heard and that was enough. There was a white-hot moment that ended with him cradled between her legs, and his one hand under her knee, pulling her leg higher.

He tangled his fingers in her hair, and he could smell the flowers and fruity fragrance of her shampoo. Lord help him, but self-control was not his strong suit, and God knows it wasn't Nikki's either.

"Nik, love, we've got to stop." Was that him speaking? *Oh, thank God.* His mother would've been so proud.

Nikki didn't say anything, just moved her mouth to the under-side of his jaw. And *Christ,* did her tongue just trace a trail from his neck to his ear? Where the hell had she learned that? No, he didn't want to know.

"Please, love." Maybe if he begged, she'd feel sorry for him.

This couldn't go down between them like two teenagers rutting in a barn. He didn't want her first time to be on the night her mother died, in a tack room with some guy who should've known better. He didn't want to see any more regret in her eyes. With Nikki, things were different. She wasn't just a girl he picked up on a Friday night and forgot about on Sunday. He wanted to start something, not end it before they had a chance.

And besides, Cole would kill him.

He grabbed her face and forced her to look at him. Her breathing was ragged, and he didn't even want to contemplate how he was going to walk out of this barn. But he had to break through to her. "It's okay, we have time. I'm not going anywhere."

Her eyes softened, and for a moment she looked so heartbreakingly young. "Do you promise?"

"With all my heart, I promise."

But Jett had been so stupid back then. The promise was made by the wrong person. It should've been Nikki he made say those words, because years later she'd packed up her things and left him without so much as a goodbye.

Chapter 13

Jett pushed through the door of Hal's Eats diner and smiled at the pleasant jingle that rang above him. He took his hat off, whistling the catchy Dixie Chicks tune he had stuck in his head.

"Morn', Jett," Ginger said, her arms loaded with two big trays full of food.

"Good morning, beautiful. Lookin' good as usual," Jett replied as he carefully leaned over the trays to plant a kiss on her weathered cheek.

"My, my, a compliment and a kiss, all before your morning coffee. You're in a fine mood this morning."

Jett grinned. "Why, yes I am, Ms. Ginger."

"It wouldn't have anything to do with a dark-haired young lady with a penchant for trouble, would it?"

"My lips are sealed."

Ginger gave him a saucy wink and went on her way. The old waitress was too observant for her own good. His mood had everything to do with Nikki.

After Nikki's confession that he'd been her first real kiss, Jett had driven home. *Her* home. Then promptly left her on the front step with only a wink and a peck on her cheek before he could change his mind.

He knew he could've pushed his advantage. Could've pushed Nikki up against the wall and kissed her like a man who knew what he was doing and did it well. But he wasn't a young man of twenty-five anymore. He had a bit more practice in self-restraint. And it was like his daddy always said—*Win the war, son, not the battle. A patient man always has his day.*

Jett was counting on it.

Jett hung his hat on the hook and slid into his favorite booth at the back of the diner. Some blessed soul had left today's paper on the table, conveniently open to the sports section. *Day just keeps getting better and better.*

"Ginger looked busy, so I thought I'd bring your coffee to get started."

Jett glanced up to find the mayor standing over him with a steaming white mug in each hand. "Why thank you, Carl. Please, have a seat."

The mayor had something he wanted to get off his chest, and Jett had a sinking feeling he knew exactly what it was. He mentally braced himself, wanting the matter over and done with. He had plans for his day. Plans that had to do with Nikki, and none whatsoever that had to do with sitting around with old Carl, talking about his daughter.

"I thought we had a deal," Carl said, squeezing himself into the booth across from Jett. "Beth said you called and canceled on her,"

"Something came up."

"Was that something Nikki Logan?"

Jett laced his fingers around the coffee cup. "I'm thinking that something is none of your business."

Carl leaned back as much as he could in the small confines of the booth. He rubbed his freshly shaven chin and pursed his lips. "Let me give you a free piece of advice, son. Your daddy has made a pretty good living out of keeping the right people happy and keeping the unhappy ones silent. I know he sees you following in his footsteps one day. He didn't put all this time and money into his legacy just to watch you piss it away."

Jett had every idea where this conversation was going. He'd had it before—with his father, for one. But Mayor Emerson wasn't his father, which meant Jett didn't have to sit here and listen to Carl besmirch his character. But getting angry with him was not the best way to handle this type of situation. And Jett had learned from the best—his father. In perfect Avery manner, he let a politician smile ride his lips and waited for Carl to have his say.

"Now, Jett, you know I don't like getting into other people's business. I think a man can choose how he lives his life as long as he doesn't hurt anyone or break any laws."

Carl leaned forward and leveled Jett with a stare that had gotten this town more funding than any other mayor, but Jett wasn't a government legislator or a socialite with deep pockets. "Cut the crap, Carl, you're starting to get me confused with a baby-toting voter."

"Fine, Jett, have it your way. This town doesn't think that Nikki Logan would make a very good wife for a sheriff."

Jett blew on his coffee to hide the tick in his jaw. "When you say town, does that mean everyone . . . or just you?"

"There's a lot more to being sheriff than just shaking hands. Nikki's a loose cannon. She's got a reputation. Rubs people the wrong way."

"Well, Carl, you rub me the wrong way, and yet, I still voted for you."

Carl's face, normally red, flushed crimson. "You know what, Jett? When it comes to the Logans, you've got a blind spot. That daddy of theirs was nothing but a gambler. Leaving that family in such straits was nothing short of a crime. Now, don't get me wrong. The whole town felt sorry for them when their mamma up and died. We all looked the other way when Cole took to drinking and raising hell in town. And I guess in the end, Cole turned out okay. How in heaven he made a go out of that ranch, I'll never know. But that Nikki's a whole other story."

Maybe Carl was right when it came to his view of the Logans. But Jett had never met a more loyal friend than Cole, and Nikki, despite all her bluster, ran even truer. "So let me make sure I'm hearing you right, Carl. Are you saying, if it's Nikki and me, then there's no place for me in the politics of this town?"

"That's what I'm saying." The conversation had ended as far as Carl was concerned. He took a sip of coffee and began the cumbersome task of squeezing out of the booth. Carl had said his piece, and in all fairness, was used to getting his way. He totally believed his carrot was big enough to set Jett straight.

But Jett had chased after the best—and what Carl was dangling wasn't it. "Well, I'm sorry to hear you say that, because I think you're wrong. I think there are a lot of people in town who'd like to see a Logan get a fair shake. People like an underdog, and no one's been more under than Nikki."

Carl put down his cup, sloshing coffee over the side. "Are you saying what I think you're saying? You want to run for office with Nikki as your wife?"

"That's right." *Ah, hell.*

"You agreeing to running for office or to marrying Nikki?"

Shut up, Jett. Keep your stupid mouth shut. "Both."

Carl pushed himself up and reached over for his hat on the rack behind Jett. Carl's face had the look of a smashed beet, but there was disappointment in his eyes that Jett hadn't anticipated. "I don't care how much money the Averys have. I'll only back a candidate who I think is good for this town. And the Logans, well, the Logans haven't been good for much."

Jett stood, no longer able to continue the conversation sitting down. "Then it will be an interesting race."

Carl placed his hat on his head like a cherry on top of a sundae. "I hope you know what you're doing."

Jett watched Carl walk out the front door, then slowly melted back into the booth. He pressed his fist to his lips, but it was too late. He'd already let his mouth run and take a flying leap off a cliff. *What the—*

What had his mom always said? *Just a matter of time, Jett, before the Logans' fondness for trouble will start to rub off.*

Damn, he hated when his mother was right.

Chapter 14

Frankie propped one flip-flop on the wall behind her and leaned back against the outside of the pool hall. She let her head fall back and closed her eyes. This was the life. This was living. It was a beautiful day, the sun was shining, the back of the buildings provided enough shade, and the slight breeze was enough to wash away the stink of the alley.

She took a drag from a cigarette, practicing holding it just like that old cowboy in all those westerns she watched on AMC. She tried a smoke ring. Almost perfect. She smiled.

She snubbed out her butt and thought about lighting up another. Sam, the owner of the pool hall, was a hopeless chain smoker, and since Texas law prohibited smoking indoors, he was constantly running outside to catch a smoke. The end result was butts with only three or four puffs off them, free for the taking.

A whole day at the pool hall was before her. She'd worked out a deal with Sam that she'd keep the place clean—sweep the floor, put paper in the stalls—in exchange for table time. Now that everything was done, the rest of the day belonged to her. Her stomach growled. She picked up another cigarette. One of the best things about smoking, other than blowing cool smoke rings, was it helped with the hunger pains.

A hand came out of nowhere and swatted the cigarette out of her mouth. Strong fingers clamped down on her arm and spun her around. Frankie wasn't one of those stupid girls who didn't know how to fight; she could take care of herself. Her knee made ready for a well-placed aim when her arm was jerked so hard she swore her shoulder squeaked.

"You knee me in the balls, kid, and I will break your arm."

Crap. She knew that voice. *Freaking Jett.* He was worse than Mike. Between the two of them, she couldn't seem to take a dump these days without getting their permission. She rolled her eyes. "Ahh, come on, don't you have better things to do then bust my balls?"

Jett looked pissed, but then again, almost every time she saw him he had a scowl on his face. "Oh, I have plenty of other things to do. Speaking of which, why aren't you in school?"

"Early release."

"At ten in the morning?"

"State holiday?" Damn. She should've gone with parent-teacher conferences.

"I'm taking you to school."

She shook her head, readying to make a plea when her stomach growled and did it for her.

"What the hell was that?" Jett's brown eyes narrowed down at her as if it was *her* fault there was no food in the fridge. "When was your last meal?"

"Well, I *was* enjoying my breakfast before you so rudely slapped it out of my mouth." The comeback would've sounded better if she could've placed her hand on her hip, but his vise-like grip held her arm captive.

"Don't try and piss me off. Better people than you have tried and failed." But his heart wasn't in the insult, as he pulled her down the street and glanced around, as if hoping someone else would come and take this "problem" off his hands.

She could've told him there was no one else.

"Where are you taking me?" Frankie dug in her heels, not liking being hauled around like some disobedient toddler with no say in where she was going.

"Breakfast," he growled.

Jett finally stopped in front of Hal's Eats, and pulled her inside without even a glance. Maybe she didn't want to eat at Hal's. Or maybe she didn't want breakfast. Had he ever thought of that?

He led her to a booth and then called out to the blue-haired waitress. "One special and a . . . " he looked over as if finally realizing she might have an opinion on her own life. "Chocolate milk?"

She crossed her arms over her chest. She hadn't had chocolate milk since she was five. "Coffee. Black."

Jett raised his eyebrows.

She always added cream and sugar, but that didn't make the same statement.

"Coffee then, Ginger. Black and strong. Apparently, Frankie has had a long night."

He had no idea.

Jett leaned back in the booth and they both waited in silence until Ginger placed a large order of French toast, bacon, and scrambled eggs in front of her. At the smell of battered sugar and fried fat, Frankie forgot all about making statements. She scooped out the whipped butter from the tiny silver cup and plopped it on top of the toast. Jett waited in silence as she made serious headway on her breakfast.

"It's been three days since you called."

Really? Had it been that long? That explained why he came looking for her.

"Sorry," she mumbled between mouthfuls. She took a sip of coffee to help wash down the half piece of toast stuffed in her mouth, regretting nixing the cream and sugar.

"Today, when I drop you off, we're going to have a little chat with the principal. She'll be calling me anytime you're late, tardy, or skip school."

She dragged a piece of bacon through the pool of buttery goo and then popped it in her mouth. She closed her eyes. *Heaven.*

"From now on, you'll report here to Ginger every morning for breakfast."

There was some syrup left in the bottom of the silver cup. She took her finger and scooped the remains into her mouth. "Or what?" She licked her knuckle. "You'll call my mother?"

"I'll call Sam and have you banned from the pool hall."

She pulled her finger out of her mouth. He wasn't smiling. Could he be serious?

"School mornings you will be here seven thirty, sharp."

She almost choked. "Holy crap, seven-thirty? School doesn't even start until nine. And I refuse—"

He kept right on talking as if her opinion didn't matter. "That goes for smoking also. Consider that your last cigarette."

He was serious.

"That's total crap."

"That's the deal."

"What if I say no?"

"Then I hope you like your mother's career choice."

The French toast grew heavy in her belly. Maybe she shouldn't have eaten all three pieces. "And what . . . what if I *can't* do all that?"

He carefully placed his hands on top of the table then folded them as if he was praying for patience. "And why is that?"

Frankie scrunched her mouth to one side and took a glance around the empty diner. No help there. "What if I got suspended?"

It was kind of sad to see such a pretty face get all droopy and depressed. "So, you need me to go and talk to the school again."

She smiled. "You didn't have lunch plans, did you?"

Jett let his forehead drop into his hands and groaned.

Nikki wasn't disappointed. Nope, she was just fine. Couldn't've cared less. Jett had called Cole, letting him know Jett had to cancel their plans for lunch. And she wasn't disappointed about the brotherly kiss Jett had planted on her last night, either. Not that she wanted anything more from him. She didn't. But the signals he'd been throwing last night made her feel anything but sisterly.

If she was any less of a pool player, she might have worried about the "favor" Jett wanted to extract from her. As it was, she had no idea what possessed Jett to set himself up for an epic fail. The thought made her uneasy. Everyone in town knew Jett as a good, upstanding guy. If hard pressed, some might admit that he could be dangerous, but only to the women who'd read more into his charming smile and bedroom eyes than was there.

But Nikki had seen there was more to Jett than sugared words and a set of broad shoulders. Underneath his savvy coolness lurked a man who didn't like to share, one who felt more deeply than he let on, one who didn't always play fair. There was a darker side that many were never allowed to glimpse. Nikki counted herself fortunate that she'd never been on the receiving end of his more intimidating moods.

Nikki shook her head. Jett wasn't her concern. She wasn't one of his groupies trying to trick an Avery into walking down the aisle. Contrary to popular opinion, she still had some self-respect. Or at least as much as a person could muster when working at a low-end strip bar for nothing more than tips and a clean ledger.

Her stomach churned at the thought of her first night working at The Pitt; that or the queasiness was Montezuma's revenge from the left-over French fries she'd eaten this morning. Regardless, she had no time to second-guess her decision to work at the roughest bar in three counties.

Well, the motto "fake it 'til you make it" had never done her wrong, and who wouldn't have guessed that a Logan was good at faking it? She put in her ear buds and cranked up her favorite emogoth music on her iPhone. She washed off her combat boots, slicked her hair back, then outlined her eyes with her favorite charcoal-gray pencil. Armed from head to toe in black with only a metal-studded wristband for color, she felt prepared to match her wits against the worst.

Cole had loaned her Old Bertha until she could get the Toyota out of the shop. If he knew exactly what the truck was for, he'd have revoked the privilege faster than a preacher's daughter could get her legs crossed. But what Cole didn't know . . .

With a kiss and a prayer, the old truck started on the first try, and within seconds Nikki was bumping down the deserted country road at a blistering forty-five.

During the summer, the days stretched on forever, and even close to six o'clock the sun resisted calling it a day, sinking in the west like the slowest of molasses. Dust coated her windshield in a fine powder, and the AC fought the humidity with a low-pitched whirl and tepid air.

The parking lot at The Pitt was nearly empty when she pulled in. Apparently, with not much of a child's menu or crayons, The Pitt did better after dark. Nikki walked in, and after filling out a few pieces of paperwork, was thrown in behind the bar for her official sink or swim. After fumbling her seventh drink, Nikki caught the briefest glimpse of Mike's crooked canine. It was hard to tell if his so-called smile was from humor or smugness. She was starting to believe he was hoping she'd walk out and save him the trouble of firing her. But Mike had no way of knowing she had a secret— burning bridges was her specialty. There was nowhere to go from here.

A pulsing dance beat filled the bar, and a young woman began gyrating on the stage. Rough-looking men filtered in, taking up the few odd tables around the stage and occupying the bar stools. All of them wore the same dirty, haggard look common to hard men. Some came by it from long miles on their bikes sucking down exhaust, and others from just not caring. Genetics didn't seem to matter, slicked back hair or none, long straggly gray beards or young and barely shaving—they all had a weariness around their eyes that said they'd seen too much and respected even less. The only looks harder than on the faces of these men were the ones coming from the women dancing on stage.

But everyone had to respect Mike or they wouldn't get served . . . or paid. Mike had no problem laying down the law with a wooden bat tapping against his palm after the first lewd comment or catcall. Apparently, Mike's reputation for keeping "Billy" locked and loaded behind the bar was well known. But Mike couldn't be there all the time. Nikki knew she'd have to hold her own or she'd sink before there was even a chance to swim. And by the gnarly, open-mouthed looks and beady eyes around her, she guessed the waters were full of piranhas.

Nikki was up to her neck in drink orders, and the bar's loud din might've permanently damaged her hearing. She had to lean far over the bar just to hear the customers speak, and only after much ogling did she begin to suspect that most were keeping their voices low on purpose. She glanced down and caught a nice peek of her lace bra as her low V-neck tee gapped. She did a mental eye roll— men. That could've accounted for the twenty-dollar tip she'd received earlier. Definitely wasn't the service.

Out of the corner of her eye she saw something fly through the air. A peanut bounced off her head. She raised her hand up as another hit her shoulder. She turned, about ready to throw a beer mug back.

"Hey, how 'bout some service down here?" The peanut thrower had a sweat-stained T-shirt under an army green vest that showed off full-sleeved tats.

Nikki put down the glass and walked over. "Whatcha having?"

The good thing about this crowd was that sophistication didn't run high—mostly a beer and whisky group.

"I been watching you," he said.

She guessed there was a smile somewhere under all the hair, but it was hard to tell amid the blond, wiry beard that covered half his face.

She threw him a bored look, but ignored his comment. Men were like children—any attention was better than none. She avoided tapping her fingers as she waited for his answer, but just barely. Apparently, some men needed more prompting than others in narrowing down their choices. "The beer on tap is behind me or I've got whiskey. The good stuff and the watered-down stuff. Which do you want?"

"I'll tell you what. I'll take whatever you've got if you come over and serve me from my lap."

This was not the first such comment made tonight and by no means would it be the last. She could ignore it, get offended, or treat it all like one big joke. She chose the latter.

"Funny, even with the beard, you don't look much like Santa."

"And if you're working here, you're not much of a good gal," he said as he flashed a strip of yellow between his nonexistent lips.

How close to the truth was that? She couldn't help it, and laughed. "What's your name?"

"Snake's my biker name, but it could be anything you want."

Dick breath? But she kept that to herself. "Snake, let me be straight with you. I serve beer and whiskey. I clean the glasses and put up with crude comments from guys like you because the tips are good and because there's a restraining order preventing me from working with children. If you want a drink or even a plate of greasy fries, then I'm your gal, but anything other than that, I'd have to be twenty years older and a helluva lot more desperate. So what'll it be?"

There was a bark of laughter from his friend beside him. Dick breath / Snake's dark eyes did a quick once over, measuring her up. His eyes narrowed and nostrils flared, but his voice was laced with humor as if he thought this was all one big joke. Maybe it was.

Nikki shifted slightly back, a tad nervous that her mouth had run off without her head again.

"I'll have a beer." Then he leaned closer. Nikki could smell the bike exhaust on him and the bar peanuts on his breath. "This ain't over. I'm just bidin' my time."

Nikki swallowed hard, but flashed her most charming smile in an attempt to smooth his ego. "Good choice."

The rest of the night was a blur of whiskey shots, sour beers, and avoiding butt slaps whenever she left the protective space behind the bar. By half past two in morning, her feet ached and her hands were chapped from washing dishes with the industrial strength soap, but she'd made a few hundred in tips so the financial pressure eased somewhat, knowing she could buy groceries and get her phone turned back on.

"You ready?" Mike asked. They'd cleaned up, and he was already totaling the receipts for the night.

"Yeah, all set." She grabbed her purse from behind the bar, more than ready to call it a night.

Mike reached behind her and got his shotgun. "I'll watch you walk out. Make sure you get to your car. "

"That's not really necessary."

Mike raised one eyebrow. "I wasn't asking permission. People know you'll be carrying cash. No use getting robbed on your first night. I won't get you back after that."

She nodded, glad he seemed to want her back at least. Of course, she wasn't sure what it said about her life that now she required an armed escort to get to her car.

Nikki followed Mike as he held the door for her. "Is he with you?" he asked with a nod toward the darkened parking lot.

Nikki took a look. Parked alongside Old Bertha was a cherry-red pickup, and leaning against the bumper was a tall, sexy cowboy. His tanned arms were folded across his chest, showing off a pair of biceps that had been hiding beneath long sleeves. His booted feet were crossed, giving the impression that he had all night.

Something warm and tingly rushed through her as she recognized the slight tilt of the hat and casual stance that was all Jett. She said goodbye to Mike and walked over to the long drink of water that would've made a lesser woman giggle. "What're you doing here?"

"I heard a rumor so outrageous, I had to confirm it for myself."

"Which was?"

"That a crazy, sexy woman was throwing caution to the wind by serving drinks to misfits and lowlifes."

"People are saying I'm sexy?"

"Like I said, it was a rumor."

"But do you think I'm sexy?"

"I think you're crazy."

"That works, too." The twinkle in his eye and the slight lift of the corner of his mouth had her forgetting all about her tired feet and aching back. "So, you're here to lecture me?"

"I'm here to see you home."

"Not sure I want that. You're a bit grumpy." She smiled back.

"I'm a bit tired."

Night had tamed the summer heat and a gentle breeze rustled through Nikki's hair, sending a shiver across her skin. A bit wanton, a bit bold, Nikki stepped a little closer. Teasing Jett was turning out to be the best part of her day. "Would a kiss cheer you up?"

She was playing with fire, and she knew it. Maybe the brotherly kiss he'd given her last night still smarted. Or maybe she just wanted to see if he'd take the bait.

He didn't

"No. But quitting this job would."

"Not going to happen," she countered.

His smile deepened like he knew exactly how this would play out, and it was all to his advantage. "Thought as much. Being reasonable was never your strong suit."

Okay, his short one-liners were starting to wear thin, which had nothing, of course, to do with his rejection of her kiss.

She stood straighter, all the playfulness gone. "I can take care of myself. You don't have to see me home."

Jett pushed off the bumper and walked over to the driver's side. "That's the thing, Texas. I do."

Jett followed her home and when she turned off toward her house, his truck was right behind her. Slightly embarrassed by the attention and what seeing her to her door implied about her character, Nikki quickly got out of the truck and up the steps. Did he really think she couldn't take care of herself? Lord, he was worse than a card-carrying NRA father on prom night. Jett pulled his truck alongside the porch and watched as she opened her door. "See," she turned letting him see the door behind her. "I'm in. You can go now."

"Good," he said over the rolled-down window. "Lock the door behind you, and be ready for me to pick you up at nine o'clock."

Nine? That was less than six hours from now. "Why?"

The porch light fell harshly on his face, highlighting the dark circles and etched lines of fatigue. There was a quick flexing of his jaw, and something flashed in his eyes that made Nikki glad she hadn't come across him in a dark alley. "Do you know how to shoot a gun?"

She shrugged one shoulder.

"Bring your father's old shotgun. It's time someone taught you how to handle one."

Nikki watched the red truck disappear into the night. In the past, she'd made her fair share of lame mistakes—pink hair, a poorly thought out tattoo, a tell-off text to a previous boss, not to mention the unflattering picture of her on Facebook. But not until she agreed to let an armed and dangerous man take her out to the middle of the desert with no witnesses could she have won the "too stupid to live" award.

Chapter 15

Nikki woke to a pounding on the front door. The crappy mini-blinds on the front window rattled and the hollowness of the door echoed along the paper-thin walls. *Christ*, it sounded as if the whole house was going to come down.

Another pounding. "Nikki, open the door right now, or I swear to God, I'll break the window."

Nikki closed her eyes briefly. Brothers sucked, and stubborn, bullheaded ones even worse.

It had been five days and four nights since she'd started working at The Pitt, and Cole, apparently, had just found out. Her lucky reprieve had ended. What did Lady Luck have against her anyway? Had she flirted with Mr. Luck or something?

Take for example, Jett. Every night after work she'd walk out to her truck and every night he was waiting to follow her home. No matter what she told him, he still showed up, followed her home, made sure she got inside. The whole thing was starting to panic her, starting to make her feel like Jett wanted something more than she was willing to give.

She hoped that once they started shooting lessons, Jett would feel more confident in letting her drive home at nights, but if anything things actually became worse. Not for him of course—all signs showed that he was cool as ever—but for her. His manner every day when he came to pick her up was easygoing, charming, the one that every gal in town, young or old, had fallen in love with at some point.

The door rattled again. Cole wasn't going away. "I'm coming," she yelled. "Let me get dressed."

She'd taken to sleeping in nothing more than panties and a tank top since the nights were so damn warm and the days off-the-charts hot. Who was she kidding? The heat originated in the afternoons spent with Jett as he taught her how to hold the gun, where to place her hands, how to stand. And of course, all this consisted of touching, lots of touching. He didn't even seem to be aware of how often his front brushed against her back, his fingers on hers, the angle of his jaw against her cheek. There'd been times when she rolled her shoulders to get more room, and he had immediately backed off. But then a minute later, he was back again, brushing up against her or whispering instructions in her ear.

It didn't take long until the back of her neck would grow warm, and her skin would feel flushed. She had a hard time concentrating. And the worst part was, she seemed to be the only one affected. There'd been times she imagined he'd been trying for a reaction from her, that he'd been doing the whole thing on purpose. Especially when he *accidentally* brushed the back of his hand against her breast. She'd almost fallen to her knees at the spark she felt. She'd turned on him, ready to call him on it, but all she got was his charming smile and a blank look.

Maybe it was all in her head. He'd never done more than kiss her on the cheek the night they went to dinner. He'd brushed off any other advances she tried to make. She was the one all crazy and irritable, and he, well, he just seemed to be as nonchalant as always.

Or was he trying to mess with her head? Nine-ball was more of a mental game than anything else. Did he know that? Was he trying to throw her game off?

She couldn't think of that now. Right now, she had an angry older sibling waiting to lecture her to death.

Nikki flung the door open just as Cole had his fist up, ready to pound again.

"What's going on?" she asked, putting on her confused and concerned look. Playing dumb would buy her at least a few minutes.

"Don't start with me. You know exactly why I'm here."

Okay, playing dumb bought her nothing.

Cole pushed his way past her into the living room. His shirt-sleeves were rolled up, fingers dark with dirt. The smell of horse, hay, and sweat filled the room. Nikki was surprised the scent wasn't as offensive as it had always been. She inhaled deeply, letting the fragrance of Texas and sunlight settle her more than she would've ever admitted.

Cole stopped, braced his hands on his hips, and stared at the ceiling as if trying for composure. "Just tell me one thing. Are you stripping?"

"What? No. I tend bar, that's it. I promise."

He turned on her. "You bartend at a strip bar, Nikki. A *strip bar*."

"You told me to go and get a job. I thought you'd be happy." Not really, but it sounded believable.

An ugly snort. "You thought I'd be happy that my only sister works at the sleaziest place in town, where the customers are nothing more than drug runners and criminals? What happens when you walk out into that parking lot at night? It's not a question of 'if' with those guys, it's a question of 'when.'"

"It's not like that." Sure, the men that frequented The Pitt were a bit rough, but other than giving her a hard time, they all seemed like pretty decent guys. Most held down blue-collar jobs, and Snake had even mentioned that his granddaughter had gotten a full ride to college. He carried her picture around in his wallet like a proud papa. She had a feeling most were like overgrown puppies, their barks worse than their bites. But trying to convince Cole of anything was harder than getting a bad tattoo removed—she would know. "Most aren't bad guys."

"And you know this how—by your vast worldly wisdom? You can't even pay your phone bill on time, and yet you expect me to take your opinion on human nature?"

That pissed her off. What, Cole had never screwed up? He'd never made a mistake? She knew better, and he should've also. But she'd fought this fight before and knew arguing would do no good. Cole could be stubborn, but her father had always said Nikki took the Logan family trait to a whole new level. "My phone will be back on soon. I can take care of myself. I don't need you to protect me anymore."

"Sunshine, you've never been able to take care of yourself. If it wasn't bailing on your rental agreement or screwing up your chances for an academic scholarship, it was something else."

That wasn't fair. She'd backed out of her rent because a weird ex-boyfriend was semi-stalking her; and her scholarship, well, she had gotten a scholarship . . . sort of. Regardless, his words cut.

Cole had never actually come right out and said she was a burden, but she'd known, of course. It was hard not to when she witnessed the tightness around his eyes and the thinning of his face when he worked himself to near death. But now, to actually hear him say that he was sick to death of bailing her out gave her a panicky feeling of wanting to run hard and fast and never look back.

Nikki turned her back on him, automatically calculating how long it would take to pack up all of her stuff.

Cole continued to pace behind her. "I don't understand. I called Mrs. Lewis, and she said the accounting position was still open. This town is desperate for new tax advisors."

Nikki started folding her blankets—the first time she'd done so since coming home. "That's not why I came back."

"What? But—"

She whirled on him. "I didn't come back to this small-minded town just to work at Mrs. Lewis's Taxes-R-Us. I'm not here to make a life and set up some white picket fence and join the Rotary Club. I'm here to pay back a debt. That's all. After that, I'm out of here."

Cole whipped his hat off and slapped it against his leg. Dust motes caught the sunlight and floated in a cloud around them. "What debt, Nikki? What the hell have you gotten yourself into?"

"It's my problem. Not your concern."

"Everything about you is my concern. Has been since Dad died."

"Well, I'm not a kid anymore, and I'm sorry. I'm sorry you had to raise me. I'm sorry I ruined your life and made you grow old before your time. But it wasn't my fault Dad died, and it wasn't my fault Mom did, either."

Something she said must've gotten through to him, because for the first time in Nikki's life Cole stood open-mouthed with nothing to say. He took a step back and ran his hand through his messed hair. "You didn't ruin my life."

The thickness in her throat made it hard to swallow. "You act like I did."

Cole looked down at his boots, crossed his arms, then uncrossed them and hooked his thumbs in his belt loops. Nikki experienced a flash of sympathy. They didn't do this. Logans never talked about their problems. It was no wonder, since neither of them was any good at it.

"Those were tough times, those years. And I know I didn't handle everything right. Didn't even come close. But God, Nikki, I tried. I tried so damn hard to keep food on the table and make sure you said your prayers at night so that you didn't end up like one of those lost souls down at The Pitt. So . . . so that you didn't end up like me."

A heaviness seeped into her chest and for a panicked second she wondered if she'd lost the ability to draw air. She swallowed and blinked against the burn behind her eyes.

"Quit." His voice broke, and Nikki couldn't ever remember a time when she'd seen her brother this close to tears. "Just quit, Sunshine. Please. For me?"

The walls closed down on her so fast that the room spun. She turned and braced herself against the back of the couch, no longer able to look Cole in the eye. She focused on the washed-out faded pillow that had been her mother's, and the hole in the couch where the stray cat she'd taken in for a day had sharpened his claws.

She searched for words to explain. The ones that would ease his pain and her guilt, but in the end she said the only words that she could. "I'm so sorry."

Chapter 16

Jett threw off his bow tie the way one would a bad polyester shirt. He just wished he could throw off the stink from his dad's fundraiser as easily. The party had all the usual attendants—money, greed, power, and influence—and lasted well into the night. Now all he wanted was a cold beer and a hot shower.

He threw his jacket onto the bed, pulling out the dozen napkins marked with phone numbers that had been stuffed into his coat pocket. He took the wad and threw it in the trash, not at all interested. Jett was used to the attention—figured out the score long ago. The women at these parties didn't want him because he was such a nice guy. It was the Avery name they'd like to brush shoulders with. The shallowness never bothered him before, but lately the whole political dance was starting to wear thin.

Tonight had been worse than usual. Tonight had him on edge. He rubbed at the coarseness of his three-day old beard, which he hadn't bothered to take care of earlier. Maybe he should've played the game better, but it had been tough watching fathers push their daughters toward him, and when Jett showed no interest, watch his brother-in-law step in and take Jett's place. Jett had always wondered how his sister, Lauren, dealt with being married to such a jackass. It wasn't until tonight he realized she didn't. Lauren spent the majority of her time with her nose in a martini and a socialite smile plastered on her face. He guessed that was one way to not feel anything anymore.

He stripped and turned the shower on full blast, wanting the water to be extra hot. He padded out to his kitchen naked and pulled a cold bottle of beer from the fridge. Back in the bathroom, he stood under the massaging showerhead to hit the spot at the back of his neck where a low throbbing had started. When he'd first bought the house, he had the whole plumbing system redone just to get adequate water pressure. Now, with his new, luxury 180° rainmaker massaging showerhead with dual air and light features, Jett was a shower snob.

He let the water sluice over his face as he sipped from the still-cold bottle. It was a total redneck thing to do—drinking in the shower. If he tried hard, he could conjure up his mother's disapproving look—the image made him smile. He loved his family, really he did, but it came as no surprise to him that his loyalty ran deeper to the Logans than even to his own blood.

Cole had never wanted anything from him, neither had Nikki. He wondered how many napkins he'd get if he was just some truck driver, making thirty grand a year, with a standard tract-home shower. Nikki wouldn't care though. She'd never put much stock in his family or their money. More than likely, for her, his family was the biggest deterrent to taking their relationship to the next level.

Nikki. The thought of her had him turning his shower to cold. He'd never been celibate this long before. After Nikki had run off, he'd been heartbroken and wandered around in a dark funk for weeks. Anger and a "screw-her" attitude came riding in hard after that. It wasn't until Katie made a comment about Jett not picking an easy one to love that he'd taken a step back. Katie always said loving a Logan was hard, and she certainly had first-hand experience. But she also said that loving a Logan was worth it. They'd never leave you, never cheat on you, would give you the shirt off their back, and once they were committed, they were yours for life.

The problem was Nikki was scared to death to commit. He knew where he'd gone wrong the first time. He'd gone too fast, pushed too hard, and like a skittish colt, she'd bolted. But the Logans hadn't cornered the market on stubbornness. Jett was used to getting what he wanted, and this time he wanted more than just a one-night stand.

Of course, happily-ever-after was the one thing she'd spent her whole life running from. Yeah, he knew Nikki was a mess. Her job situation more than proved his point. Yet he followed her like a lost ship would the North Star. Jett studied women the way others studied foreign languages. Nikki might have been a challenge, but Jett could still read her. Her words might say one thing, but her body told him a different story—Nikki loved him. It was in the way her body moved, the hope in her eyes when she thought he wasn't looking. The shudder in her breath when he held her. The way her heartbeat sped up to match his.

Nikki belonged to him. Hell, the whole town already thought they were together. He just had to get Nikki to realize it. And if he had to coerce and bribe to accomplish his goal, well, he hadn't been raised as a senator's son for nothing.

Jett knew he had to speak to Nikki in her own language. Connect with her on a level she understood. Use her own warped sense of honor—the one that would let her walk away from a promise to him, but never a promise made across a pool table. The one that had her willing to come back home to pay a debt to a sleazy strip joint owner, but unwilling to take a chance on the two of them.

So Jett had learned to play pool. Not just play, but play well enough to hustle a hustler. The last two years of his self-imposed celibacy had been rough, but he'd kept busy flying back and forth to Vegas, stacking the odds in his favor. He aimed to play the smartest nine-ball of his life. With stakes this high, he couldn't afford to lose.

But the key to playing good pool was focus, which hadn't been a problem with Nikki miles away and no visuals to get him distracted. But now, having to watch Nikki's backside sway as she walked, the tight T-shirts that showed off—if memory served him correctly—a pair of the most beautiful breasts he'd ever seen. Her dark, just-rolled-out-of-bed hair, turquoise eyes that sparkled green in certain lights, blue in others, and full and juicy lips—he was a man on the edge.

Jett got out of the shower and wrapped a towel around his waist.

Even showered and clean, he couldn't shake the panicked feeling that rode low in his gut. He finished off his beer and headed to the kitchen for another. There was more to this thing with Nikki than having an itch that couldn't be scratched. He felt the desperation of a match already lost, because no matter how well he played Nikki, she was a flight risk.

He could smell a runner a mile away, and Nikki reeked of it. She had just enough money in her pocket and just enough of a mess to leave behind. He wasn't stupid. He saw how she was sleeping out on the couch, not even bothering to unpack. No, there was nothing long term about Nikki. And that pissed him off even more than her asinine job or the mouth she had on her.

He eyed the digital clock on his bedstand—two-thirty flashed in neon red. Nikki would be getting off from The Pitt right now. He should be there making sure she got home safe.

Dark parking lot. Deserted bar. Mean drunks.

One thing he'd learned in Vegas—gambling on the edge was a sure-fire way to lose. A person had to know when to cut bait and when to cast his pole someplace else.

Nikki, in jean cut-offs and a tight shirt, stranded on the side of the road with that piece-of-crap truck and no cell phone.

She wouldn't be stupid enough to walk home? Would she? Yet stupid seemed to find Nikki like a defense attorney found loopholes.

The smartest thing he could do was walk away from Nikki. He could feel the wild beast inside of him start to growl. The one he always kept locked down, the one he kept hidden under his polish of charm and wit. Nikki had that effect on him—always had. She called to that primal part of him that he didn't like to see or feel. Didn't like to remember he had.

He groaned and threw his wet towel across the room. Sometimes the beast won out over the man.

Not bothering with underwear or socks, he pulled on the first thing he saw. He paused, keys in hand, phone in his pocket, and caught a glimpse of himself in the full-length closet mirror. The term "dead man walking" didn't even come close. His face was pale underneath the three days' growth of blond scruff. His eyes were red and puffy, mouth bracketed with deep grooves. He was nauseous from lack of sleep watching over Nikki the last two weeks, and near crazed from the lack of something else.

He wasn't a gambling man, and here he was, placing all his chips on the one person who was the polar opposite of a sure thing.

Then his image shattered, and it took him a moment to realize the red stuff splattering on the glass at his feet was coming from the blood on his fist.

Chapter 17

"I'm ready to go, Mike," Nikki said to the open door at the back of the bar. Her socks were wet in her boots, she'd spilled some beer on her sleeve, and her lower back was on fire. But the bar was clean, and her tips safely stuffed in her back pocket. All in all, a good day.

She heard the wheels of Mike's chair before she saw him, his black reading glasses pushed up against the sun-spotted expanse of his forehead. "Is that boy of yours out there waiting for you?"

Nikki wasn't sure what Jett would think of being referred to as a boy, but Mike had his own way of thinking. Anyone who still had all their hair was considered a young 'un.

Jett had been there every night since she started working at The Pitt, no matter what she said to try and discourage him. She threw up one shoulder in response to Mike's question, not letting on how much she wanted her answer to be yes. "Not sure. Probably."

Mike put his glasses down on his nose and peered at her from above the rims. "If I know Jett, he'll be there."

Nikki hid her sudden need to smile. She wasn't ready to admit that the best part of her night was seeing Jett in the parking lot after work.

Mike was settled in his office chair, already on his second cup of chamomile tea. She knew he had no desire to walk her out.

"I'm sure you're right," she said, then threw her apron in the "2b washed" pile and got her purse from behind the bar. "See you tomorrow. And Mike, make sure you get home soon. Don't stay too long."

"Have a good one," he said, already rolling out of sight. Mike didn't take babying by anyone, much less a twenty-four-year-old girl.

Nikki got the tips out of her pocket to put the wad of folded bills in her purse. Her thumb fanned the thickness; tips were good here. A gal had to put up with a lot of smack, but if you could dish it out and not take offense, the money was good. A few more days and she could get the car out of the shop. A few more weeks and she could start to make a dent on what she owed Mike.

And then what? No matter. She'd figure it out.

Nikki pushed through the front door and out into the night. She stood still and took a lungful of air that wasn't laced with beer and stale sweat. The clear black sky was a blanket littered with sparkling glitter and the moon hung fat and happy in the center like a well-fed toddler. Nikki wanted to reach out and touch it the way she had as a child.

The memory flooded back of her father and her walking home from the pool hall late at night. When she'd been too young to stay home by herself and her mother had wanted a night out, her dad would usually end up with her. Not that Nikki had minded. He'd taken her to exciting places, dark smoky places, but where most of the men were really nice and usually gave her as much soda and French fries as she could eat. There'd been some nights, if her dad was in the middle of a winning streak, that she'd curl up on a chair or in a corner and fall asleep. But there'd also been other times when they'd walk home together, and he'd tell her stories that his grandfather told him about how the sun was jealous of the moon because when people looked up at the moon, they smiled, but when people looked up at the sun, they squinted.

He told her the story about two foolish girls who wanted to marry stars, but who, once they had, weren't happy living so high up in the sky away from home. Then the conversation always turned to the horse ranch he wanted to start and how the family would be so much better off once he got his big win. As a child, she loved to hear his stories, his hopes and dreams; now as an adult, the memory made her sad. Sad because he never got his dream? Or sad because his dream was what crushed their family?

Nikki shook her head. What was with this melancholy that seemed to follow her ever since she'd gotten back home? Was it any wonder she hadn't wanted to stay? Any wonder why she couldn't wait to leave?

Yet, as she scanned the parking lot looking for Jett's truck, a renegade thought sprinted across her mind. Jett was here. Jett was home, and her home could be anywhere he was.

Not seeing his truck, Nikki tried to brush off the sinking disappointment at his no-show. It wasn't like he'd told her he'd be here. And hadn't she told him every night not to come? Still, his absence had her kicking herself for her stupid "Jett and home" thought.

She briefly considered going in and asking Mike to walk her out, but the lot was empty except for her pickup and Mike's. Tired, she wanted to get home, and of course, didn't see the motorcycle parked on the other side of her truck until she was almost on top of it.

"Hey there, good-looking."

Nikki jumped, her heart doing a painful stop and start. She struggled to place the shadowy figure on top of the bike even as her eyes adjusted to the night. It wasn't until her brain registered the name "good-looking" that she made the connection.

"Christ, Snake, you scared me." Her fingers rested at the base of her throat, feeling the pounding of her pulse beneath her necklace.

"I wanted to talk to you. Thought I wait, sees if you want a ride home." His words were a bit slurred as he tongued the tobacco wad in his lower lip to the opposite side. He swiped at a piece of long gray hair that had slipped from his ponytail.

"The bar closed about an hour ago, Snake." She had no idea what he'd done to get that biker name, but hoped it had to do with the tattoo curling up his arm and not with how he reacted when disappointed. "What have you been doing out here this whole time?"

He answered her question with a lift of his arm, took a sip from a metal flask, then leaned heavily against the silver glint of his handle bars.

For a moment, he was so still she thought he'd fallen asleep. She should walk away, go back to the bar, get Mike to take Snake home. Snake would be pissed in the morning about having to leave his bike here, but he was in no shape to drive. She turned to go.

"Wait, don't leave."

Nikki looked back, and then sighed when she saw what Snake was attempting to do. He had tried to swing his leg around to get off his bike, but his boot had gotten caught, and he was wobbling precariously. She rushed forward to steady him.

Snake's arm went around her; his face buried itself in her hair. "You's so pretty, Texas. Smell good, too."

"Don't call me Texas," she snapped. Only one person got to call her that. And at the moment, that person was on her hit list.

Nikki groaned. Lord, Snake was heavy. Was he even trying to stand on his own two feet? "Geesh, Snake, unhook your boot already."

He had to be over two hundred pounds of barley hops and fried food. If he didn't get both his feet on the ground quick, grandpa or not, she'd let him drop.

"Maybe you can drive me home, Texas. Or maybe I can go home with you. Yeah, that be better. Sometimes the girlfriend gets a little testy when I bring home other girls."

Ya think. But she didn't want to get into a discussion; the fumes on his breath could start dry kindling on fire.

"Last time . . . yeah, last time was bad. She shot her."

"Your girlfriend shot your other . . . girlfriend?"

"No, girlfriend shot my dog."

"Your *dog*?"

"The dog never liked her. But she's fine, only missing a foot."

"The girlfriend or the dog?" She groaned. She should know better than to get into a conversation with a drunk.

Snake was still balancing on one leg, but instead of helping her he batted at her with his hand. She assumed he'd meant to stroke her cheek, but it was more like pawing than a caress.

"Ouch."

"Sorry. There's three of ya. Trying to figure out which one yous is."

"I'm the middle one. Just stand on your own two feet, please."

"Oh, yeah," he said, like he'd forgotten what they were doing out here in a dark parking lot.

To his credit, Snake tried. He wiggled his foot this way and that way, sawing the black leather of his boot against the chrome of his bike. But Nikki and her good intentions were no match for two hundred-plus pounds and a lot of liquor.

They both went down. Nikki fell to her knees. Her head cracked against Snake's jaw. And for a split second, Nikki's only thought was she'd never make fun of the "I've fallen and I can't get up" commercials again.

Get off! That's what Nikki would have screamed if she'd had enough breath to fuel her words. As it was, Snake's excessive girth had sprawled out on top of her, and Nikki's face was kissing tire-trampled gravel. Dirt had a certain smell, not entirely unpleasant, but the taste . . .

Then there was a grunt and she was free. It took a moment to push up to her knees, but not nearly as long to turn toward the sound of something solid hitting glass.

The moon shone bright and the light filtered through the finger-like branches of the trees as it illuminated the two men struggling. Or better yet, one man struggling and the other, slamming a head into the windshield of Old Bertha.

Crack.

There was no contest. Snake was bigger, taller, and outweighed Jett by more than fifty pounds, but Jett was like nothing she'd ever seen. Jett was crazy.

The cool, calm, charm boy had lost his head and . . . his hat. His hair was wild, shirt undone, sleeves rolled up exposing forearms, corded and veined, as his hands lifted Snake's head, then slammed it back down again.

The sound turned to a dull thudding, and Snake's moans stopped altogether. A dark liquid that looked like chocolate, but Nikki knew was blood, spread across the windshield.

"Jett. Stop!"

How long had it taken for her to find her voice? Too long by the looks of Snake's limp body. Jett looked up and found Nikki's gaze. Even in the soft light of the evening, Nikki could see him. His teeth were bared, sucking air as he panted, biceps straining against the faded cotton of his shirt. It was too dark for her to see the color of his eyes but it didn't matter. Crazy had its own scent and the air was thick with it.

Jett released his hold on Snake's hair and shirt. The body crumpled to the ground. Jett stepped over him like he'd step over road kill. He walked toward her. Nikki was still on her knees, and scrambled to her feet, her flight response firing like it never had with Snake.

Jett stood before her. His hair was longer than she'd realized and darker when wet with sweat. His shirt was unbuttoned, showing off a wide expanse of smooth chest and giving her a prime view of another button undone—the top one on his jeans. The waistband hung low, flaunting a certain set of sexy abdominal muscles only very fit men could flaunt. And if she didn't miss her guess, she'd say Jett was going commando in more ways than one.

And that's when her mouth went dry.

She broke her gaze and looked past him. The black lump on the ground didn't move. Then she whispered the one question she'd never thought she'd have to ask Jett. "Did you kill him?"

He didn't blink, didn't even grimace, but held his stance like a caveman who'd just brought home dinner. "I hope so. Save me the trouble later."

"And I hope *not*. What were you thinking? He wasn't going to hurt me, at least not on purpose." Nikki made a move to go check if Snake was still breathing.

Jett's hand clamped around her arm. "Get in the truck."

The growl in his voice had her searching his eyes, and she didn't like what she saw. Butterscotch indeed, what a tame word compared to what was staring back at her. She'd seen kerosene that color, right before it burst into flames.

Nikki jerked out of his grasp, then hid the meaning behind the gesture by wiping at the dirt she was sure was smeared across her face. *Time to go.* Quickly, she started to rummage through her purse, trying to find her keys.

"Uh uh, not that truck." He took her by the arm again, opened his passenger side door, and nudged her toward the seat.

And for the second time that night, Nikki thought of making a run for it. She'd only seen Jett like this a few times before, and she could recount them all. The time he pulled her out of Johnny Town's pickup, both drunk, but only one of them with his clothes on. When a bunch of drunk cowboys had ganged up on Cole after hours at a bar, beaten him senseless, and had stolen his wallet. And when she was gathering all her clothes to run back home after he confessed that he loved her, always had.

Nikki got in Jett's truck, and he got behind the wheel. He took his phone and threw it on her lap. "Text Mike and let him know some guy is passed out in the parking lot. Mike can handle it from there."

Nikki nodded, not at all reassured by Jett's concern. Something was riding him tonight. He didn't normally act like this, and not knowing what to expect made catching a lift with him all the more disturbing. When she'd been a kid and gotten in trouble at school, her mom would be called to come and pick her up. She remembered sitting on that long bench outside the principal's office waiting for her mother's disapproval. The whole way home her stomach would be in cramps, sticky sweat would wet her palms and the back of her neck, imitating the feeling of throwing up.

This ride was way worse.

To give her something to do, she rummaged in his glove box for some gum. She'd never actually seen Jett resort to violence. As a man known for his even temper, he always had self-control, even in the worst possible scenarios. Cole's nickname for him, Cool man, which had been adopted by the town, spoke of a guy who could defuse just about any situation with sugared words and logical arguments. And on the rare occasion when a situation did call for fists, it was usually with Cole. But who could blame him? The Logans could piss off an angel.

Even if she told someone what had happened, they'd never believe her. More than likely they'd blame her. She was the one with the reputation for fighting, which had started with Billy Rodriguez in the second grade and lasted right on through high school.

Nikki risked a glance toward Jett. Maybe he'd gone crazy. He looked crazy. Her GQ cowboy had been replaced by a seething, spitting fire dragon. His eyes were bloodshot with dark circles underneath. Hair messed, jaw scruffy. She couldn't remember ever seeing Jett not clean-shaven. It scared her to see something raw underneath the polished exterior. Scared her, or made her heart beat faster in a way that had nothing to do with fear.

And something had her wondering exactly what Jett's breaking point was? Did she have the guts to find out?

It wasn't until they pulled into a circle drive that Nikki looked up. A rush of warning flooded her belly. They weren't at her house. He hadn't driven to her home, but instead, to his.

Jett didn't wait for her, just got out of the truck and headed inside. Nikki scrambled to follow. Jett's house was nothing like hers. If there'd been railroad tracks in this town, his house would've been on the side where the houses weren't trailers and the homes had manicured lawns instead of a rusted-out car and a pit bull. Even the small porch was freshly painted, and the front door had a real security screen that kept out more than just the mosquitos.

Nikki walked through the door, which he'd left open. The AC kicked in and on the whirl of cool air floated the scent of leather from the butter-cream couch and lemon furniture polish. It said a lot about the man and the lifestyle Jett lived that he thought nothing of choosing dark wood floors and white leather furniture when he lived in a dusty cowpoke town. Immaculate and utterly stylish.

Nikki closed the door behind her and followed Jett into the kitchen. She watched as he popped open a bottle of beer, stood right at the sink, and guzzled the whole thing down. The long expanse of his throat had images running through her mind she preferred to not think about, so instead of torturing herself she turned and walked away.

Nikki walked over to one of the expertly lighted and framed modern art pieces on the wall. She stared at the bold strokes across a white canvas, and shook her head. Why people would ever spend money on things like this blew her mind.

She continued down the hall. It had been a few years since she'd been here and last time, there'd been rooms that Jett hadn't finished furnishing. Curious, she opened the first bedroom door. She peeked inside—hardwood floors and a bench press in the center. Free weights along one wall, punching bag hanging in the corner, a chin-up bar. Nikki arched an eyebrow. Interesting. When had Jett taken up boxing? Maybe that explained what happened with Snake earlier.

Never one to waste time worrying about a little rudeness, Nikki walked across the hall to the other bedroom, curious to see if there were any other surprises in store. She wasn't disappointed.

She gasped as she took in the spare bedroom, which had been changed into a miniature pool hall. The walls were painted steel gray, floors diagonally planked with dark wood, a few barstools scattered about, and in the center the pool table. She didn't even have to look at the logo stamped on the dark cherry wood to know it was a Diamond Professional, the one used at professional pool tournaments. She recognized the diamond inlaid sights and rounded rail top with no metal ornamentation to catch clothing or damage cues. She'd drooled over pictures of the flush rail design that made shooting out of the pocket just as easy as shooting off the rail.

The skin between her shoulder blades tightened, and her heart went into a crazy stutter. She'd always wanted a table like this. Growing up, her father had taught her on a homemade table with six coffee cans for pockets. It wasn't until he'd won a table in a three-day rubber match that they'd had a respectable one in their home. Here, within her reach, was a table her father would've broken his left leg to own. That she herself had obsessed over in the glossy catalogues. And here Jett had bought this table on a whim. A simple spur of the moment impulse to try something new.

Nikki couldn't help herself. She stepped forward and let her fingers caress the smoothest of felt. Proficiency at pool might be a sure sign of a misspent youth, but pool had also been her friend, her comforter, her religion. Like most hustlers, she'd worshipped at the altar of the green, or in Jett's Diamond Professional case, the royal blue felt. Deep down, pool players were gamblers—a person couldn't divorce the two. Most players she knew would gamble on anything from a cockroach race to how many times a coin would land on heads. In every hustler there was a risk taker, a con man, a place where right and wrong, truth and lie bent to their advantage. But just like a hustler sizing up another player, Nikki could tell Jett was none of these things. He was a straightforward shooter. Honest. A what-you-see-is-what-you-get kinda guy. So why would Jett, a charmer, a womanizer for sure, but deep down an all-around nice guy, have a Diamond Professional in his spare bedroom?

Every time Nikki had seen a pool table, especially one this beautiful, she'd felt an itch to pick up a stick and send a ball home to its pocket. But now as she looked at this one, then at the cues that lined the wall, all she wanted to do was run.

She turned to go and almost ran smack into Jett. He filled the doorway, casual, easy, but she could almost see the waves of tension rolling off him.

With beer in one hand, shirt draped open, eyes still hard and dark, he was a sight to behold. His kerosene gaze raked over her, and she felt the need to grip the solid support of the cherry wood beneath her hand.

He took a long pull from the bottle. "We have a game to finish."

She watched as he walked into the room, decreasing the square footage by half, and picked up one of the sticks that lined the wall. He chalked the tip, the sound of rubber against the blue chalk like a self-satisfied sigh after hot sex. The rack was already set, balls one through nine in a tight diamond formation awaiting the break that would scatter them across the blue in some haphazard way that begged to be angled and steered back into order.

Nikki's dad had always told her that the best pool players had an internal radar that alerted them to trouble. That was how a hustler knew which mark to go after and which player to avoid. There was a level of risk that every pool player thrived on, but there was also a level that made a smart player decide to pay up and go home.

"I believe it's my break," he said.

She had been up five games when they'd left The Smoke House, but as the lights had shut down, she'd lost her concentration and choked the last shot. She'd given Jett the table, but at that time wasn't too concerned. That night she'd watched Jett closely, and, yes, his skills had improved, but she was confident he still wasn't her equal across the table.

Then again, she hadn't seen Jett quite like this. Gone was the cautious man who gentled each ball into its pocket. Instead, a hard stroke broke the balls apart, three balls sinking with the initial break. Jett pocketed the balls with speed and force that sure worked a number on her confidence.

Every pool player had seen it. The lucky ones even experienced it. Some called it the zone, but to Nikki it was more than just a single-minded focus on the game. To her it was when the balls seemed guided by a magnet or remote control: misses were simply not an option and the cue ball was willed into the perfect placement for the next smooth shot.

She watched as Jett worked the table with force and energy that took no prisoners and gave no mercy. This Jett was furious, untamed, and totally unpredictable. From his pummeling of Snake to his angry vent at the table, this wasn't the Jett she knew. It wasn't that she was afraid of losing, there was no shame in choking a difficult shot, she was afraid of winning against this Jett. In a world of pool hustlers, predominantly occupied by men, Nikki had learned when a mark would lose well and let her leave with her winnings . . . or not. Every internal signal screamed that this game had too much risk written all over it. It was time to put her stick up and live to play another day. Nikki inched toward the doorway, taking a lazy, one-armed stance against the door jam. "I'm gonna use your bathroom."

It was the oldest trick in the book. If a player found he was in over his head, he would request a bathroom break while propping his cue stick up against the table. Then he'd take off out the back window, leaving his cue as collateral for the bet. Nikki didn't have a cue stick to leave, but that didn't matter one iota to her. Besides, she wasn't backing out of the game, just backing out of the game *right now*. Later, when Jett evened out and regained his composure, and she wasn't all alone without any witnesses, she would play him fair.

Jett looked up, his gaze as intense as a double shot of espresso. "The closest one is in my room. You remember the way."

She did, not that she wanted to, but with his stare pinned on hers, she had no choice but to make her way across the hall into his bedroom. She'd been in his room once before, two years ago during a drunken one-night stand that had turned into one big mess. Maybe it had been the tequila that night that had her forgetting the little details of what his room revealed. Tonight she had no such blinders.

The master bedroom showed Jett to be a neat freak. There was a massive wood bedframe and a black armoire, but no clothes on the floor, no pile of magazines on the bedside table, no personal touches, just everything neat and in its place. On the wall above his bed frame was a large modern painting by Twombly that used to hang in the living room. The green chalkboard-like painting with large loopy scribbles still drove her crazy. Why anyone would pay decent money for a print that looked as if a two-year-old had gone crazy with a piece of chalk was beyond her. Even though she knew that the original in the Met museum would go for over two mil and this piece was only a print, it had still cost way more than Nikki would ever fork over. Confused, she'd asked him about it once.

"Why? I don't get it."

He laughed. "That's what I ask every time I see this painting."

"Then why buy it?"

One shoulder came up in a half-hearted shrug. "I think that's the point. You're not supposed to understand, but to think about what it represents."

Nikki didn't get it. Maybe a person had to have money to burn to appreciate the finer intricacies of a chalk scribble. "And what does it represent?"

"To me, it's about a guy who was completely fearless, did his thing, stayed true to who he was no matter how much his work was hated. It's easy to keep going when you're loved, but takes a lot of courage to go on when you're not so popular. I guess," a sad look crossed his features, "I'm jealous of his freedom."

Modern art had always annoyed her, but maybe she was missing something. Maybe studying what Jett found so fascinating would help her understand this "new Jett," who was busy slamming balls and felt the need to have a punching bag in the next room.

She took a step in and her boots crunched on the carpet. Startled, she looked down at the broken pieces of glass beside a shattered closet door.

"What?" she whispered under her breath.

"A fist met the mirror."

"Christ." She jumped. He was close, close enough that she could feel his breath as he spoke.

She was getting tired of being startled tonight. Turning toward him, and giving in to temptation, she let her gaze drink him in.

"Christ," she said again, but this time for a completely different reason. His brown irises looked dark against the bloodshot red of his eyes. His chest was wide and smooth, and Nikki couldn't tear her gaze away from the slight indention between his pecs. She wondered if it was the same width as her thumb or . . . her mouth.

Her breath quickened, and she had to force out long exhalations so as not to give away her reaction. She pressed her lips together, trying to find a safe place to rest her gaze.

"Have I ever told you that I've had entire fantasies just about your lips?"

"Christ," she gasped, her heart falling away to some lower extremity.

They weren't touching, but he was close. "You keep saying that." His voice was smooth like the sun after a long winter and had about the same effect.

She knew playful Jett, the nice guy who'd let her sleep with him and then let her walk away the next morning. This Jett wasn't that guy. So she tried for levity. "Would you believe me if I told you I've found religion?"

He crowded up against her. She took a step back, pressing against the wall. She had to tilt her head to look him in the eye. Had he always been this tall? Jett never loomed, he charmed, but he was looming now. She could smell him. Not just the soap he used or the fabric softener of his shirt, but him. His skin smelled like sweat and the underlying bite of iron from the blood on his hands.

"No."

She trembled—couldn't prevent it. The tingle she always got that signaled danger ran rampant through her veins. And for the first time in her life she didn't know if that meant she should run . . . or stay.

His mouth came closer, a mere whisper away from hers. Kerosene heat ignited in his eyes, and in that moment Nikki knew what it was like to be burned. "But say it again, because I love the way your mouth looks when you lie."

Chapter 18

"Say what again?" she asked, licking her suddenly dry lips. "That I've found religion?"

A low humming sounded in her head; she just hoped it drowned out the thudding of her heart. Where did he get off saying things like that to her? *He loved the way her mouth looked . . .* What did he want from her? Because all his talk did was reduce her intelligence and have her contemplate promises she had no business making.

The scar at the corner of his eye stood white against his tan skin, the bruising under his eyes finally fading. He threw her a wicked grin. "Any lie will do."

Her breath caught, but she smiled back just the same. She was swimming in dangerous waters, but since when had she backed down from a dare? She never played the part of the scared mouse very well. When cornered, her instinct was to turn and fight. She locked her gaze with his, refusing to look away. For emphasis she parted her lips with her tongue. "Fine, how about this one? I love you."

Being this close, he didn't have a prayer of hiding his reaction. He flinched as if she'd hit him. And maybe she had. That was below the belt, cold even for her. But Jett had been in control of this relationship and she was getting sick of his hot and cold signals.

Funny how his smile could morph into something else altogether when he bared his teeth.

"My mistake," he said. "I haven't seen it as often—but your mouth is even sexier with the truth falling out of it."

She bared some teeth of her own. She'd thrown that out to hurt him. To push him away. There was no way she was going to let him turn this around. "Or so you believe."

"So I know."

"Over-confident much?"

He laughed deep in his throat, the sound anything but joyous. "You think I don't know you? That I don't know when you lie? I've known you your whole life. And I know when you're telling the truth . . . and when you're choking on it."

Nikki swallowed hard. Her palms dampened, and other body parts as well. He was close—physically and emotionally. No way was she going to let him know how close. He let his body press up against her, but her gaze could only focus on one thing. Apparently his oral fascination was contagious. "How?"

"I know your tell. When you lie, you bite your lip."

"Then what does it mean when I bite yours?" She didn't wait for an answer, just bent her head and sucked his bottom lip between her teeth—hard. It was a little rough, a little severe . . . way too exciting.

He slammed his hand against the wall by her head and jerked back. His thumb came up and rubbed the mark that she'd left behind. "This is your only warning." His eyes darkened to black. "I bite back."

And he was telling the truth. Jett was sick of babying her. There was something raw and brutal inside of him, and he wasn't sure he didn't like it.

He watched almost outside himself as his hands reached up and encircled her neck, his thumbs stroking the underside of her jaw. Nikki opened her mouth for a breath to tell him, he was sure, to go to hell. He didn't give her the chance. Took her lips; stole her curse.

And who would've thought that curses could taste so sweet? A little naughty, a bit spicy with the flavor of his spearmint gum riding her tongue. And maybe he was crazy—he sure had lost his mind over this girl—but he loved the scent of his gum in her mouth. Loved that she took something of his. Claimed it as her own.

Nikki might talk big, but she didn't know the first thing about how to kiss. And that alone made him very, very happy. Jett took pride in the fact that he was a good kisser. Slow and smooth. Given the time, he could love the panties off any woman. But this wasn't his best, hell it wasn't even good. This was a fight for control. A fight for domination. Didn't she know he didn't want to argue? He'd willingly submit as long as she was under him asking him to.

But she wasn't asking now, she was struggling. He pulled back.

She wiped her lips with the back of her hand. Fire had her feline eyes snapping. "I don't like the taste of anger in my mouth."

He wouldn't have been surprised if she spat. She didn't like it, huh? Didn't like anything real? "Isn't this what you have a reputation for, Texas? Isn't that what they say? Nikki likes a little quick and nasty behind the Tasty Freeze?"

She blinked hard, but otherwise stood her ground. And since when had he stooped to her level? There was a smudge of red in the corner of her mouth. Lipstick? Whatever it was, it made Nikki look a tad used, a tad too young, and a whole lot of scared. Something sick dropped into his belly—guilt? Or was it the beer he'd drunk on an empty stomach? Either way, if this was a seduction, then he was going about it all wrong. He didn't do this. Didn't crowd women against a wall in his bedroom. Didn't have to. They all came willingly enough. "That was my tongue in your mouth, not anger. I may get drunk. I may get rude. But rarely do I get angry."

Nikki blew her hair out of her face, her eyes hardening. "I bet Snake would say otherwise."

Snake had been a gut reaction. Snake had been a red-hazed moment that began when he saw Nikki trapped underneath him and ended with Nikki shouting Jett's name.

But he wasn't that person, and he wasn't *this* person, looming over a woman. He made to wipe the red off her mouth, then stilled at the sight of blood on his knuckles. His or Snake's? Didn't matter, since he remembered Nikki didn't wear lipstick. If she ever did, it wouldn't be this shade of red.

If shame were a color it would be black, because that's what swarmed his vision. He took a breath, stepped back.

There were no two ways about it. He'd lost it, and the sick part was he wasn't sure how to rein himself in. Or if he could. She could run if she wanted. He wouldn't stop her. Funny thing was, all of a sudden he didn't want to chase, he just wanted to take her to his bed and pass out with his leg thrown over her hips for assurance. But one look at Nikki and he knew he had a better chance of holding back the hounds of hell with a squirt gun.

"Go, Nikki. I'm tired. And . . . I'm sorry." He let his hand drop to his side. "But you're wrong about one thing. It wasn't anger. It was fear."

Then something changed; she changed. The beer must've hit him harder than he'd thought because her eyes appeared wider and, dared he hope, softer?

"Oh." She whispered the word on a breath, a suggestion of a smile on her lips. "I've come to acquire a taste for fear."

And he groaned because she didn't bite her lip at all.

Nikki never understood the adage, *Work first, play later*. She never held with eating your vegetables first and your dessert last. If you knew something good was waiting for you, why not jump straight to it? Delayed gratification wasn't all it was cracked up to be.

And that's exactly what she was thinking when she pulled Jett's mouth down on hers. Like she would during a winning rack of pool, Nikki was already four steps ahead to where they'd both be naked, doing naughty things in his bed. The problem was he wasn't moving very fast, never had. *Quick, fast, now, Jett*—before they both realized what a bad idea this was.

She groaned and rubbed herself against him. Her breasts ached, and she wanted his mouth *there*, just for a moment, to ease the pain, and then he could go back to kissing her.

But he wasn't getting the hint. Lord, had he always been this obtuse? Seemed like they'd been down this road before. Well, she knew exactly how to speed things up. Nikki reached down and started to pull her shirt off. She got as far as baring her midriff when Jett ran his hands down her arms and wound his fingers with hers.

As gestures went it was sweet, and maybe a little bit endearing. But she didn't want sweet.

He pinned her arms by her sides. His thumbs drew circles across her palms, all the while never easing up on his kiss. Nikki had been kissed by other guys besides Jett. There'd been that shy freshman in her dorm, the obsessive junior professor, but none of them had been like Jett. With his tongue in her mouth and his teeth nipping at her lips, his kiss was raw, a prelude to what she hoped they were going to do in bed.

She wanted to let him know she was a sure thing, no need to convince. No problem here. And she was going to tell him, yep, just as soon as she found her breath and a smidge of intelligence to form a sentence.

Then just as quickly, he backed off, eased up on the intensity a bit. *No! Not yet.* Instead of bites and licks, his mouth turned to tender brushes on the corner of her lips, eyelids, cheekbones. Oh, he was still kissing her all right, but now there was no urgency behind it, as if he'd decided he had a whole night or a whole lifetime.

He nipped at the corners of her mouth, drew a line with his tongue across her bottom lip. She made to capture his mouth, but he anticipated her move and nuzzled her neck instead. She lost all pretense of control, which was a good thing since her knees were only holding their own because his body was pushed up against hers, arms nailed to her sides. "Jett . . ."

His tongue found the hollows of her ear and wicked chills flushed her skin.

"Jett . . ." There was a plea that hadn't been in her voice before. This had to stop or, better yet, progress to the next level, because she was about to climb his body and impale herself if he didn't hurry.

Nikki made to tug her hand out of his, needing to touch him, needing do something. Instead, his fingers tightened their grip. There was a moan, and she refused to believe it was her. But just in case, she pressed her open mouth against the tanned expanse of his throat. The salty tang of sweat and skin had her breathing in deep. She was rewarded with a low growl that vibrated against her lips. *Not so cool now, huh, Jett?*

Her freedom was short-lived as his fingers tunneled through her hair and held her head hostage. He feasted on her lips, then broke off. "I need to ask you a favor."

At least his breathing was as ragged as her own.

Her brain was a bit fuzzy, but she couldn't help a smile. He was just waiting for permission—apparently the gentleman in Texans ran deep.

Fine, whatever. "Yes, yes, okay, yes."

Jett chuckled. He was at her ear again, and her knees were about to embarrass her. "You don't even know the favor yet."

Weren't they talking about the same thing? They had to be. But then, all of a sudden, she didn't care because she remembered the top button of his jeans was undone, and her hands were free.

There was a rainbow-colored moment when logistics failed her. But what she *did* remember was a rather loud curse and lots of fumbling hands. In the end she wasn't any better off than when she'd started. Jett's hands were back to pinning hers at her sides, but the heat of his body was absent, no longer flush against her own. Now at arm's length, he was bent, resting the top of his head on her chest. She could feel the hot pant of his breath fan the bare skin of her stomach.

"I wanted . . . I wanted to ask you . . ."

Was it because he was bent over or did he sound like he was in pain? She hoped so since she was. Besides, Jett wasn't making any sense. Hadn't she already answered this? Maybe he hadn't heard. They spoke at the same time.

"Yes, Jett. Dammit, yes."

". . . to dinner . . . "

Dinner? Was that what they were calling it these days? *Whatever.* She'd agree to paint his house if that's what he wanted, as long as they both got naked and wound up in his bed.

"At my mom's."

Now that made her pause. She must've missed a critical part of the conversation, but she knew what she wanted with Jett had nothing whatsoever to do with his mom.

"Ahh, your mother doesn't even like me."

As far as comebacks went, it was pretty lame, but apparently they both weren't thinking too clearly since he lifted his head and had to close his eyes for a moment to regain his composure. "No worries. My mom loves everything I do."

Some other stupid girl, one who would've cheered on the football field and let her boyfriend cop a feel under the bleachers might take that comment to mean Jett was in love with her. Might even think there was a future for them, but she'd never been that girl.

"Say yes," he whispered by her ear.

His mouth was wicked, making her lose the thread of the conversation *again*. Oh yeah, he was good. She felt like she was drunk, and she hadn't been the one who downed the beer. She groaned, then softly banged her head against the wall once . . . twice.

He didn't have to worry because it was *his* mom. But to Nikki his mom was worth a few worries; his mom meant sweaty palms, and a churning stomach. His mom was . . .

But Jett had a few tricks up his sleeve, and Nikki was beginning to realize his reputation hadn't been exaggerated. How could he give so much—his lips on the column of her neck, the dip of her breast bone, everywhere—and yet be so stingy?

His mouth was back on hers, but just barely. He was such a tease. "It's just one word. Here, I'll help."

And help he did. He abused her mouth with his as he imprinted the word he wanted on her tongue.

"Yes," she moaned against him.

With that one word she earned her freedom, whether she wanted it or not. His hands cupped her face. His gaze bored into hers. "Thank you."

Jett kissed her then, but quick and light with the sting of a farewell behind it. Then he had her by the elbow and led her back toward the living room. Jett grabbed his car keys off the side table and placed them in her hand. He flung the front door open, and she was thrust out onto the porch. Nikki turned to stare at him, stupid in her confusion.

Jett was a mess. His normally neat hair was destroyed; shirt torn at the collar, red marks along his throat, but there was a sly smile that penetrated even her sluggish, lust-filled blood.

"Take my truck, go home, pick me up at six tomorrow night. And don't be late."

"Wh—"

His lips were quick to cut off her words, and then just as quick to leave. Nikki stared at the front door as it slammed in her face. She stood for a full moment, knowing she'd missed something, but not sure what.

It wasn't until she was driving Jett's truck home that she realized today was Saturday—which made tomorrow, by default, Sunday. And she'd just agreed to a tradition as old and ingrained as oil and cattle in Texas—Sunday family dinner.

Nikki slammed the brakes, and the truck lost traction on the gravel road. Dust filtered in through the open windows and filled her mouth as she screamed the mother of all obscenities into the night air.

A mile back from the road, Albert and Mable sat on their front porch swing, sipping on a cup of chamomile tea for him and scotch on the rocks for her. Mable turned to her husband of forty years. "My God, Albert, what is all that howling about?"

"Sounds like a cat in heat."

"Lord, that's a horrible racket. Can we spray her down with the hose?"

"Only thing that can calm a feline like that down there is a tom."

"Well, heaven help us. I hope he finds her quick and puts us all out of our misery. I ain't sure I could stand much more of this."

Chapter 19

Nikki started calling Jett the moment she woke up. It didn't bother her in the least that it was seven in the morning since it was his fault she woke from a sweat-drenched dream, gasping for air. Yep, seven in the morning, and she already knew she couldn't go through with a Sunday dinner at the Avery house.

By ten o'clock she'd called five more times, texted seven, but it wasn't until three o'clock rolled around that she realized Jett was avoiding her calls. She knew he didn't want to give her an easy out from dinner tonight. Of course, they both knew she could just not show up, and then she could be the one to avoid his phone calls.

And call he would, because she had his truck. Nikki smiled to herself, and wondered how long it would take for him to come pounding on her door.

Her smile faded. She wouldn't put it past Jett to show up at her house and drag her to dinner, kicking and screaming, dressed or not. She looked down at her T-shirt and boxers—maybe she should be more careful for what she wished for.

What was she so afraid of? No one knew about the conversation she and Mrs. Avery had over the rolled-down window of her Mercedes and a thick padded envelope. Nikki hadn't told a soul, and she was pretty sure Mrs. Avery hadn't either. What did she care what the ice queen thought of her? There was no reason to feel any shame. If anyone should be ashamed, it was Mrs. Avery. Besides, Nikki had changed. She wasn't the same insecure girl who had accepted that envelope. She was a college graduate, and Cole was a respected horse breeder now. They were no longer white trash. They've pulled themselves up. Made something of the Logan name.

Except Nikki knew first-hand that towns never changed, and a bad reputation was like a blood stain on a white blouse—some things marked a girl forever.

Jett would never let this go, and she couldn't hide forever. Might as well get the meeting over with. At a quarter after three she decided to get ready; forty-five minutes later she had to pop open a beer to give her courage. Only after a whole hour, and reviewing the entire contents of her closet, was she finally dressed.

Cold sweat pooled under each arm, and she'd taken to stuffing tissues under each arm to keep from pitting out another shirt. As it was, this was her third.

Nikki stood in front of the full-length mirror inside her bedroom. It wasn't lost on her that she'd finally "moved" from the couch to her room, but she'd had no choice, she simply had nothing from her college days that would be appropriate to wear. Well, she found appropriate and went right on through to hideous with the simple black flats and a long khaki shirt that she'd bought years ago. A short-sleeved, high-necked white shirt she'd worn for the first and last time to her mother's funeral. And it only got worse. Her gaze traveled up. There was nothing she could do about the copper streaks in her dark hair, and her mother's pearls and coral lipstick had made the I'm-a-Sunday-school-teacher outfit look even more awful.

She bit her lip and closed her eyes to quell the sting. *Great. Now she felt like crying.* Well, it wasn't going to happen. She didn't have waterproof mascara on, and it had taken way too long to fix her eyeliner.

Nikki pinched the bridge of her nose instead, and gave herself another once over. She looked like a twelve-year-old playing dress up in her mother's clothes. Funny, that was how she felt . . . like she was playing. Playing at getting a job, at coming home, at this thing with Jett. She refused to call it a relationship. It wasn't really. It was more of a summer fling, but did a summer fling include dinner with his whole family?

And Nikki wasn't stupid. An invitation to dinner meant meeting the whole Avery clan. His three sisters, their husbands, and there had to be a butt-load of kids by now. Yeah, if the Averys ever wanted to adopt a family mascot, Nikki would suggest a rabbit.

Mrs. Avery, Jett's mother, would've put the roast in the oven before they left for church, the dining table set with a real tablecloth, and she was sure there wouldn't be a plastic cup in sight.

Yeah, flings didn't include family dinners at the Averys. Who was she kidding? Apparently only herself, since she'd called Cole earlier for last-minute advice. When she told him about Jett's invitation, he'd barely spit out the warning, asking her if she really wanted to spend her evening trying to figure out which fork to use? And then he started to go on about contacting Mrs. Lewis concerning the accounting position when she finally hung up on him.

Nikki reached for the bottle of beer on her dresser, her second, then lowered her hand without touching it. Her stomach was already in knots, and even though the Logans had a reputation for loving and living hard, she still had enough pride not to show folks how right they were.

And just like that she heard her mother's voice as if she were standing right next to her. *Nikki, doll, you have nothing to be ashamed of . . .*

If she closed her eyes, she could breathe in her mother's scent. And not the sick chemical smell that her mother died with, but the one she had years before, of purple violets, summer grass, and maple syrup.

You're wrong. There's so much to be ashamed of—wanting to run, leaving that last night, resenting so many days of your last years.

No, Nikki doll, you are a child of God and of mine. You have a good heart, a tender spirit, and have always loved big. As long as you can look yourself in the eye and tell the truth, you could never shame me.

The pain in her gut was as real as any physical blow. She crossed her arms around her middle. Could she do that? Could she look herself in the eye and tell the truth? Hell, she couldn't even find the truth, but whatever it was, it sure wasn't this Sunday-school look.

With the back of her hand she wiped the coral off her lips and threw the pearls back on the dresser table. Nikki had lied her way through life. She had no qualms about that, did what she had to. But between her and Jett there'd always been truth. For some reason, under all the BS she fed him, Jett could always tell what was real. He could always see her. He would see through her attempt to make her outside change who she was on the inside. Because every Logan knew, no matter how pretty you dressed up trash, blood is stronger and it always tells.

Jett flung his front door open at the first tentative knock. "You're late," he growled, but let his gaze linger. Nikki was in combat boots with a clingy black dress that showed an awful lot of leg. Some type of metal belt was looped low around her hips, hair in her face, eyes outlined with black, and lips sexy bare.

And there was a very real moment where he totally forgot he even had parents, much less that they were waiting on him for dinner.

Then he noticed the sleeves of Nikki's dress, and how she had pulled them over her palms as if she were cold. And how her turquoise eyes were sharp and seemed lost in her pale face. She was scared to death, but had come anyway. There was a part of him that didn't believe she even showed up.

But here she was, standing on his front porch in a dress that hugged a body he hadn't seen naked in two years, and then only through the haze of tequila shots. He didn't think—she'd be pissed, but he'd deal—just grabbed her around the waist and had her back up against the outside wall.

Her eyes widened. "Jett . . . "

He loved to catch her with her mouth open so he didn't have to waste precious time teasing her lips apart. Last night pushing Nikki out his front door was the hardest thing he'd ever done. He'd stood with his back up against the door, praying she wouldn't leave, that she'd knock, call his name, anything so he could toss his plan aside and toss her into his bed. And then he wouldn't let her walk, much less run, out of his bed for days.

He'd woken up this morning with the taste of her in his mouth and the feel of her whispered *yes* against his lips. All day he'd been nervous, wondering if she'd show. He'd seen her total of fifteen calls and texts, but he wasn't fool enough to answer. If she wanted to back out, she'd have to do it to his face or . . . against his body.

Which he hoped would be as hard for her as it was for him. Had he thought he liked her dress? He hated it. The skirt prevented him from dragging her knee up to his waist. Right now, her calf just teased around his knee. He filled his hands with an ass that had swayed through his dreams ever since he watched her walk away from him. He smiled against her lips. Jesus, he was in a good mood. There was a lightness he hadn't felt until Nikki showed up. "Be a good girl," he teased, "and tell me you're wearing a black thong under this dress." Why he wanted to torture himself he had no idea.

She pulled back, her face incredulous, her eyes feline-serious. "Underwear? Oh dear, I think I forgot."

Jett stilled, his playful mood suddenly gone. "Texas, I'm not kidding, you'd better be lying."

If she wasn't, he'd take her right here and now, neighbors be damned.

She fought a smile. Then very deliberately bit her lip.

He clenched his jaw and took a huge step back, no longer having fun. "When did you get to be such a tease?"

She laughed, seeming to love the power she wielded over him. If she only knew.

"I learned from the best," she said. "Payback is a—"

"Yeah, yeah," he cut her off. "Just give me the keys." He took them out of her hand and then led her laughing all the way to his truck.

They drove most of the way to his parents in silence, since it took the whole hour to get his good humor back and cool his heated blood.

Nikki, Jett knew, was quiet for a whole other reason. She was nervous, not that he blamed her. His family was . . . formidable. He was the only son, and the only one not married. Yeah, it wasn't like that topic hadn't been beaten to death over the dinner table.

"Nik, it's gonna be okay." He tried to reassure her, but she continued to stare out the window at the acres of pasture and miles of barbed-wire fence.

Nikki had met his whole family at one time or another. His parents hadn't always lived one town over, and they still made the trip for special town occasions, and had come often when Cole and he and gone to the same high school.

Even though Cole had been to his family home a handful of times, Nikki hadn't.

Jett knew he should've warned her, but the Logans had such a hang-up about money. Hell, Cole was the most prideful SOB he'd ever met, and that was saying a lot.

As the scenery outside changed from cattle ranches to rolling manicured hills, Nikki's knuckles bleached white with each passing country estate.

"Where did you say your parents lived?"

"We're almost there," he said, not answering her question.

After a few minutes, he pulled into a wide, cobblestone drive, and by Nikki's sharp intake of breath, he knew he had a fight on his hands.

"You have a fountain in your front yard?" Her voice was tight, yet she never altered her forward gaze.

"No, I don't. My parents do." But even he had to admit the large statue of the Virgin Mary weeping copious amounts of water was a bit of overkill. Taste and money didn't necessarily run hand in hand.

But how could he explain to Nikki that even though his father had always done well, it hadn't been until Jett had been in middle school that his father's business had really taken off. That was when the family moved from their home in Grove Oaks to this, well, this house.

He still remembered the fight he'd had with his mother over changing schools. His mother had wanted him to go to some preppy private school, but Jett would have none of it. It wasn't until his father stepped up and agreed it was good for a man to never forget where he came from that his mother finally gave in.

How was he supposed to explain to Nikki that money didn't make the man, and to him, all this meant nothing?

He looked over at her, willing to at least attempt a conversation, but it was too late. There was already a look on her face, and he knew, to her, this meant everything.

"In order to go to dinner, you have to at least get out of the truck."

Nikki had been sitting in the passenger seat for ten minutes while he'd been standing there like an idiot holding her door open, waiting for her.

In all fairness, maybe he should've warned her, at least given her a heads up. Though he knew if he had, he would've seen the back of her quicker than he could've formed the word goodbye.

But he needed her to meet his parents, because if he had a prayer of pulling off what he wanted, he had to have the whole dinner with his family under his belt. And maybe that was the problem—Nikki was smart and by her deer-in-the-headlights look one would've thought he'd just asked her to marry him.

Lord, would he ever grow balls big enough to ask *that* question? If he did, he'd better be prepared for a rejection.

"It's just dinner, Texas. I'm not asking you to cross political party lines."

"Why, is that a problem?" She wouldn't even look at him.

"Only if you're a Democrat," he laughed.

If possible, her face grew even paler, and he decided to leave the jokes till after dinner.

"Jett, I don't belong here. I'm not even smart enough to know what fork to use."

The way she pulled on her sleeves, he wouldn't doubt there'd be a hole in both of them before the night was over. If only she could see herself the way he did. He loved the way she was—tough, funny, with just enough of a go-to-hell attitude to give his mother a heart attack.

Okay, that wasn't fair, but he loved the fact that she was totally different from his family. But he couldn't tell her any of that, and the hell of it was he didn't know if it was because she was scared or . . . he was.

He put his hands on her knees and turned her around to face him. He tugged her forward, so her dress bunched up a little higher on her thighs. He ignored the view and was so proud of himself when he looked into her eyes instead. "You think smarts has anything to do with how to BS your way through a dinner party? Hell, I've had dinners with senators who could pick the perfect wine, but couldn't poke their way out of a paper bag without a GPS."

He made small circles on the inside of her knees with his thumb.

No matter what, he couldn't seem to stop touching her. "Look at me. No, come on, look at me."

Nikki lifted her head and peered through the dark strands of hair that fell across her eyes.

"Do you trust me?"

"No."

"Okay, that was quick. I'll try not to be wounded." He took a deep breath. "Let me try this one—have I ever lied to you?"

Silence.

He'd take it. "It's going to be okay, Nik. I promise."

A flash of hurt crossed her face, then disappeared as she reached up and cupped his cheeks. "I've long ago quit holding people to promises they've no power to keep."

That stung. He'd made promises to her. Ones he hadn't kept. Ones that had fallen to the wayside just as easily as the dust from the tack room where they'd been made.

Of course she'd been hurt; he'd known that. Nobody became a mess like Nik without being kicked around a bit, but the protective instinct she always called up in him roared to the surface. He lowered his forehead to hers, but it was through clenched teeth that he shoved the words out. "Well. I'm telling you, Texas—hold me to it."

Chapter 20

Nikki's boots echoed on the tiled floor that was laid out in some type of mosaic in the entryway . . . foyer? . . . parlor? She had no clue. She also had no idea what the going rate for chandeliers was, but she had a good guess that the one hanging above the spiral staircase cost more than her college education.

Jett closed the door behind them and threw his keys on the side table. "Hello?"

"In the dining room, honey. Come on back," a woman called out, much closer than Nikki would have liked.

Jett grabbed Nikki's hand and began to drag her down the hall. Nikki hadn't come to terms with what this thing was between her and Jett, but not wanting to complicate matters further, she tugged her hand out of his. It would be better if they looked less like a couple, and more . . . more like friends.

Jett snatched her hand back and gripped it so hard, her knuckles rolled over each other.

"Ouch," she mouthed.

"Then don't pull away," he whispered back, lips plastered in a stiff smile.

She'd seen that smile, knew its origins, and she was so screwed.

Yet all she could think was she never should've removed the wad of tissues under each arm.

A person's first impression of the Averys could be of a warm, rather loud, down-to-earth family, but the dinner table told a different story, which was exactly what Nikki expected. Cream-colored tablecloth, crystal wine glasses, and numerous sets of silverware, but the table's intimidation was broken by colorful plastic plates and multiple sippy cups. In some abstract way, she'd known Jett's family was big, but over the course of dinner when every adult lap was occupied, hers included, the abstract had a way of becoming a noisy reality.

One little boy in particular—Kyle? Kalli? some K-name—had claimed Nikki's lap as his own perch. She shifted a little so he wouldn't be touching her as much. The tow-headed little boy had demolished her chocolate cake with his fist, and then proceeded to wipe the frosting in his hair. And people said that kids were cute? Underneath the sweet scent of sugar and chocolate was the moist bite of ammonia she was sure had something to do with his heavy diaper.

Nikki ducked a swipe of sticky hand as he bounced up and down, excited at his idea of a new game. She just hoped the smile that was stuck on her face was believable because if this kid left a damp spot on her dress, she'd throttle him—Avery charm-boy smile be damned.

Nikki glanced around for Jett, wanting to send out an SOS. Sticking to his promise, he wasn't far, but was in no position to help. Two little girls—twins?—were standing on either side of him, securing braids in his hair with pink butterfly clips. Unlike her, he seemed to be enjoying it.

One of the sisters' husbands walked by, owner of the boy, maybe? Father? Uncle? Didn't matter, it was another adult.

The soggy boy on her lap took to pounding the table with a steak knife. Really, where were his parents?

"Hey," Nikki called out, waylaying the adult midstride. "I think he needs some help."

The man stopped and looked down. It was Ken, right? Yeah, she remembered because he looked totally the opposite of his namesake—the Mattel doll. Middle-aged paunch, thinning brown hair—if the Ken doll had morphed into this as he'd gotten older, Nikki didn't blame Barbie for divorcing him.

"Oh, wow, he's a mess. Here, let me take him. Maybe I can hose him off or something."

Relieved, she handed him over. "Or drop him into the deep end of the pool?" she laughed.

Ken gave her a stare.

"Kidding." Sorta.

"Come on, kids, let's move this party outside," Ken yelled above the din. It took a while, but finally all of the children and most of the men vanished, and quiet once again reigned.

"Ah, thank God. I love my grandbabies, but all together they can make more racket than a fox in a hen house," Mrs. Logan said from the chair at the end of the table. Even after several children had used her lap as a jungle gym, her hair still swooped down into an impeccably smooth pageboy, and her royal blue blouse was barely rumpled, though there was a damp spot on the shoulder. She swiped at the stain with her napkin, then shrugged. "One more designer blouse bites the dust." But she was laughing when she said it.

Jett was said to have taken after his father in looks, but he'd gotten his high cheekbones and eyes from her. Not his smile though. No, Jett's smile was nothing like hers.

In the end, it was the eyes that did Nikki in. When Mrs. Avery locked gazes with hers, it was with those same coppery eyes that Nikki had warmed herself under. Like a fish being lured by a fancy hook, Nikki opened wide and took the bait.

"Jett, honey, I would love some cabernet with my cake." She held up a glass filled with the wine from dinner. "All your father brought out was the white. The wine opener is on the counter somewhere. Do you mind?"

Jett's gaze went to Nikki's, making sure she was okay with his departure. And stupid, stupid her, she nodded her assent because really, what could go wrong during a five-minute trip to the kitchen?

As soon as Jett left, Nikki found herself the focus of four pairs of piercing eyes, belonging to Jett's three older sisters and his mother.

"So I hear, Nikki, that you graduated from some college. U of S, was it?"

"Yes, ma'am. Magna cum laude," Nikki said. It was the one feather in her cap, paltry as it might be. She looked around at the bleached blondes at the table, and the diamonds adorning their wrists and ears, and immediately regretted saying anything. What was a feather anyway, among so many crown jewels?

"Oh, that shouldn't have been too hard since it's a state college and all." Mrs. Avery smoothed an imaginary hair back into place while she sipped her wine, the chocolate cake untouched in front of her.

"Ranked in the top ten for business," Nikki said, still believing their talk was an actual conversation.

"Ah, but you didn't go to school for business, did you?"

"No, ma'am." Nikki took a sip of water, her face suddenly flushed. She took another as she glanced around at the four women sitting at the table. All were beautiful, as if one could expect any less from an Avery. If there ever were an ugly baby born into the family, they'd probably just refuse to take it home from the hospital. One sister, Mary Ellen, sat nursing a tuft-headed infant, and the other two mimicked their mother by sipping their white wine with ice. All while Mrs. Avery sat and presided over her subjects.

And suddenly, Nikki realized she'd been set up. Well, no one had ever accused the Logans of being smart.

Johanna, the oldest sister, flipped long, platinum, straight hair that one could only get from a professional blow-out off her shoulder. "I did read that U of S was rated number one, but for something else," she smirked. "The highest rate of STDs in the country."

"Johanna!" gasped the other sister, whose blond hair was also flat-ironed straight. Her name was Lauren, if Nikki remembered correctly. "Sorry, Nikki. We haven't medicated Johanna with her daily Prozac, so she's a little cranky."

Nikki gave her a small smile. Even though she appreciated Lauren's gesture, Nikki knew there was no stopping this train wreck. Besides, from what she'd heard around town, Lauren had her own problems—straying husband, infertility. In comparison, staring down the queen was a walk in the park, or at the very most a sprint through hell.

"Is that true?" asked Mrs. Avery, her pencil thin eyebrows winging up, though all facial expression stopped there. No doubt, regular Botox injections blocked any ripple of emotion from crossing her porcelain-smooth forehead.

"I wouldn't know," Nikki said, this time leaving off the ma'am.

"I find that hard to believe. You have a reputation and it . . ."

Mrs. Avery paused as if to draw out the tension, but Nikki could've told her it wasn't needed. ". . . precedes you."

Then Mrs. Avery broke off and glanced around the room.

"What's that tapping sound?"

Nikki slid her hand under the table and stilled her leg. Her boot immediately stopped rattling against the chair.

"Oh, I've embarrassed you. I'm sorry," Mrs. Avery said.

How could Nikki have thought that Jett had his mother's eyes? When she got lost in Jett's gaze, she started dreaming of possibility and hope. Now, looking into Ms. Avery's, Nikki was slammed back to reality. It was something she wouldn't forget again.

Nikki allowed herself the one small luxury of a quick close of her eyes. She knew this game. Had played it since the eighth grade, perfected it in high school, and had left it behind with relish in college. Nikki smiled and allowed her thoughts of iced-over ponds and glass snow-globes to come across in the winter blue of her stare.

"Please, no need to be embarrassed on my account. I should've been prepared for petty insults. But of course, Jett assured me that his family would welcome me, being his guest and all."

Lauren looked as if she was going to cry. While Mrs. Avery folded her hands and turned her mouth up at the corners, not allowing a hint of emotion to affect her perfect Snow White features.

"Jett is the most kind-hearted of all my children, and as such, has a tendency to overlook certain facts. But I don't think even Jett would consider your sleeping with the entire football team petty."

"Oh," Nikki said, allowing her eyes to show mock horror.

"You're right, the football team would've been petty, but since it was the chess team, well, that just makes me ambitious." Nikki put an expression of condescension on her lips. "Of course, you know all about that."

That broke Snow White. Two red spots rose high on Mrs. Avery's cheeks, and even the Botox had a hard time keeping her forehead smooth.

"And what is it that I know about? Being ambitious or making your way on your back?"

"From where I'm sitting—" Nikki did an exaggerated look around. "It seems like you did pretty well at both."

Mrs. Avery nodded as if conceding the point, but she was in no way calling a retreat. Her French-manicured nails made a rhythmic ping sound as they tapped the wine glass. "The Logans have always been a sore spot between my son and me. He always held a heightened sense of loyalty to your family, one that I never understood. I must seem very cold to you, Nikki, but maybe when you have a family of your own, you'll understand. A mother always wants the best for her children."

Snow White was back in full composure as Mrs. Avery leaned away from the table. She sighed as if resigned to some dirty task in front of her. "I know what you see when you look around this house—wealth, prestige, power. But all this came from a lot of hard work. Let me tell you a secret that most men don't realize. Business deals aren't made over a handshake across a conference table. Business deals are made over a perfect roast and a second glass of cabernet. So let me ask you, Nikki, are you the woman who could raise Jett up in this world or bring him down? Because your mother may have had some class, but she married beneath her. Blood always tells, Nikki—and in the Logans more than others. So you may have some ambition, but in the end, if I can help it, all it will get you is this invitation to dinner and a glass of very expensive wine."

Chapter 21

Nikki stood. His mother stood as well. Nikki's insides rippled with tension, but she made sure all outward signs broadcasted control.

Nikki allowed her eyes to flash, and Mrs. Avery picked up on the signal—she wasn't through with Nikki yet. "You'll ruin his chances, you know. He was groomed since he was a child for a seat in the senate. He could be the next senator from Texas. He could be more if he had the right wife."

It wasn't until the dream died that Nikki even realized how hard she'd been holding on to the hope of happily-ever-after.

But the Logans were never known for their smarts—just their pride.

"I'll keep my eyes open for when she comes along." Nikki flipped her hair out of her eyes, and out of habit, pushed her chair in. Let no one say her mother hadn't taught her how to act at a dinner table.

Jett walked in from the kitchen carrying a bottle of wine. The light in his eyes that warmed the brown to butterscotch faded along with his smile. "What's going on?" His voice was calm, tired even. Resigned?

Regardless, the monotone was something Nikki had never heard from him before.

"Nothing," Nikki said quickly. She might have grown accustomed to this game, but Jett hadn't. Not yet anyway. "I was just leaving."

Jett looked from his mother to Nikki and then back again. "Then I'll take you home."

Nikki stepped away from the table. Jett started to follow.

"Wait," his mom called out. "Jett, is this what you really want? You can't be a senator and have a wife with a criminal record."

There was a twitch in Jett's jaw, but when he replied his tone was still southern-respectful. "The dream of politics was never mine. Still isn't. But other than a few parking tickets, Nikki's record is cleaner than yours."

His mother didn't even have the grace to look ashamed. "Of course. I forgot the things you'd do for a Logan."

"You forget a lot of things, Mother."

"That's where you have it wrong. It's not I who has to forgive and forget. I can look the other way if it makes you happy. It's this town that will never forget her reputation, nor forgive." Her blond pageboy brushed her shoulders as she raised her chin. Nikki's mind flashed on an image of a general issuing an order to his troops.

"Then maybe it's time this town remembers the truth and not just the rumors," Jett said. He braced his hands on the table, his voice having lost the soft Texas drawl he was known for.

"No, Jett." Nikki tugged on his arm. It wasn't hard to see where this was headed and panic edged up her throat.

"What truth is that?" His mother's eyes narrowed. "That it wasn't the football team she screwed, but the chess team? I don't think that's going to make a bit of difference."

The baby started to fuss and Mary Ellen bounced the infant on her shoulder. Johanna maintained a stiff smile while Lauren looked as if she was going to lose her dinner. She wasn't the only one.

"How about none," Jett said.

"Jett, please. Stop, let's go. It's not worth it." Nikki pulled in earnest now.

"How could you possibly know that?" his mother countered. "What? Because she said so? Please, Jett, I didn't think you were so naïve."

Jett dug in and didn't move. If the mountain won't come to Mohammed . . . then time to get in front of the mountain and push like hell. Desperate, Nikki wrestled herself in front of him, hands fisted in his shirt. "Shut up, Jett! Don't say another word."

It took a moment, but he finally realized she was there. "What! Don't say the truth, Nik? You think I don't know?" Jett turned to his mother. "I know because I was her first."

Mrs. Avery laughed, the single strand of diamonds showing off the white column of her throat. "Why, because she told you so?"

"No, because a man knows when he takes a woman's virginity. And since she held on to it until the age of twenty-two, longer than anyone else here, I think that's a pretty good indication of the truth."

Nikki stepped back, and faltered for a second. She grabbed the back of a chair for balance as black spots popped around her vision. There was a gasp somewhere in the background, along with an echoed, "Oh my God."

Nikki's façade, her protection, her jaded exterior, was ripped away in one sentence. Her mother had always told her the truth will set you free. What she'd forgotten to mention was it also had a way of eviscerating you.

Shame burned her face at the thought of all the comments and attitude she'd flung at Jett. He'd seen through her the whole time. "I thought you didn't know," she whispered.

The night they slept together they'd both been drinking, and she'd hoped the Cuervo had rubbed out the details.

"How could I not?" Jett said as he reached for her. And she realized in that moment that he'd waited a long time to speak in her defense. Fool. He knew a thing.

She flung his hand away. "You never said anything."

"You never wanted me to."

The black spots faded and the warmth of shame turned to the flush of anger. "At least you got one thing right."

"Fine," Mrs. Avery said. "Maybe she didn't sleep around, but Nikki's reputation is not all made up of lies."

Jett turned toward his mother. "If you have something to say, Mother, just say it."

Nikki watched the scene as if she were an outsider looking in. She watched as Mrs. Avery took a breath and tilted her head as if delivering a fatal judgment to her loyal servants. "I paid her off. That's why she ran last time. Because I gave her thirty grand to get out of your life forever. And she took it, Jett. Took the money and never looked back."

Disbelief and hurt crossed Jett's features and in that moment Nikki would've given anything to go back and do things differently. He shook his head. "No. I don't believe you."

At least his first reaction was to have faith in her. She'd have to remember that, hold it dear in the days to come.

"How do you think she paid for college? How would a Logan come up with thirty grand just like that?" She snapped her fingers.

"I don't know, Mother. I never asked. Student loans or grants maybe." Jett's brow furrowed as he defended her. Her white knight until the end.

"She doesn't love you, Jett. She just wants you for your money."

"Nikki?" Jett looked at her and the doubt she saw in his eyes almost brought her to her knees.

Her mother was wrong, after all. It wasn't the truth that mattered, but what you believed.

"What do you think happened, Jett?" Nikki held on to the back of the chair to keep herself upright. She couldn't break down now. If there were even a small chance for them, even one in one-thousandth odds, then he would have to believe her.

He took a step back and raked his fingers through his hair. "I don't know, Nik. I just don't know what to believe."

Nikki nodded. She wasn't surprised. What got her was the pain that was slicing through her insides. After all she'd been through, she would've thought she could have protected herself better.

She stood there and took a moment to search deep inside herself for the strength to turn on her heel and walk. There, underneath the disappointment, the hurt, the unfairness, was what all Logans turned to when their world came crashing down. Nikki turned and walked toward the front door. Jett's keys winked at her from the front table, and with an almost steady hand she grabbed them.

Everything inside her wanted to run out the front door. But she was a Logan. She would square her shoulders and walk out with her head high because she had something that, even with their deep pockets and perfect platinum hair, the Averys could never have— Logan pride. And right now, she wouldn't trade that for all the crown jewels in the world.

* * *

Lauren watched Jett run after Nikki, watched her mom's hand tremble as she took another sip from her wine glass, watched her sisters fall into shuddering silence and avoid eye contact. And suddenly Lauren felt sick.

She wasn't sure which was worse, the looks on her family's faces or the look on Jett's. What she saw in her brother's eyes was nothing she'd ever seen on an Avery—love. It was different from what they felt for their children or each other. Yes, as a family they loved each other. But Jett had gotten hold of the brass ring. The ultimate fantasy. He'd found the person who completed him. Found the one he wanted to spend the rest of his life with.

Lauren crossed her arms over her stomach, her eyes catching the large rock her husband had given her. How had John proposed again? Oh yeah, through an email. He'd been seven time zones away, or at least that was his excuse for such an unromantic gesture. He'd outlined their marriage like a merger—joined assets, stronger political connections, powerful family names. She'd been such a fool to say yes. No, she'd known he didn't love her, wasn't that big an idiot, but she at least hoped for mutual respect. She wasn't even sure when the cheating started. Was past caring at this point. Had she ever? She did a mental shrug. Maybe in the beginning.

But they'd gotten along relatively well. Both subscribed to the unwritten rules. She'd overlook his philandering ways, and he'd maintain their perfect image. From the outside she had the dream: a handsome husband, important charity work, beautiful house, vacations in the Hamptons.

All that was missing was children. A year ago, they'd both decided it was time to start a family. Lauren had picked out the preschools, looked at names, and started interviewing nannies (the right ones always went fast). She even endured her husband's attentions month after month. And month after month there was no pregnancy, no plus sign on the slender white stick. They tried for a year before they went to the doctor. It was never spoken out loud; they were too polite for that, but they both knew it was because of him. He'd slept around enough with no illegitimate children. Who else's fault could it be? She'd never forget the look on John's face when the test results came back. Nothing was wrong with him. He was fine. Which could only mean one thing.

That was the first time she heard the screaming. She remembered looking around the room and wondering who was making such a racket, but no one else seemed to hear the noise. Not the doctor, not the nurse, or even John. She realized the crying was coming from her. From inside her head. The constant scream of a woman raging against the hurt, disappointment, and total unfairness of what life had dealt her. Lauren had done everything she was supposed to. Married for her family, made all the right social connections. Yet, she was the one who was being punished. She would be the one growing old without children around her. No family. No babies.

That had been the only time in the history of their marriage that Lauren had been glad she'd married John. She'd never have wished this fate on someone she actually liked. Now, at least he would be miserable right alongside her.

It wasn't until after John told her he was leaving her for his pregnant mistress of two years, saying he couldn't stand the thought of not having a family, that the screaming inside her head became a constant presence.

Lauren looked around the table. Her gaze rested on her mother, whose face was abnormally pale, two spots of color high on her cheeks. Mrs. Avery hadn't always been like this. Proud, polished, cold. Lauren barely remembered the event that had separated their lives into the "before" and the "after." There were pictures, possibly a video buried in a box somewhere, of the child her mother had lost. Seeing Jett had to be a painful reminder of Sarah, Jett's twin, who had died at such a young age. That kind of thing had to change a woman. Some families grew closer over tragedy; theirs drifted further apart.

"I think I made a mistake," Mrs. Avery muttered into her wine glass.

Lauren wanted to tell her that was part of being in the club. That was what the women in her family did. One big Avery mistake after another.

Jett's phone vibrated against his cheek. It took him all of two seconds to push himself up and check the caller ID. Unknown.

Not Nikki then. Not that he would expect her to call. No, that would be way too mature, considering that she'd taken his truck and he'd had to borrow one of his dad's cars to get himself home. That was, of course, before he drove by Nikki's house and had even called Cole on the off chance that Nikki would be with him.

"Leave her alone," Cole had barked. "And besides, if she was here I wouldn't tell you a fool thing, anyway."

Damn Logans.

Maybe he would've been better off if he'd listened to his mother all those years ago when she said trouble always followed the Logans.

Ahh, his mother. Just the thought of her made him sick. The dinner hadn't been a good idea. He'd rushed the whole thing—again. Sure, after Nikki had run off, his mother had apologized, possibly even meant it, but the damage was done. Nikki was on the run.

The phone buzzed again, bringing him back to the present. Against his better judgment he answered it.

"Jett, it's me, Mike."

His gut tightened.

"Down at The Pitt."

"Yeah, I know." Pride had kept him from chasing after her. Now it was anger that would drag her back.

"I thought of calling Cole, but well, it seemed . . . it's just that someone needs to come get her. And I'm not a damn babysitter. But I thought I'd let you know I close in twenty."

"Be there in ten."

In two minutes flat he was in his truck and roaring down the road. It was crazy to go the speed he went on those dark country roads where anything, a cow or a deer, could meander across. Hitting a three hundred pound animal going sixty-five miles per hour was not a pleasant way to die. But Jett took his chances. There had been an edge to Mike's voice; he wasn't a person to call over nothing.

Nik was in trouble, but tonight he wasn't going fix any of her problems. He was going to make some.

Lauren couldn't remember the last time she'd been in Grove Oaks. High school graduation? Maybe. Regardless, it had been years. After the catastrophe that had been the family dinner, she couldn't stand the thought of sitting in that house for one more minute. With some lame excuse of a headache to her mother and sisters, she'd left. But instead of heading home, she took the opposite way and just drove. When she first started driving, all she wanted was to go back to the last place she'd been happy. When was that? Before her marriage? No. College? No.

As if her heart knew what the answer was before her mind did, she looked up and found herself in front of O'Brian's Bar & Grill in Grove Oaks. When she'd been younger, the owner's son, Ron, had let her and her friends come and drink after football games and on weekends. O'Brian's had become their unofficial hangout. Drove the owner crazy, but Ron had had a crush on her, so he'd let them slide.

She smiled at the memory. Where had she taken the wrong turn? In high school, she'd been so sure of herself. Happy and confident that her life would end up just as she'd always wanted—with a loving husband, kids, white picket fence, and a large yard. She never had any huge aspirations when she was younger. All she wanted was to be happy. And maybe that had been the problem; she'd never wanted anything enough for it to matter. Except being a mother. Children mattered and having that dream taken from her had woken her up like a five-alarm fire.

Suddenly needing a drink, she parked the car and headed into the bar. The place looked exactly the same, and Lauren took comfort in the fact that some things never changed.

The bar was long and polished to a high shine, the smell of food and sawdust filled the air, and even this late at night, the place was half full of people sitting at the bar, playing pool or darts, lounging in the dark corners of the booths. A previously recorded golf game played on the TV in the corner. The tournament looked sunny and bright on the screen, and she absently wondered about the location. Maybe she'd pack her bags and go.

Lauren found a corner stool far away from the crowded pool table. "Vodka and club soda," she said to the middle-aged bartender.

"Lauren, is that you?"

She glanced up into the freckled face with the slightly receding hairline, but couldn't place the kind-looking man.

"It's me, Ron. Remember, from Groves High? You and your friends used to come in here after the games and drink beers and strawberry daiquiris."

The memory made her smile. Now she'd never touch beer unless it was light, and strawberry daiquiris were about half her calories for the day. Back then, though, she hadn't worried about calories. Just about having a good time. "Hi, Ron. It's been a long time. Almost didn't recognize you."

"Yeah." He looked a little embarrassed as he ran his hand over his hair. "I've gained a little around the middle and lost a little on the top. But you look great. Haven't aged a day since high school."

Lauren took a sip of the drink Ron placed in front of her. That's what monthly skin peels and daily Pilates classes do for you. Too bad the other areas of her life couldn't be fixed as easily.

"So what are you doing in town?"

She glanced around the bar, despair weighing heavily on her chest like one of those long-ago asthma attacks she had as a kid.

"Getting drunk." She looked back up at Ron, saw the kindness in his face and something else . . . pity? "So keep them coming."

Nikki had no idea what time it was, but it must have been close to two since only a few desperate diehards were left, and of course, herself. And that made her—what?

She shook her head. Everyone already knew what that made her. Just time she wised up to it herself.

A man with a shaved head, goatee, and hard eyes had his hand on the inside of her knee again. She brushed him off—for the fourth time.

What did he think? That she'd changed her mind and wanted his hand up her dress in the middle of The Pitt? Maybe when she'd first got here, she'd had some vague, crazy plan of doing something out of revenge. Something in the way of throwing her middle finger to Jett and his mother. But now, now she was tired, and maybe deep under the haze of booze there was a little intelligence left. She should go home, sleep it off, but didn't think she could find the door.

Nikki took another long pull from the bottle in her hand, having changed from tequila shots to beer. *Shoulda stuck with the shots. Then I would've been passed out by now.*

Goatee-man whispered something about getting out of here. A hundred cutting remarks tickled her tongue—another family trait. The Logans were mean drunks.

She looked up at Goatee-man. His tattooed arms were big,

knuckles scarred. Black eyes that wouldn't blink over kicking a dog or a woman, so Nikki swallowed her words. Her problem: she was scared. Goatee-man had three friends at the bar who would back him up.

Her stomach rolled. The tequila? Maybe. But she didn't think so. She'd had this feeling before, the night her mother died. It was like all those drowning dreams she had. There was a point when the water crashes over your head and you know you're in too deep. No way out.

She sat on a sticky wooden table, boots on a chair, with Goatee-man on one side, crowding her, stroking her hair, and the distant floor on the other. The ground looked a long way off, but she'd have to risk it. Her boot slid, heavy, off the chair as she tried to push her way to standing.

"Whoa, baby. Where you think you're going?" Goatee-man asked, his hand suddenly on her thigh, pushing her butt back up on the table.

Nikki didn't want to look back into his eyes. Her heart raced—an effect of the alcohol?

"I need to get up."

"Oh no, baby, you just sit right here and have another drink."

Her tongue was thick, and she had to drag it across the roof of her mouth a few times, but finally found the words. "Get off."

"I been paying for drinks all night. Think I'm gonna need some kinda compensation."

Nikki went to push him off, but his fingers bit down harder. She didn't feel it now, but knew there'd be a bruise on the inside of her thigh.

She darted her gaze past Goatee-man to Mike, but he'd left her to the wolves. She couldn't really blame him. There were four bikers and only one of him. Mike had his limit as to how many times he'd bail her out.

How did she always wind up in the middle of a disaster? But that's what she did—make a mess, burn a bridge. And wasn't that what Jett had always mumbled under his breath—no one could stop traffic and screw up faster—every time he'd pulled her out of a jail cell and got her back home.

And maybe he was right because there was a blaze of destruction behind her—Mrs. Avery, her own mother . . . Jett.

Maybe Goatee-man was all she deserved. Lord knows it was all this town had ever expected of her. Yeah, maybe it was time to start living up to her potential—a welfare check and a trailer. And Goatee-man here would probably get her there quicker than most. Yeah, this was her life, and there was nothing left to do but accept it.

Jett wasn't sure what to expect after Mike's call, but visions of Nikki being hassled by drunken men, shaking and cowering in fear, crossed his mind. Of course, if he'd been rational, he would've realized that this was Nikki, and she never did the smart thing.

He burst through the door, willing and ready to take on the world if need be. Instead, there was Nikki, sitting on a table, feet propped on a chair, head thrown back, laughter bubbling out of her throat. She had no fewer than four biker guys surrounding her, and all of them with blatant arousal in their eyes.

When she'd left the dinner table, he'd taken a few steps after her, but then let her go. Had Nikki really taken money from his mother? The fact that his mother had tried to pay her off was one thing, but that Nikki had taken the money was quite another. He'd never expected that from her. Didn't think she cared about money, but maybe the lure of getting out of this town had been too great. The thought turned his stomach. Had he misjudged her? Had the Nikki he thought he'd known most of his life been a lie? He couldn't believe he would have misjudged so badly, but now with the cream expanse of her throat exposed, and her finger outlining the ridge of her collarbone, the rolling in his gut solidified to something a bit more tangible. His game plan a bit more direct.

He was going to kill her.

Chapter 22

No one had ever labeled Jett a hothead. Nope, when he got angry, his rage never ran hot. It burned cold.

Jett was sure that when he came through the door, the bar hadn't quieted, the music hadn't stopped, the sound of glasses clinking together hadn't ceased—but at this moment he couldn't hear a thing. He did see Mike's eyes widen, and his mouth move slowly as if to form words. But if Mike spoke, Jett couldn't tell. There was some small part of his brain that was grateful he hadn't brought his gun. Not because he didn't want to use it—he did. No, because with his gun, the killing would be too easy, over too quick.

His hands tightened into fists. It was a good thing he could still count—four drunken bikers to one of him. No, no gun, but he would've traded his inheritance for a bat.

Nikki's head came up as if sensing his presence, and she met his gaze from across the room. For a moment surprise flashed in her cat-like eyes, then just as quickly they turned money-hard.

Fine with him. She wanted some action, he'd give her more than she could handle.

The trip across the sticky concrete floor took forever, and yet in one step he was there.

Usually, Nikki could meet him eye to eye, toe to toe, but from her sitting position he towered over her. He loved every blessed inch he had on her.

"How did you find me?"

"A bitch in heat leaves a scent."

He had to give it to her. Didn't even blink.

"I expected that from your mother," she said, "but not from you."

"Like they say, blood always tells, and it's sure true for the Logans. They can't seem to find their way up from the bottom of the pile."

He didn't even feel the sting of the slap. But that was Nikki for you. She'd let you drag her through the mud all you wanted, but no one could say jack about her family.

"Hey, the girl's with me," said a man to his right.

A shove to his shoulder had him breaking his glare on Nikki. Jett looked to the side and up and up. Damn, that boy was big. His head was shaved and his mouth was carved out of a rectangle of facial hair, but it was the size of his chest and the length of his arms that gave Jett pause.

Apparently, what was said around town was true. Nikki had the loyalty of an alley cat, and yet, always landed on her feet. And Nikki being with this guy finally meant she was ready to live up to her reputation.

So be it. If she was willing to put out, then damn it, he was going to be first in line.

Jett looked back to the brute of a man who was trying to claim Nikki. Even though the number of fistfights he'd been involved in kept rising, he could guarantee every damn one of them involved a Logan.

He glanced back down at Nikki, blue eyes snapping, even if they were a bit dulled down by drink, as she wobbled precariously on the table. Her dress inched up higher and higher on her thighs, and he couldn't help but ask if this girl was worth it.

A huge shaved head came into his line of sight. "That girl is going home with me."

Jett didn't even turn his head, just looked straight at Nikki and smiled. Hell, no. If anyone was going to find out whether she was wearing a black thong or not, it was him.

And everyone knows if the odds aren't in your favor, then you've no choice—fight dirty.

Jett swung his fist, smashing a cheekbone. An upper cut to the big boy's stomach and a hard kick to his knee, and Mr. Shaved-head went down.

Yeah, big-boy went down just in time for his three friends to join the party. Jett ducked a fist, but got one in the rib. Someone came from behind and got him in a chokehold, while a rat-faced dude started to work on his midsection. These boys might've spent the night drinking, but by no means had it slowed down their reflexes. Their fists were like a jackhammer in the gut, up one side and down the other, delivering bone crushing pain.

He heard someone scream. He hoped it was Nikki, hoped she felt guilty about being the cause of him pissing blood for the next week. Black spots circled his vision, and it became clear to him that there was a possibility his life was going end in this sink-hole bar, fighting for a girl whom nobody—including herself—thought was worth it.

But he'd always loved a challenge. With Nikki, he just had to work a lot harder.

Using the man behind him as leverage, Jett kicked up and caught the rat-faced biker in the nose with the steel toe of his boot. A grunt. Blood sprayed out in an arc. A body thudded to the floor.

Jett threw a hard elbow. There was a loud grunt and the hold on his throat loosened. That was all he needed. He turned, fisted his hand, and threw a punch. Jett was free.

In the dim haze that was his brain, he was aware that one plus two was three, and that number four was still out there. His eyes swept the room and came to rest on Mike standing over number four with the top of his bat resting on the biker's windpipe.

"I thought I'd help you even the odds," Mike said with a smile.

Jett was never so happy to see that crooked canine flash.

"I wouldn't have minded a little more evening-out a whole lot quicker." Jett coughed, sending spasms of pain through his sides.

"And I wouldn't have minded a lot less blood in my bar, but life is what God throws at you."

Jett bent over, trying to catch his breath. "And here I thought the Devil was the cause."

Mike looked over at Nikki, who had made her way to the back wall, visibly shaken. "When it comes from her to you, the Devil is most definitely involved. But going from you to her—it's all the

Good Lord, because anyone can see you're that girl's only saving grace."

"Stop crying," Jett growled. They were driving home in his truck, him bleeding all over his shirt, her sobbing silently into her hands.

Well, almost silently. He could hear her quick catches of breath interspersed with random sniffing. He could only remember Nikki crying one time, the night he'd found her in the barn after her mother had died. He hadn't liked it then and didn't like it now.

What he wanted from her was anger. He was angry, and he wanted to fight. One would think that getting the crap kicked out of him would've used up all his energy. But the fistfight with the men at the bar had been a poor substitute for the fight he really wanted—the one with Nikki.

"I said stop."

"I'm not crying." She wiped her face with the back of her hand. "And if I was it wouldn't be because I felt bad over you getting hurt."

Liar.

"Good, because I'm not hurt," he lied back.

So much for always having truth between them.

Nikki sat up and blew her nose into a napkin she'd found in his glove box. The girl never had a tissue when she needed it. "I'm leaving, Jett."

He stared straight ahead. "Big surprise, Nikki. Big surprise."

"I have enough money to fix my car, and Mike pretty much told me that I was more trouble than my outstanding debt."

"I would've fired you too."

"I couldn't get another job in this town."

"Nope, not with your reputation." He knew that wasn't true. There were people who were ready to support Nikki, but if she refused to see that, then there was no point telling her.

"Cole seems happy with his new family. He doesn't need me around messing things up."

"Yep, he wasn't even concerned when I called earlier to say you were missing." That one hurt, he could tell. He took the turn into his drive a bit too sharply, his back tires shredding the gravel.

Nikki grabbed the door handle. "Well, see then, there's no real reason for me to stay."

Jett parked the truck, reached over Nikki and flung her door open, then immediately hated himself for that gesture. She could damn well get her own door. "Nope, no real reason at all."

He stepped out of the truck, and it took everything he had to wait patiently for Nikki. Then taking her elbow, he led her into his house. "No reason that I can see, except for one."

Nikki walked ahead of him to the middle of the living room and turned to face him. "And what reason is that?"

Jett leaned back against the front door, reached behind him, and turned the deadbolt. There was only a dim glow from the kitchen. Jett flipped on the living room lights, so Nikki would be in no doubt how this whole thing was going to go down. There would be no shadows to hide in, no doubts about what he meant.

Nikki blinked hard in the sudden brightness. Or was it from the savage look that was written on his face? Then Jett smiled because he didn't actually give a damn which one it was. "Because it's payback time. And you owe me. Now take off that dress."

Chapter 23

As far as dares went, that one was pretty brutal. Of course, it was up to Nikki whether she wanted to accept it. To him the point was moot because either way that dress was coming off.

Her make-up was completely gone, washed off with tears and the corners of her sleeves. Her hair was pushed back from an ashen face and a pair of greenish-blue eyes. How had he ever thought of summer when he stared into those eyes? Now all he saw was the cold hardness of winter.

Her chin went up. "To pay back favors with sex would make me nothing more than a whore."

Her tongue was always sharper when she drank, but tonight he brought his own arsenal of pissed off. "Call yourself whatever you need to in order to get the job done."

If tequila turned Nikki mean, then what was his excuse?

Pain? Insanity? Or was it that the adrenaline had long ago worn off, and now he felt every one of those punches. He'd gotten the crap kicked out of him, been left humiliated at his parents' after she'd gone off and taken his truck, and had lost all hope of making this thing with Nikki work. Hell of a record, even for Nikki.

And for what? She was leaving tomorrow. He knew damn well she'd be gone as soon as she'd slept the night off. Had he really thought that he could get Nikki to stay? Nothing short of a marriage contract and a vow would've done that. The Logans were stubborn as hell, but loyal to the end, and once they gave their word, they kept it. It was getting to the making of the promise that was tough. No, his chances with Nikki were gone. All there would ever be for them were drunken one-night stands and mornings of regret.

But stupid idiot that he was, he'd take it. "It's time to see if you can make good on that black thong."

Then he knew. Was it by the flex of her jaw? The hardening of her eyes? Or maybe it was the fire in his blood that told him she'd taken the challenge. Lord knew his blood ran hot enough when it came to Nikki.

She widened her stance for balance and crouched down to untie her boots, still a bit unsteady on her feet.

"Leave the boots." He hated those boots. She wore them in defiance. A way to snub her nose at everything Texas and everything him. So this time he was going to take her with the boots on, from behind, and show her that Texas always ended up on top.

She looked up at him, a question in her eyes.

Apparently, she needed clarification. He was more than happy to give it. "On your way up. Just grab the hem . . . and pull."

And she did just that.

There was a slight rustle of cloth and an uncovering of caramel skin. Then the black knit dress was thrown at his head, and a scantily clad Nikki stood in the middle of his living room. His mouth watered, and he could feel his senses heighten as he caught her scent—tangy and sweet, innocent and jaded. Since the beginning of time it was the combination that men killed for. Lord knows that thought had crossed his mind more than once when it came to Nikki. But if he gave in to temptation and touched her, his control would go the way of his anger, so instead he kept his distance and circled her.

And to her credit, she didn't flinch. *Damn Logan pride.* Well, Nikki had met her match because he could be just as stubborn. "And now the bra."

Manuel "Cash" Rodriguez was nursing his beer in a dark corner booth when he saw her walk in. Lauren Avery. He'd heard she was married to some oilman's son, so the last name might've changed, but from where Cash was looking, not much else had.

Platinum blond hair, trim figure, and such perfectly tailored designer clothes that even he could tell they were expensive. Lauren Avery, the Ice Princess. Geesh, how long had it been? Ten years? Eleven? Even from this distance he'd bet the nickname he'd given her in high school still stuck. So, he'd been a little bitter then that he spent four years sitting behind her in homeroom, and she never learned his name.

He wondered if she'd remember his name now. Judging by the way she was downing those drinks, he doubted it.

Cash took another sip of his beer and tried to focus on the golf game, but instead his gaze drifted right back to the petite blonde at the bar. Damn, she was pretty. For some reason he'd always had a thing for her. Maybe it was because she'd been so far out of his league. As a poor Mexican who lived on a two-bit ranch on the outskirts of town, he'd never had a prayer of catching the eye of Lauren Avery, aka every teenage boy's fantasy.

He should go over there. Say hi for old-times' sake. Buy her a drink. He wasn't the same shy, scrawny kid he'd been in high school. Over the years he'd gained some muscle, started riding bulls. Some women even thought he was hot. Instead, he sipped the dregs of his now empty beer and placed the bottle down in disgust. *Coward.*

He could face down an eighteen-hundred-pound raging bull with nothing but the shirt on his back and a cowboy hat on his head, and here he was afraid of a half-pint girl with designer jeans.

He shook his head. Got out his wallet and threw a bill on the table to cover his tab. When he looked back up, Lauren was gone. Even as disappointment growled through him, he took her absence as a sign. He didn't have time for distractions, even distractions as pretty as that one. In the morning he was heading out of town again for the next rodeo on the circuit. His next ride was important. If he rode well, he'd secure his spot at the championships in Vegas.

Cash settled his hat on his head as he headed toward the door. He nodded to Ron on his way out, all the while scanning the bar for a certain blond-haired, slim-hipped woman. Once outside he headed toward his truck, and that's when he saw her. She was sitting in the driver side of her Lexus, door open, car light on, trying to get the key into the ignition. Cash stopped and watched for a moment, then sighed. Avery or not, that woman was in no condition to drive. He walked over and squatted down to her eye level so he wouldn't scare her. "Ma'am, do you need some help?"

She looked up, startled, even though her reaction time was a bit slow. Cash had forgotten how big her eyes were and even more so with tears streaming out of them. "No, I'm fine," she said, swiping at her face with her arm, missing the black mascara running down her cheeks.

Christ, she was a mess. His Ice Princess seemed to be melting right in front of him, which now made him wish he was back in the bar watching yesterday's golf game. "Well, you're obviously not fine," he said. "So let me give you a lift home. You can pick up your car tomorrow."

That did it. She started shaking and a few more sobs came out. "I . . . I don't want to go home."

Okay. Now what?

Cash never carried a hanky, that was his grandpa's generation, but he always had a bandana handy for when he found himself working outside or needed to wipe something off his hands. He pulled out the handkerchief, shook it out the best he could, then handed it to her. She took his bandana and blew her nose loudly.

Hers now.

"Well . . ." His knees were starting to hurt from crouching for too long. Past riding injuries had a way of making him feel older than he was. "Where do you want to go?"

She sobbed again, and lowered her forehead to the steering wheel.

After all the time he'd spent dreaming about Lauren Avery, this was never part of the fantasy. Cash looked around for some help. Was there anyone who'd be willing to take a hysterical woman off his hands?

The parking lot was empty.

Cash drummed his fingers against his knee. "Do you want to come home with me?"

As far as pick-up lines go, that was one of the worst. To be fair, he wasn't really trying to pick her up. All he wanted to do was get to his own bed, possibly throw her on the couch, and call a taxicab for her in the morning.

Her head came up. He took the handkerchief out of her hand and cleaned off the running eye make-up. She took a deep breath and then seemed to study him for a second. "Do I know you?"

And just like that he was back in high school and his heart sped up with the possibility of her knowing his name.

He swallowed. "Yeah, we've met. Sat behind you in homeroom."

"Oh." She nodded. Her nose was red, her eyes all dewy from tears. How anyone could look so good after bawling their eyes out was beyond him. "I sorta remember. It's Jake, right?"

She'd been drinking. Her memory was affected. He could cut her a little slack. He shook his head.

She furrowed her brow. "Johnny? Jimmy? It starts with a J, I know it."

It was like his pride took a head-first dive off the Grove Oaks Bridge. He'd sat right behind her for four years. *Four years.* Gave her his pencil every time she forgot hers, which was practically every day.

"Can you give me a hint?"

Not on your life.

And there went any desire he had to take her back to his house.

"Here." He straightened, knees creaking, and held out a hand for her. "Let me take you to your mom's house."

Jett walked behind her, wanting every angle of Nikki burned into his mind. Like he'd ever forget her standing in his living room in the most tantalizing black thong and bra he'd ever seen. There wasn't a tan line in sight, just pure cream-colored skin. Her legs, long and lean, were defined with muscle—strong legs, runner's legs, legs that would wrap around him and squeeze. His gaze followed the strip of fabric that covered the slit in her behind, and it took everything he had not to grab her by the hair, throw her over the arm of the couch, and replace that thong with his . . .

And yeah, he was turned on, maybe more so than he'd ever been in his life. But he also wanted to see her break. To see a flush of red across her cheeks, to show just a damn bit of shame. But not Nikki. Instead, he watched her toss her hair out of her eyes, straighten her spine, narrow her gaze.

And all of a sudden his ribs started to hurt, his jaw throbbed, and a sick feeling spread hot in his belly. Christ, what kinda game were they playing? How did they get to this place where she was angry and jaded, and not even bothered by standing in his house almost naked? Where he, on the other hand, was finding it difficult not to foam at the mouth.

"What's next?" Her voice was all throaty and thick, but there was no mistaking the resentment underneath.

Of course, she pushed. She'd always push.

His pride wanted him to hold the line, teach her a lesson. Show her that flirting with danger only got you hurt. But his line was starting to blur, and he was forgetting what side of it he was on. He didn't do this. He loved women, would worship at their altar if there was one handy. He loved their skin, their scent, the soft lines of their bodies.

And he was never at a loss for words like he was now.

"Cat got your tongue, Jett?" she taunted. "Where's the Avery charm when you need it?"

His charm? What charm? His skin was so hot he couldn't remember his own name, and one part of him was so hard it hurt. But he took her words as she intended—a challenge. And he was sick of her always winning. "You seem to be having a problem following simple directions, so I'll repeat. Take off that bra."

He saw her stiffen as if he had done her physical harm. Who knows, maybe he had. But he got what he wanted—a perfect view as her hands reached behind her, her fingers shaking as she unsnapped the bra. The lacy undergarment dangled from one hand. Then Nikki turned and faced him.

He didn't objectify women. Nope, he did not. But that was sure hard to remember when a lace bra hit him in the chest.

Her breasts were full and tipped with taut rosy nipples that swayed with each panted breath. And he wanted to be there, on his knees, to catch one sweet tip in his mouth.

Break, damn you. Say my name. Cover your face. Anything.

"And now the panties."

Her eyes snapped to his, wide and frightened. And for one moment that was enough, and he made a move to go to her. Then her eyes slanted into her famous "screw-you" glare, and her shoulders rolled back into that proud stance of hers.

"I'll hate you for this in the morning." Her voice was clear and calm, completely devoid of any trace of drunkenness.

"You'll hate me regardless. So it doesn't make a damn bit of difference."

Her nostrils flared. Then she quickly turned her back on him, which was impressive really, since the room must be spinning for her right now.

Nikki's fingers fluttered at the sides of her thong, then she hooked her thumbs underneath the fabric on each side—and hesitated.

Black swarmed Jett's vision. He couldn't get enough air and had to lean against the wall to keep upright. Then in a move so sexy Jett would remember it when he was old and gray, she turned her head. Met his eyes. Pulled her thong down as she slowly bent *all* the way over.

And when she carefully slipped the panties over her boots, there was no mistaking the view or the fact that she was more than ready for him.

There was a loud buzzing in his ears, and a sharp pain as he banged his head against the wall. Then he did it again just to keep himself upright.

"I assume you want your payment rendered in the bedroom." She had stood up and now faced him with a smile on her face that was hard and a whole lot dirty.

Jett watched her sway down the hallway in her black boots, a hand on the wall for balance. He was sweating, sweating and sick with a need so violent his mouth was dry with it. On shaky legs, he made himself walk to the kitchen sink. With the faucet on full blast, he washed the blood from his hands and splashed cool water on his face.

It wasn't enough.

He took the faucet and wetted his whole head, the back of his neck, and then stayed under the cold water until he could breathe without lust blacking out his vision. He flung the wet mess of his hair back, hearing the water spray the cabinets behind him.

He'd never brought a woman home and made her strip in his living room. Never taken advantage of a drunken date. Never treated a woman like a whore.

He opened the fridge and pulled out a beer. Unscrewing the cap, he downed the entire contents in less than ten seconds flat. He felt the beer hit his stomach and hoped it put out the flames in his gut.

If he went through with this, Nikki would be gone in the morning, and he'd be left staring at the man in the mirror. But could he stand what he saw?

Because if he walked down that hallway, he wouldn't be the man he'd always thought he was.

Jett buried his face in his hands and groaned, but he found he couldn't lie to himself even now. His head came up. The bottle was tossed in the trash. His feet resigned to their destination.

With each step down the hall a realization settled in—Nikki and he weren't as similar as he once thought. Because underneath that broken exterior, Nikki had strength. It took courage to show the world the truth, even if it was her version of the truth. He, on the other hand, was way weaker then he'd ever believed. He thought she would never break him, never make him stoop to this level. Because a real man would walk out the front door, not look back, leave Nikki her dignity. And a real man would feel a whole lot worse that he was damning them both to hell.

When Cash pulled up into the Averys' circular drive, the ridiculous looking fountain in the front had been turned off, but was still lighted for ample effect. He crossed himself, not at all sure what the proper protocol was for passing non-weeping deities.

He turned toward Lauren, who'd been alternating silence with hiccups for the last hour. He threw his kind smile at her. He never would've nicknamed her the Ice Princess if he'd seen her like this— hair pulled back, bandana crumpled in her fist. "We're here."

She made no move to get out of the truck. Was she waiting for him to hop out and open the door for her? Really? Wasn't driving over an hour out of his way in the middle of the night enough chivalry from a guy whose name she never bothered to remember?

"Did you know that I haven't been kissed by anyone since I got married?"

He raised his eyebrows. They'd been riding in silence for over an hour, and she wanted to talk to him about kissing *now*? What he wanted to say was, ah yeah, that's what being married means. You stop kissing other people. Instead, he just nodded. She'd finally stopped crying, and he didn't want her to start up again.

"Not my husband though." She stared straight ahead as if it didn't matter who was sitting beside her as long as it was a warm body. "My husband has been kissing other women for almost as long as we've been married. Doing other things too, but the kissing I've seen with my own eyes."

Cash squirmed in his seat. He didn't want to hear about this. Really, really, didn't want to get sucked into this woman's problems. Because that was what she was. Just some woman he'd picked up at a bar. Not at all the same person he'd had a crush on for over four years of his life.

"You know that I've been drinking, right? Which is a shame because I really want to remember this."

She turned toward him and, damn his heart, but it did a bucking action in his chest. She was just so pretty. Put together so nicely, like a trophy somebody could win. Even with her hair a mess and her face without any make-up, he knew she was out of his league. But that didn't mean he still didn't like to look at the merchandise.

She pressed her lips together. Took a few steadying breaths, then suckered him with the full power of those golden eyes. "So I guess what I'm trying to say is . . . will you kiss me?"

Cash actually glanced out the driver side window because, really, she had to be talking to someone else. Lauren Avery did not ask Manuel Rodriguez for a kiss. No way. Not in the real world, anyway.

She pushed her hair behind her ear, and damn if she didn't look like she was seventeen again. "If you don't want to, I understand. It's just that I've never done anything crazy. And I'm starting to think I should've had more crazy in my life. I think I want to start feeling things. And you're kinda cute, and I thought maybe you wouldn't mind giving me a goodnight kiss, so I could have something else to think about instead of my loser soon-to-be ex-husband."

He cleared his throat to help cover up his girly gasp. But damn, he was actually nervous. His heart sped up, palms a little sweaty. Was he actually going to do this? Take advantage of a drunken girl who was sitting in his truck?

Hell, yeah!

He tried to be smooth—he'd mastered a little technique over the years—but he was halfway across the cab before she had a chance to change her mind.

She came at him just as quick, as if he was some bad cough syrup she wanted to down. But this was his adolescent fantasy, and he was going to enjoy every moment. He slowed things down. Took her mouth with his, cradled her face in his palms. He tasted the vodka from earlier, and then totally lost himself in the scent of her hair.

She was unsure at first. So was he, but when she leaned in a bit farther, he took the inch and ran with it. Without over thinking, he grabbed her around the waist and straddled her across his lap. The kiss turned long and heated.

And then she trailed her hand across his chest and over his shoulder, and squeezed. He was so glad that riding bulls had kept him in shape and kept his reflexes sharp. He was glad to have both in this situation. Her shirt was eye level and he wasted no time in slipping the delicate buttons through their tiny holes. With her shirt undone he pulled it down her shoulders, revealing a white conservative bra that was in stark contrast to the sexy woman moaning on his lap.

Cash didn't want to scare her off, but at the same time he was already thinking of how he was going to get the pants off her and the condom from the back pocket of his jeans. But Lauren had other ideas.

The kiss ended, and when she pulled back there was color in her cheeks and a soft look in her eyes. "Thank you. That was good," she sighed. "It's been a long time and that was really, really good."

His pride surfaced from the cold lake it had been dropped into, and shook its mangy head like a wet dog. He grinned like a fool.

"And you know what?" She smiled that special Lauren smile like she had a secret that nobody else knew. "I remember your name."

Whoa, he'd only felt this kind of adrenaline rush when he was getting into a pen with a top-rated bull. He let out two quick breaths and waited.

"It's Hosea."

He almost laughed. Almost. "Get out."

Chapter 24

God is vengeance, God is wrath, God is the punisher of all sinners, and yet sometimes . . . God is merciful.

When Jett entered the bedroom, Nikki was sprawled out across the whitest of sheets, black hair in a mess around her head. One arm thrown across her eyes, the other over her head in careless abandon. Her damn boots had left a trail of dirt smeared across his thousand-thread-count sheets.

Her soft snores filled the room, and his lust died a slow painful death. Because even he couldn't keep it up for a beautiful corpse. And that was what Nikki was, dead to the world, passed out from the Cuervo and whatever else was in her system. He hated his life.

Wasn't that just like Nikki? Even damning them both to hell couldn't go according to plan.

He weighed his options, cursed, then cursed again. He'd gone way past gentlemanly behavior. He took off his shirt and boots. Then grabbed her arm and dragged her over to one side of the bed and crawled in next to her. He lay down on his back and stared up at the ceiling. "Damn, girl, what did we almost do?"

Nikki just moaned and turned to hug her pillow in answer.

The way he saw it, two things could happen tomorrow: Nikki could wake up remembering what had happened and leave hating him, or she could wake up not remembering and leave hating him. In either scenario, she would end up running.

But he wasn't going to be sad about it. He'd taken the gamble, knew the risks, and had rolled the dice anyway.

No, he wouldn't be upset. This pressure in his chest had nothing to do with watching her pack up her bags and drive out of town again. No, he knew he could live without Nikki. He'd done it once before. The problem was it just wasn't nearly as fun.

Or messy, he reminded himself. Without her, things would be much simpler. And that's what he wanted, right? Simpler.

The funny thing was, if it had been anyone but Nikki, he would've already had a ring on her finger. Didn't Nikki know that he was a catch? His family was well off, he knew he was a good-looking dude, and women had never told him no. He could charm any woman out of her principles and her clothes faster than other men could get turned down. So why didn't he just do it already? Find some other girl.

Jett let his head roll to the side and stared at Nikki's beautiful backside. He'd been right—her skin did look like cream against his sheets. He couldn't help himself; her skin drew his touch as if electrically charged. He let his knuckles move down the sloping curve of her hip, the small of her back, the dimple above each cheek.

He'd never given up on anything in his entire life. Of course, he'd never had to fight for anything as hard as he had to for Nikki.

He knew some people hadn't been as blessed as he had. Some had to work for everything, like Cole. And some worked just as hard and still lost it all, like Nikki. He could understand the pessimism born of such a life. But he wasn't a pessimist. Life hadn't denied him yet, and he wasn't going to let is start now—despite Nikki.

The specialized ringtone from the *Jaws* theme song broke through Jett's thoughts. His gut tightened in response. There was a moment, a sweet hope that he would mute his phone. Ignore the ring, turn over, and bury his face in the scent of Nikki's hair.

That hope burst as quickly as he reached in his pocket and pulled out the mobile. He pressed the screen with a grunted hello.

There was a rustling on the other end of the phone, then a soft whisper. "Jett?"

Her voice was all little girl and a lot scared. Jett closed his eyes, recognizing that combination all too well. "I'm here, Frankie."

There were a few moments of silence, but Jett didn't rush her.

"He's here. And she's . . . "

Frankie's voice trailed off, but that was all Jett needed to fill in the ellipses.

He was Stella's dealer. Though the actual person changed from time to time, the *he* was always the same. He was a boyfriend of some sort, which allowed Stella to do her bartering from her back . . . or her knees.

An ex-con, a businessman, a methed-out truck driver, Jett had seen them all in the dead, broken-down stares and the greasy combed-over hair. Stella's relationships all started the same way. With laughs, kisses, and "this is the one." Ended the same way also. Screams, curses, more than likely fists, and no one remembering there was a thirteen-year-old girl locked in her bedroom with nothing but a prayer and a well-placed phone call to Jett for help.

"How bad is it?" He needed to know if he should go alone or call the sheriff to meet him there. Either way he was going.

"Bad." Her voice cracked on the one word. Frankie might be young and scared, but she was a long way from innocent. If she said it was bad, then it was.

"I'm on my way. Stay in your room. Stay low. And don't come out until I come get you. Okay?"

"Roger, that."

Jett couldn't help a sad smile. Here this girl's life was a living hell, and she still tried to find a way to make him smile. He hung up the phone and turned to glance at Nikki. Why was he the crusader of lost souls? Why did every damsel in distress work her way deep into his heart?

Jett groaned as he pulled himself out of bed and pulled on his boots. He didn't need a psychology degree or a couple hundred therapy sessions to answer that question. It was the same reason Cole fought, why Nikki ran, and why Jett saved—skeletons in the closet. His just happened to be a little girl made smaller by the white hospital bed that surrounded her—his twin sister.

He had a hard time remembering exactly what Sarah looked like. The only vivid image he carried with him was of wide brown eyes in a scared face. A crooked line of freckles that marched across the bridge of her nose.

His family never talked of her. He guessed it was too painful. She'd died just after their fifth birthday. The official diagnosis had been leukemia—but even at such a tender age he'd already formed his own truth. He'd always been stronger than Sarah, and if he'd been allowed in the hospital, he could've helped her fight. Maybe could've saved her.

Now, at the age of thirty-one, the thought was ridiculous. He knew his logic as a little boy was flawed—except, as he brushed away a strand of hair that had caught on Nikki's lip, he was still trying to save wide-eyed girls with freckles across their noses.

But he couldn't save Nikki if he wasn't here. If she ran away.

A sudden rush of panic flowed through him at the thought of Nikki not being here when he got back. The night she'd run off the first time had left a wound in his heart he had no desire to re-open.

Then a thought hopped across his mind like a bird pecking in the wet sand. He swallowed hard to shake it off, but it was too late. The thought had already grown wings and the resulting flight had him sighing with relief. He leaned over the bed and traced the path along Nikki's spine with his finger as guilt tried to weigh in with his decision. Fear was stronger, and in the end he could justify anything.

He rummaged through his bedside table searching for what he wanted. He pulled out his gun and a pair of fur trimmed handcuffs some girl had left behind. One he shoved into the waistband of his jeans. The other he closed around his bedpost.

Really, she'd never find out. She'd be passed out at least until morning, and he'd be home way before then. This was the only way of putting his mind at ease, even if what he wanted fell into that gray area between legal and illegal.

Still, his conscience fought with valiant effort as he fingered the handcuffs. Then Nikki moaned and flung her arm up by the bedpost, and Jett smiled. Well, if that wasn't a sign then he didn't know what was.

Chapter 25

Nikki knew she must be alive because there was an ice pick stabbing her from behind her eyes. Her tongue was fat and dry, and felt twice its normal size. And that was all before she had enough courage to open her eyes. *Time to get brave.* She cracked an eyelid. *Too bright.* She slammed it shut. The hangover was present and vicious; it was better to sleep until the worst had past.

Nikki pulled the covers up over her head and snuggled into the pillow. The bed wasn't familiar, but it wasn't the first time she'd woken up in a strange place—of course it was the first time she was naked. The thought had her peeling open a lid. Naked? *Crap.*

Piecing together the puzzles of last night would come later rather than sooner, and since it wasn't her favorite part of drinking the night away, she voted for later. Yeah later, though there was a problem—she had to pee.

She rallied enough to push herself up, but her hand was caught. She let her gaze travel up her arm and stop on her wrist. Information downloaded into her brain like slow, dial-up internet.

Jett's room. Jett's bed. No clothes on, and her hand was handcuffed to the bedpost.

What the—?

She tugged on her arm, not believing her eyes. The metal rattled against the wood post. She blinked, then kept blinking. This was a dream, except when she pushed herself to her knees and pulled with both arms, reality started to cement itself.

"Jett!" she yelled, proud her voice wasn't in full panic mode yet. What the hell had happened last night?

Her memory was a black hole that no amount of probing could illuminate. But she tried anyway, which made the ice pick in her head dig deeper. It took a moment to realize Jett hadn't answered. She laughed even though it made her head pulse. He was in the kitchen making them breakfast.

"Jett!"

He must be in the shower. She strained for the sound of running water. Nothing. The house had the settled quiet of abandonment. Nikki twisted around, looking for a sign that he was still here, boots, clothes, phone.

Nothing. Flashes of icy heat broke over her skin.

Nikki looked around quickly, considering her options. There was a window close to the bed that looked out to the front of the drive, enabling her to see whether Jett's truck was still out front. Nikki looked around again, but still bit her bottom lip and hesitated.

She was of a mind that there was good naked and ugly naked, and there were some things a person should never do naked: fix a bike, barbeque, cook bacon. The maneuver she made, balancing on one knee and stretching her boot out to push the blinds back so she could check the driveway, was unequivocally in the ugly naked category.

With the quickest of glimpses and a flexibility she never knew she had, she realized that the driveway was empty. Empty, as in no truck. As in Jett wasn't here.

He'd made the fifteen-mile trip to town to get doughnuts. Maybe some coffee.

And left her chained to the bed?!

Calm, Nik. No need to panic.

She sat back down and struggled to take several deep breaths. With oxygen came reason. This was Jett. He'd be back. He was as dependable as the sun and as sure as the waves of the ocean. All she had to do was wait until he got back, and he'd unlock her.

And only then, only when calmness reigned, would she find the gun he kept and shoot him in the belly.

*   *   *

The night had been hell, and the morning wasn't shaping up to be any better. Jett sat in the passenger side of the patrol car, waiting for Sheriff Harry to give him the okay to leave.

The whole situation had been a complete cluster meltdown, and all Jett wanted to do was crawl into his bed and forget the whole thing had ever happened.

The situation with Stella and her current, or he hoped soon-to-be-ex, boyfriend had gotten sticky. In the end, after much persuasion and a few harsh words, Stella had agreed to press domestic violence charges, and Sheriff Harry had finally gotten Meth-head, Stella's latest, in the back seat of his patrol car. Harry was finishing up with some paper work and had asked Jett to stick around. Said he had something he wanted to talk about.

Jett was more than ready to call it a night, or by the look of the sky, morning, but he knew Harry's job was hard, and Jett didn't want to make it any harder. So he waited, eyes burning, ribs aching, jaw sore. He'd just sit in the sheriff's car, rest his eyes for a minute.

Harry tapped Jett's shoulder, startling him awake. "Do you have a moment?" he asked.

Jett rubbed at the stiffness in his neck. Sure, he had a moment. Didn't matter he hadn't really slept in close to twenty-four hours. Didn't matter dealing with lost girls and white-trash moms wasn't anywhere close to his job description. Instead, he simply nodded and stepped out of the car.

"Frankie okay?" Jett had checked on her earlier, but still had to ask.

Harry nodded his head. "Fast asleep. Stella's passed out also, but that's no surprise. Good thing that girl has you to look out for her, because that momma of hers leaves much to be desired."

Jett had heard all of this before, and was in no mood to rehash the deficiencies of Stella Johnson as a mother.

"I heard you were thinking of running for sheriff? At least that's what old Carl is in an uproar about." Harry pushed on the brim of his wide, tan hat and rubbed at the deep grooves in the center of his forehead. Jett wondered if he was taking his migraine medicine.

Jett might've remembered making some vague threat to that effect, but running for office was the last thing on his mind. Right now, all he could wrap his fuzzy brain around was the need for sleep.

Harry nodded and rubbed a hand over his face. He looked tired; years of service had left their mark. "Carl wants me to run one more year. Says that's best for the town, but I'm tired, Jett. I've put in my time, and now I'm ready to spend the rest of my days on my fishing boat. If the town really needed me, then I'd do it, but the thing is, I think the sheriff's position needs some new blood. And I think you'd be perfect."

Jett shook his head. He didn't even have any law enforcement background. Heck, he couldn't remember the last time he'd held down a job, but he had been on the town council for years, and he knew they'd let him complete the law enforcement academy if he was elected. But still, it was a lot of work.

"I guess what I'm trying to tell you is I'm ready to step down. You'd more than likely run unopposed. Heck, not sure there's anyone in town who wouldn't vote for ya. You're likable, intelligent, and have some crazy notion of wanting to help people. Having a badge on your chest would put you in a better position to do that. And with that rather large donation to the Track and Field Club, you're a shoo-in."

Jett sighed. "I wasn't the one who donated that money."

"Well, in that case, I'd still take credit, since everyone in this town already thinks it was you. Nobody else has thirty big ones to spare. Even if they did, it would be socked away for retirement or their kids' college funds."

Jett's gaze snapped to Harry's. "When did you say that donation was made?"

Harry shrugged. "I didn't. But it had to be around two years ago."

A suspicion spiraled in Jett's gut. "Two years ago, over the summer?"

Harry looked up as if his memory could be enhanced by studying the clouds in the sky. "Yeah, it had to be. That's when Maggie called to tell me about it."

"And totally anonymously?"

"Three stacks of 10k in a white envelope. A simple note explaining it was a donation. You usually don't see that kinda cash unless its drug money or a payoff, you know what I mean?"

And Jett did. He knew. How he'd ever thought otherwise was beyond him. The Logans would never accept charity. They were too damn proud. And there was no way Nikki would accept a payoff. She was just too damn stubborn to be put off that easily. It was just like her to thumb her nose at his mother by accepting the money and donating it to a charity his mother would never support. A charity that supported kids who loved to run, the way she did. Only Nikki had never gotten the chance to go out for Track and Field. Jett still didn't know where she'd gotten the money for college, but he'd bet his last dollar that Mike had something to do with it.

Jett felt sick. He owed Nikki an apology. A big one. He'd make it up to her by . . . *Oh. My. God.*

The world spun, and Jett had to brace himself on the car door to steady himself.

Harry grabbed his arm. "What? What's wrong?"

Jett didn't answer, too consumed with patting down his pockets, trying to find his phone. *No. No. This wasn't happening.* "What time is it?"

Harry muttered something, but a sick panic started a low roar in his head as he stared at his phone and tried to process what the forty-one missed phone calls coming from his house meant.

It meant she was going to kill him.

Nikki had to pee so bad she was seeing yellow. And it didn't help matters that every quick movement of her head sent her into a dizzy spell that competed with the tilt-a-whirl at the fair. She bent over and tried to combat the spinning room with slow breaths. There was no way she was going to get sick. She'd suffered enough indignities than having to add puking all over herself to the list. Her eyes caught on a small wastebasket. Maybe. She strained to the far left, inching the decorative wicker basket closer with her fingertips just in case, but the nausea passed and she slumped against the headboard with relief.

It had been when she was tearing the room apart—or as far as she could reach—looking for a screwdriver or anything else to dismantle the bed frame that she'd noticed Jett's house phone was within reach. She'd spent the better part of an hour calling his cell.

Forty-one times to be exact.

Forty times until she'd realized Jett wasn't coming for her. After that, her options dwindled rapidly. Thanks to speed dial, there were only so many numbers she'd memorized, but she knew her brother's. It was a mark of her desperation that she was willing to call Cole and ask for help. With blood pounding in her ears and a hand covering her face, she'd dialed his number.

He hadn't answered.

I'm going to die here.

That was when she lost it. Things went a little hazy as she ripped off the sheets and flipped the mattress on some small hope that she could unscrew the headboard from the frame of the bed. That was what she told herself to justify her little psychotic episode, but really she was frothing at the mouth to tear something apart with her bare hands.

In the end, all the tantrum had accomplished was to leave her sprawled across a bare mattress, half on the floor and half on the box spring, and dripping with sweat.

Exhaustion finally succeeded where anger hadn't, and some sense returned. Her wrist ached, her throat felt like she'd eaten a bowl of sand, and she still had to pee. An old weight, heavy and cold, settled like a familiar pet on her chest. Her heart beat like a slow fist against a steel, barred door. The feeling was so much a part of her, it was hard to remember there'd been a time when she'd ever been free of it.

His death would not be enough. A gut wound was too nice.

Nikki tugged on her wrist. Her other hand clawed at her throat. She might as well have been caught in a noose for all the air she could gasp.

Focus on the anger.

She had to or else the other feeling, the worse one, would come up and drown her.

The one that whispered in her head that she was caught, and maybe would be for days. And whispered that she couldn't run. Trapped just like her mother, in this town, in this bed, all alone . . .

No, she shook her head. No, anger was better. Anger was strong. Fear was weak. She'd been judged a liar, a cheat, a nobody, and a slut. What was one more name? One more snicker? She could handle it. She'd lived through worse, and she was out of options.

Her only hope was that the whole town wouldn't end up knowing. Nikki reached for the phone, closed her eyes, and pressed zero.

"Herber County operator, what is your emergency?"

"I need some assistance at the Avery house."

"Is this at Jett Avery's residence?"

"Yes."

"What's the nature of your emergency? Do you require an ambulance?"

"No."

"Is there a crime in progress?"

"No."

There was an exasperated sigh. "Honey, this could go on all day. Why don't you just tell me what's going on?"

"I have an emergency that only Jett can handle. I was hoping you could radio the Sheriff since Harry and Jett usually eat at Hal's—"

"Oh, please honey, if I had a dollar for every time I heard that one. This is not an escort service, so I suggest you get yourself out of his house and back to your mamma, where you belong."

"No, I really—there is an emergency. I'm," *oh God*, "stuck."

"Stuck how, honey?"

Nikki closed her eyes and took a deep breath. "Stuck on the other side of a pair of handcuffs."

"Ohh... Ohh well, that does changes things, wait—Nikki? Nikki Logan, is that you?"

She wasn't going to cry. She just wasn't.

"Nikki honey, it's me, Laura Kelps. We sat next to each other in English class."

"Oh, hey, Laura. Good to hear from you." She pulled the wastebasket closer to her and waited patiently to throw up.

"Good to hear from you, too. Didn't know you were in town. You knew Neil and I broke up, right? Damn SOB, shoulda known in high school. But you and Jett, I didn't know you were, you know, a couple."

"We're not." Since he would be dead as soon as she laid eyes on him.

"Oh... OH! Well, I just assumed that the handcuff thing was mutual. You'd never guess the stuff I hear doing dispatch. There was one time—"

"Laura." She did not yell. Her voice just sounded like that because her throat was dry. "Can you please radio Harry and tell him to send Jett home? He's not answering his phone."

"Sure thing, I'll get someone out there right away. You just hold tight. Oops, sorry, just a figure of speech."

Panic broke free. "No! No one but Jett. Just send Jett!"

It was no use. She'd already been put on hold.

A rash of nerves spread across her skin like tiny spiders or a deadly infectious disease. And being nervous always made her have to pee. She sat up on her knees and rocked back and forth. It was no use; it was either now or now. She had never known mortification until she positioned the wastebasket in the middle of the bed and had the thought of someone coming to rescue her and finding a bucket of urine by her bed.

Out of the corner of her eye, Nikki caught sight of Jett's hat, which had been knocked off the nightstand.

And despite the blinding pulse of her head, the incessant demand of her bladder, and the rising flush of shame, Nikki smiled.

This wasn't Jett's everyday Stetson. No, this was his going-out-hoping-to-get-lucky hat. This was his black, beautiful, and by the look of it, brand-new hat. She reached for it and stroked the soft felt. She hoped it had cost him three hundred dollars. She only wished it had cost him thirteen hundred.

Nikki put the Stetson upside down in the wastebasket and patted it into place. Then she squatted and sighed with blissful release as she found a whole new use for Jett's lucky hat.

Chapter 26

Jett had never been electrocuted, but at the sound of the dispatcher's voice crackling in through the patrol car's radio, he was pretty sure the effect was about the same.

"Hey all, we have a woman in distress at Jett Avery's residence."

Harry made a move as if to answer the dispatcher's call, but Jett was quicker, and a hell of a lot more motivated. He dove head first into the front seat, nearly ripping the handset off the dash in his rush to answer. However, he had the presence of mind to gather his calm before he spoke. "Hey, Laura, no problem. Harry and I are heading over there right now. Got it covered."

"Jett, is that you?" Laura's voice transmitted with a bit of static, but Jett could detect the censure nonetheless. "Nikki said she was handc—"

"Got it, Laura." Jett cut her off, fully aware they were broadcasting this conversation across county lines. "Thanks, we're all good here."

Jett climbed into the passenger seat while waving Harry to get in and start driving.

"Handcuffed," Laura said loudly, blowing through Jett's attempt to control the conversation. "Who do you think would do that to such a sweet girl?"

Jett must have lost the thread of the conversation since he was busy convincing Harry with rapid hand movements to turn on the sirens. *Sweet?* The Logans were a lot of things, but ... "We are talking about Nikki Logan, right?"

"Well, hell yeah, Jett," Laura said. "How many women do you got handcuffed up at your place?"

Jett was about to say "none" but another voice cut in. "Hey Laura," said Deputy Bert. "I'm right here. I'll check it out."

Jett slammed his head against the back of the seat. As if Jett's day wasn't bad enough already.

"Sounds good, Bert," Laura said. "Nikki sounded upset. Let me know if you need the fire department."

"No," Jett shouted, then fought desperately for control. "I mean, Bert, I'm only ten minutes away." It was probably closer to twenty, but who was keeping track?

"Negative," Bert answered.

"Bert!"

No answer.

"Bert, dammit, I know you're still there." Jett turned to Harry. "Tell him to stand down. Or at the very least wait until I get there."

Harry gave him a sheepish shrug. "Now, I can't really be doing that, can I? What if that poor girl is hurt? I wouldn't want to be responsible for that delay."

"She's not hurt! She's—"

"Oh, man," said Meth-head from the backseat. "Can't you slow down? I get carsick riding in the back. Dudes, I'm serious."

"Quiet," Jett snapped. He had to think. The sweat caused by the ninety percent Texas humidity was nothing compared to the flop-sweat he was breaking out in now. And then he thought of what Cole would do to him when he found out. Not to mention Nikki. Well, he wasn't above begging. Jett talked into the handset. "Bert, please, if you ever considered me a friend, I'm asking you to wait for me before you go into my house."

There was silence and then a wheezing static that came across the radio. Jett threw a confused look at Harry, who just shrugged.

It took a full minute to realize it was the sound of Bert, who had a pack-a-day and a can-of-snuff-a-week habit, laughing. "Ah, Avery, you and me friends? That's a good one. Maybe you should've thought about that before you slept with my wife!"

"What! Sue? She wasn't your wife then."

"I was dating her."

"You were on a break."

"Damn," said Meth-head from behind Jett. "You stole that dude's wife? That's just wrong."

Jett slammed the receiver against the dash, once, twice, three times. This was not happening. He was an Avery. Things like this didn't happen to him. He could calmly talk his way through anything. "Bert, seriously, that was over ten years ago. There is no way you are still upset about that. Besides, she ended up marrying you in the end."

"Yep, she did. But doesn't mean I'm not still pissed about it," he said, and then there was that static wheezing again. "I'm pulling into your drive right now. Time to find out what you've been hiding, Avery."

"Let him have it, dude," yelled out Meth-head from the drilled out holes in the Plexiglas.

Jett twisted in his seat and pounded on the barrier between them. "You have no idea how close you are to death, do you?"

The young man widened his glazed-over eyes as if offended.

Jett ignored him. "Bert? Bert?" he screamed into the hand piece. Silence.

Jett swore. Swore again. Then threw the receiver at the windshield.

Harry raised a bushy eyebrow. "You break it, you buy it."

"I can afford it, Harry. Just drive. And not like an old man. Drive like you stole it." Jett leaned forward and panted in the charged silence, totally out of ideas, and out of his head.

To Harry's credit he stepped on the gas, but after a few minutes he turned to Jett. "Sorry, son, but I'm gonna have to agree with the meth-head back there."

Jett glanced over. "About what?"

"You shoulda never slept with Sue."

Harry pulled into the driveway, and before the patrol car even stopped moving Jett was out and running toward the house. He slowed as he approached Bert, who was leaning against the front hood of his patrol car, ankles crossed like he'd been there all day.

Bert saw Jett and then carefully spit brown on the ground by his feet. "That's some pissed off woman you got in there."

Jett nodded, suddenly not in as much of a rush. "Did you, um, release her?"

"You kidding?" Bert gingerly touched the small cut above his eyebrow. "Got this courtesy of a lamp thrown at my head. She said to send you in and nobody else."

Jett nodded again, then mentally took an inventory of his bedroom. "Does she have, you know, any other weapons?"

Bert spat again. "You mean, other than her tongue?"

"Yeah, other than that."

"She can flay a man to bare bone. Not sure anyone needs more than that." Bert tongued the lump in his bottom lip to the other side. "Not that she didn't look good doing it. And, just to let you know, I might've taken a bit too long with my admiring. Nikki's a mighty fine-looking woman. Mighty fine."

Jett's eye started twitching. "I'll be sure to let Cole know."

Bert laughed. Funny that it didn't sound any better in person than over the radio. "I don't think I'm the one that Cole's gonna be mad at."

Jett nodded and rubbed the spot between his eyes. "So she's still naked?"

"She'd gotten the sheet wrapped around her, but I saw plenty."

Jett resettled his hat, trying to get a small part of him comfortable, instead of feeling like the soles of his feet were on fire. "I don't suppose you'd be willing to keep that part to yourself?"

Bert smirked. "Not a chance."

"Okay. Just had to ask."

"I can respect that."

The conversation at an end, Jett supposed there was nothing more to do except walk on in. He'd been in tough situations. He could do this. He had smooth-talking politicians running in his blood. He came from a long line of charmers and womanizers. He could do this. Make this right. This was not beyond him.

"Oh, one more thing," Bert said. "I'd leave your gun here with me."

Jett groaned. Then handed Bert his gun. He walked into his house on legs heavy and wooden. His gut sick like he'd swallowed a rock.

Inside, the house was dead quiet. Jett followed the trail of Nikki's discarded clothes from last night. Down the hall the trail turned from clothes to books, shattered glass, and a broken lamp. He did a quick mental assessment. Dare he hope everything that had been worth throwing had already been hurled down the hallway? Was it safe to assume she was out of ammunition?

The door to his room was open, and as he picked his way over the debris down the hallway, he got a clear visual.

His mouth went dry and for a blissful moment he forgot that they were fighting. Forgot Nikki was going to run. Forgot that they had no future. All he saw was a mostly naked woman kneeling on an overturned mattress with one arm outstretched and handcuffed to the bedpost. The other was listless at her side. Her head was bowed, hair fallen forward. One breast was covered by a sheet. The other was rosy tipped and thrust forward.

His eyes drank in her body like a man lost and desperate in the desert. Curvy, full, and totally Nikki. He knew enough about women and the current fashions to recognize that full hips and a round bottom wasn't the "in" thing like the gaunt, airbrushed models on glossy magazine pages. But the way Nikki's waist nipped in and then flared out into curves sought after by some of the world's most talented artists, the way the flat expanse of her navel perfectly showcased the classic dark vee between her legs, made him forget how to breathe.

Easy boy. Easy.

He loved women, their bodies, their laughs, the elaborate way they did their hair. But gazing at Nikki, he realized she put every other woman he'd ever had to shame. And he realized something else. He hadn't worshipped this body in the way it deserved. He hadn't spent the time to kiss the spot behind her knee, to nip at the webbing between her thumb and forefinger. To trail his tongue along the delicate dip of bone at the base of her throat.

Nikki deserved more than a night dulled with tequila and a careless no-strings attitude. And he promised himself, and whatever god looked after lost souls and damaged hearts, that if he were ever given another chance, he'd never forget again.

Her head was down, hair a mess, but he must've made a noise. A sharp intake of breath, possibly a small groan—God, he hoped not—and she looked up.

He watched her take him in, watched her upper lip part in a small curl, eyes snapping with wicked, blue lightening.

He was suddenly very glad he'd left his gun outside. All thoughts of lust were dampened like a randy dog sprayed with a garden hose. There was only one message in her eyes—murder.

Slowly he put his hands up in the same manner a man does when he comes across an armed and dangerous criminal or . . . a cornered animal. He didn't want to consider which one Nikki resembled.

And he wasn't even at a loss for words, because really there was only one thing to say. "I'm sorry."

She hissed, and only the handcuffs prevented her from lunging at him. Jett walked toward the nightstand and pulled out the drawer. He pushed aside some how-to-play-pool manuals and some CDs, and lifted up the key that had been there the whole time.

The knowledge that her freedom had been within her reach didn't seem to pacify her any. Her eyes widened and nostrils flared, she shook with rage, and he had a very cowardly thought, but possibly a very smart one. He could throw her the key and make a run for it.

Instead, slowly, very slowly, he reached over to unlock the cuffs. The lock sprang open, and she lunged forward. He caught her clawed hands a mere inch before they mauled his face. He twisted his leg to block a well-aimed knee—he did want to have kids one day.

He lost his balance among the curses thrown on his head and turned so he landed on the bed with her on top.

Nikki fought like a madwoman; he'd expected nothing less. He had to give it to her—the obscenities she strung together were creative, thought provoking, and showed a flare for the fanciful. And of course, there were multiple "I hate you's."

Nikki was no match for him in brute strength, but it took everything he had to keep her from hurting him and herself in the process.

He tried to reach her, he really did. "Nikki, wait. Stop."

But she wouldn't stop until she had her pound of flesh. He knew her too well. Her pride would accept nothing less.

He clamped his legs on either side of hers to protect his manhood. His hands were wrapped around her wrists, and he shook her. "Stop! Nikki, stop. Listen to me."

How many times he shook and shouted her name before she focused on his words, he wasn't sure. Her gaze finally cleared. Motions relaxed into bridled anticipation. The rigid curl of fingers folded into restrained fists.

This was the best he was going to get. "I'm sorry."

"I'm gonna kill you."

Did he deserve it? Yes. His decision made, slowly he loosened his grip on her wrists, and as calmly as he could, laid his hands down by his sides. "I'm sorry, Nik, I really am. Whatever you do, I deserve it. Do your worst."

She straddled him on either side with thighs that quivered with pent-up energy. Her breath came hard and furious as her breasts heaved. He could almost hear the blood rushing through her veins, or was that his?

She raised her clenched fist.

He braced for impact, but he didn't look away. No, he wanted her to see him. To see he meant her no harm. Not this time.

She stilled, her fist trembled, and she tried to swing. He saw the blow coming, saw the moment it would connect with his jaw and then saw the moment when her face crumpled because she couldn't carry through.

She screamed. Loud and deep. A sound born of frustration and pain, and then threw herself off him and onto her side.

In one of those weird, twilight moments of life, he lay there, staring at the ceiling, and saw the room from a whole different perspective. He looked down from outside himself and watched a man fully clothed, breathing hard, lying next to a naked sobbing woman curled in on herself as if a vital part had snapped. If it hadn't been him lying next to Nikki, if it had been someone else lying cold and still next to that shattered woman, he would've killed first and asked questions later.

But it was him, no one else, and he had to try. He didn't know if she heard him as he spoke her name or even felt the tentative touch on her back, but he did it anyway. In a moment, maybe ten, she would pull herself up, wipe her face, lift her chin, and resent any comfort he gave.

Any moment she would walk out that door, never look back, and he'd have lost her forever.

But now, in this little pocket of time, she just looked like the scared eighteen-year-old girl who had wept with guilt and grief over the death of her mother. And just like then, he couldn't lie there and do nothing.

He pulled a blanket from under the mattress and tucked it around her, then pressing her back to his front, he gently murmured into her hair. His words were inconsequential, yet the tone was the same as on that forever-ago night in the barn.

Her sobs . . .

I promise. So sorry.

. . . so deep . . .

Please. I never meant to hurt.

. . . so old . . .

Please. Love you.

. . . so violent . . .

Sorry. So sorry.

. . . and so, *so* damn many.

It was their litany. Her shuddered inhale, his exhale of whispers. Over and over, like the synchronizing of two swaying pendulums sharing the same space. A rhythm all their own. His words, her tears. Over and over. Again and again, until there was nothing left except . . .

His regret and her pain.

Chapter 27

The violent shudders that had racked her body finally eased into exhausted hiccups. Through it all he held her and tried his hardest to keep her from flying apart, knowing he'd be the last person she would want to see her exposed. He knew she was vulnerable. They both were. He knew she was afraid, but she didn't need to be afraid alone.

He would never let his fear of her leaving prompt a rash decision from him again. If she ran, he would stand it. But he knew now, one could never catch a wild thing. Nikki would only stay if she was free to go.

He wrapped an arm around her middle and felt her stomach quiver beneath his palm. "Shh, just breathe Texas, I'm here. I'm here. You're okay now."

He knew this wasn't about him, not really, this was about being left alone, helpless and afraid. Powerless and unable to run. Nikki's worst nightmare.

The afternoon sun crept through the sky and shone through the plantation shutters in alternating strips of dark and light. Shadow and sun. And didn't that describe Nikki and his relationship—two sides of one coin, love and hate, passion and anger, running away or staying to fight.

The bars of shade rode the curve of Nikki's hip, played in her hair, tangled with her body. He had held her for hours, and somewhere in the middle she'd stopped crying, and they lay there. Him tense, her spent.

"How could you do that to me? You out of everyone, you should know." Her voice was scraped raw.

Jett squeezed his eyes shut, wanting to block the words as easily as he did the light. If his heart wasn't already broken, it would've been shattered by her words.

"I'm so sorry. I wasn't thinking. Nikki, please believe me, I never meant to hurt you."

She shook her head. "I trusted you. You promised you'd never leave me. That you'd take care of me. That's what you said that night in the barn."

She remembered? He hadn't even been sure she'd heard him.

"But what I don't understand is why. Why would you do that to me? I thought you loved me?"

"I do, Nik. God, please believe me, I do love you. But I got scared."

"Scared of what? What do *you* have to be scared of?"

Scared? He was terrified. This was his Nikki. Someone he needed in such a fundamental way that his body considered her as vital as air. "You have to know that I love you." His fingers tunneled through her dark hair—funny how the copper streaks were starting to grow on him. He rested his forehead on the base of her neck. Whispered the words against her skin. "I do. But I got scared that you'd leave. And it was stupid. A split second decision and . . . "

And one he felt he was going to regret for the rest of his life.

Desperate, he had one play left. One trick shot still up his sleeve. He hadn't wanted to do this now, but he was out of options.

Now he knew what desperate meant. It was holding water in the palm of your hand while walking across a desert. It was taking your last full breath as the water rose above your head. It was convincing a woman to go against every survival instinct she had and getting her to trust you enough to stay.

"Nik, one more chance, please. Stay with me, live with me . . . "
He took a breath for courage. "Marry me."

Silence. He felt her body relax, her breath hitch, muscles melt under his hold, and for one measured beat, his heart soared because there was hope.

Then just as quickly, he was back to palming water in the desert. She rolled out of bed, taking the blanket with her. Like a queen with her head high, robe dragging behind, she'd dismissed him. He watched her go down the hall, pick up her clothes, then disappear into the bathroom with a soft click of the door.

With nothing more to do, Jett sat up on the side of the bed, head in hands, and waited.

The door opened. He glanced up. Nikki was fully dressed, face scrubbed free of any trace of makeup, hair slicked back behind her ears. She didn't even look at him, just brushed at a wrinkle in her dress and turned to walk out the bedroom door.

"What?" Jett called out after her. "That's it? It's over? You don't have anything else to say?"

She stopped, but didn't even bother with a glance over her shoulder. "You're gonna need to buy a new hat."

Nikki held her composure all the way down the hall, across the living room, even managed to open the front door after two attempts. Her body seemed to function on automatic, her insides anesthetized to any emotion, which was good because before, when she'd been trapped inside, it hadn't been . . . good.

Lying in Jett's room had broken her wide open, like an explosion of rock and brick, blood and pain. As if she was still a little girl trying to hold back the bursting dam with nothing more than her two bare hands. Lying there helpless had done something that the death of her dad, the loss of her mom, the whispers of the town hadn't been able to do. Being tied and not able to run had chiseled her down to not only who she was, but how she'd become that person. It was painful to realize she wasn't nearly as strong as she'd always thought. Not nearly as tough.

So she'd let Jett hold her. Soaked up his words like prairie grass would the morning dew. Let him cradle her. Make love to her with his words. Let herself believe like she'd believed her father's promises, her mother's praise, her brother's devotion. And then like every time before, she'd woken up and seen them all for what they were—lies.

Nikki stumbled off the front steps like a drunk after a hard night, but caught herself before falling. She looked around for her car, but remembered it was still at The Pitt. There was no way she'd go back inside and ask Jett for a ride. There was no way. So she started to walk, and then just kept on going.

Dusk was gathering strength, though the heat of the day didn't want to relinquish its hold. Her black knit dress clung and chafed her skin, and it wasn't long before sweat beaded between her breasts and ran down her spine—the same path Jett had traced earlier with the tip of his finger and the breath of his words.

Suddenly walking wasn't enough. She had to run. Along a dusty road in nothing more than a knit dress and combat boots, she ran. She was sure she looked ridiculous. Wouldn't be the first time. Her stride widened, her dress rose high on her thighs, and still she ran. Her skin grew hot and soon was slicked with sweat. Heated air burned a path to her lungs, dried out her throat, but still she ran. A fire billowed in her chest; her legs grew heavy from the weight of her boots, but it wasn't enough.

More, a little more. She had to be able to outrun the pain. It had worked before, would work again.

Her body found the wall—the place where muscles begged to stop and shut down. She mentally shrugged. Pain didn't scare her, not anymore, because the physical pain was nothing compared to the scorched land that used to be her heart.

She pushed until there was nothing left except sweat and heat and muscle. And the only noise in her head was the rush of blood past her ears.

"Hey, you trying to give yourself a heart attack?"

And the world came crashing back into focus.

Cole's truck had pulled up beside her.

"You better let me give you a ride before you pass out."

Nikki stopped and braced her hands on her knees, panting in the thick air. She had to squint to see past the glare and into the shaded interior of the truck. It was Katie. Right, because Cole probably wouldn't have stopped, except maybe just to lecture her. As Nikki was debating what to do, Katie reached over and flung the door open. And suddenly Nikki felt stupid.

"Come on, Nikki," Katie said, obviously realizing that she

needed some encouragement. "You can't run all the way home, especially in that outfit. You'll cause traffic accidents all up and down this road."

Nikki rolled her eyes, but realized that Katie was right, and pulled herself into the passenger seat.

The AC was on high, but was no match for the outpouring of sweat coursing down Nikki's face. Katie reached behind her, rifled through a diaper bag, and came back with a wet wipe.

The cloth smelled of wet cornstarch and baby formula, and she grimaced as she mopped up her face.

Katie laughed. Soon Nikki did the same, even though the entire situation was anything but funny. And suddenly Nikki was embarrassed about all the missed dinner invitations and the Tupperware containers of food Katie had left on her porch that Nikki had never gotten around to saying "Thank you" for.

She'd been raised better than that. Since when had she started to think it was okay to treat people like they didn't exist? Nikki had so few friends in this town; could she really afford to alienate the ones she did have?

"Katie—" Nikki swallowed. "I'm sorry about the dinners and . . ."

"Ah, no problem." Katie waved her hand, dismissing the apology. "I knew you were busy."

They both knew that wasn't true, but Nikki nodded anyway, glad for the excuse Katie had thrown her way. The natural pause in the conversation drew out until it was uncomfortable. Nikki folded her hands and tapped her fingers together. That had always been the problem between Katie and her. The only thing they ever had in common was Cole.

Nikki studied Katie out of the corner of her eye. She'd always been beautiful, fun, quick to smile. She had a temper, sure, but what person wouldn't when living with a Logan? Katie also had a passion—horses. She lived and breathed the horse ranch even more than Cole did, and it suited her. Unlike Nikki, Katie had always known where she fitted in, where she belonged. And then when Cole and Katie had made it official, it had been even harder to be the one on the outside looking in.

But Katie was trying, and Nikki owed it to her to at least do the same. "You look good, Katie." And she found that she meant it. She hadn't seen Katie since she'd gotten back into town, but it was evident that the last two years of Katie's life had treated her well. Her sun-lightened hair was pulled back into a messy ponytail, and she wore jean cut-offs, and a tank top that showed off tanned, muscular arms and legs. Of course, Katie had always been pretty, but now the after-effects of the pregnancy had given her boobs and curves that Nikki was sure Cole was happy about.

Katie blushed. "Yeah, who'da thought the new love of my life would be bald, fat, and cry a lot?"

In a gesture that made her seem like she'd been a mother her whole life, and not just a few months, she reached behind the seat and stroked a bald head over the top of the car seat.

Nikki turned and peered over the plastic car seat decorated with smiling cartoon cars and huffing, old-fashioned trains. Nikki was ashamed to realize this was the first time she'd actually seen the face of her nephew, and the thought of how that might've made Cole feel was a sharp stab to her heart.

Jimmy had his fist in his mouth, slobber trailing down his chubby arm. His head seemed overly large for his body, so she hoped for his sake he'd get hair soon. He had eyelashes that she supposed would be the envy of all the girls in the town, but other than that he looked like every other baby she'd seen. Then Jimmy rolled his big blue eyes up to her and let out a laugh as if seeing her was the best part of his whole day. And Nikki's heart was caught. It was like looking into Cole's eyes, her mother's, and, if she remembered correctly, her grandmother's. This baby seemed to have the best of Cole and Katie put together, and for the first time Nikki understood that Jimmy was an extension of her family. That this little boy, in some small way, was connected to her. That this baby had a permanent place in her heart, and she was surprised to realize she wanted to have a permanent place in his.

Jimmy grasped her finger in a soggy little fist and tried to bring it back to his toothless grin. She smiled despite herself. When was the last time someone had looked at her that way? Then she remembered . . . Jett when she walked into the diner her first day back, when she'd come to his house in this little black dress and stood on his front porch, when he'd touched his forehead to hers and told her to hold him to his promise.

She thought she had cried all her tears, but apparently there was a bottomless well somewhere inside her. She blinked and turned back around. "He looks like Cole."

"Yeah." Katie shook her head. "I wanted a little girl, a mini-me, but I should've known the Logan gene pool would leave its mark." She smiled back at Nikki. "But I don't really mind that Jimmy's got his father's eyes. I'm kinda partial to them myself."

"I hope that's all he got."

"Yeah, really. I sure don't need two stubborn men in my life."

They both laughed, and the constriction around Nikki's heart eased a bit. She took a deep breath, suddenly aware of how sticky her dress had become. She peeled the fabric from her skin to let the cool air in, but it was useless.

"So, where are you coming from?" Katie asked.

Nikki didn't want to talk about Jett. The news would spread fast enough as it was. "Can you drop me off at my house before going home?"

"Sure." Katie nodded. A few more moments of silence rolled by. "You okay? I mean really, are you okay?"

Nikki was far from being okay. She was about as far from okay as a person needing to be committed in a mental hospital would be. Maybe she should just make her reservation now. She'd bet they'd do her laundry for her, let her pick out what juice box she wanted for lunch. Instead, she glanced at Katie. "Yeah. Yeah, I'm fine."

Of course, that was up for debate since Katie had seen her running hell bent for leather in combat boots and a little black dress as if her hair was on fire. But she was willing to pretend that hadn't happened if Katie was.

"You know, I used to look up to you," Katie said.

Nikki's gaze meandered over to Katie as she prepared herself for a new line of bull.

Katie laughed. "No, really I did."

"What in God's name for?"

"Your courage."

Nikki laughed. "That's where you're wrong. I'm not courageous. That's you. You're the one who risks life and limb to rehabilitate crazed horses."

Katie shrugged and shook her head. "That's with horses. With horses it's easy. Horses might bite and kick at you, but it's nothing personal. At least with most horses. Now you, on the other hand, don't give a flip what some people in this town think or say. You've always just lived life to your own standards, and to hell with what a few old biddies think."

"You mean, what the whole town thinks."

"No, Nikki, only a few people. And that's your problem."

Nikki sighed. "I only have one?"

Katie just talked right over her. Apparently, she'd dealt with the Logans before. "You were always so hard on yourself that you never gave anyone in this town a chance. You thought everyone had condemned you for being a Logan, and you didn't see how the town wanted to support you. They still do—if you would ever give us a chance. It's as if you don't think you deserve happiness or, God forbid, any kindness. But let me tell you, anyone who cared for her dying mother as well as you did deserves more than a few good things in life."

Nikki fingered the necklace around her neck, the feeling of shame as tangible as the small diamond in her grasp. "I didn't do that good a job. Of taking care of my mother, I mean."

"Don't," Katie said. There was a hardness to her jaw that spoke of a stubborn streak that wasn't exclusive to the Logans. "You can't lie to me. I was there. I saw how you held that family together. And I might love your brother, but I know he was no angel. You were the strong one when he fell apart, took to drinking. If it wasn't for you, your mother wouldn't have had those last years in her house where she wanted to be. She would've ended up in some state care home where no one would've taken notice of her. In the end, she was at peace. You did that, Nikki. And really I'm jealous."

"What? Why?"

"You had all that time with your mother. Time to talk and just be with her. Time to say goodbye. I never knew my mom. I remember being so desperate for a mom to talk to that I'd pretend I was you. I would pretend I would come home from school and my mom would be a captive audience and would hang on every word I'd say. I would talk to her about Pa, horses, and most of all, Cole. Pretend that she had this great advice for me, and even get upset sometimes when I wasn't living up to who she thought I should be."

Nikki was shocked. She didn't know what to say. To think someone was jealous of her life. That someone wanted what she had.

Was it true? There were nights she'd sat on her mother's bed and talked about the boy she liked at school or how she fought over something stupid with her best friend. Her mother was always there when she got home, always wanted to know how her day was in painstaking detail. It was just such a part of her life that Nikki never thought there were others who didn't have that. Like Katie.

Katie brushed at her cheeks with the back of her hand. "I thought the worst part was growing up without a mom, but now, having a son of my own, what I wouldn't give for her to see him. You know, just once, so she could hold him, and I could tell Jimmy one day his grandmother knew him and loved him."

Katie turned toward Nikki, her gaze a mixture of loss and hope. Nikki found that she couldn't breathe, and so instead looked down at her boots. "And that's why I know family is more important than anything in the world. And I know Cole is tough sometimes and he doesn't say it, but he loves you. You are his last connection to your parents and he is your last connection, too. Here—" Katie reached into the purse by her feet and tossed an envelope in Nikki's lap. "I've been carrying that around for weeks now, wanting to give it to you in person, but . . . "

Nikki looked down at the envelope in her lap and wondered what could be inside, but she had a sickening feeling that whatever it was, she didn't deserve it. "Katie, I'm so sorry."

"No, stop. We already went over that. I get it. I really do."

Nikki peered inside the envelope and pulled out a check. She had to read the amount three times before she could speak. "What? Oh my God, Katie. No. No way. I can't take this. Besides, Cole has done enough for me, I can't take his money."

"Now you've offended me. It's not Cole's money, it's mine. My mom's life insurance was socked away in a money market account for years. It was set aside for my tuition to vet school, but well, those plans were changed. But the way I see it, this money was always intended for college. Wouldn't be right to spend it on anything else. And since you're the only sister Cole and I have, I thought you should have it."

Nikki still didn't understand. "But I have my degree already."

"Yeah, but that degree came with a price. The way I figure, this should be enough to clear yourself with Mike. And *when* you quit your job at The Pitt, I might get a dinner conversation about something other than Cole asking me what the hell is wrong with you."

"How—how did you know?"

Katie's brown eyes twinkled as she arched a brow. "Did you really think you could pull something like that off in this small a town without me finding out?"

"Does Cole know?"

She shook her head. "No, but when he gets over being royally pissed off, he'll put two and two together. So I think it's best that this whole thing is taken care of before then. Better for you and Mike both."

Nikki fought hard for something to say, but her throat tightened and damned if she didn't want to cry again.

Katie reached over and squeezed Nikki's leg. "There's a stipulation, though."

Nikki's heart sank like a stone. When would she ever learn—there were always strings.

"We're family. So next time you're in trouble, you come to us first. That's what family does. Deal?"

What was it with her, today? She couldn't seem to go a whole thirty minutes without welling up like some baby. It was like her tears had found a way out and now they were determined to make up for years of lost time. It took her a whole four attempts before she could form the words without breaking out into a sob. "Thank you, Katie. Thank you."

Jett felt like hell. And sure enough, he looked like it. His eye—bloodshot with a dark bruise smudged underneath. His lower lip—cut and twice its normal size. And his torso looked as if someone had used him for boxing practice. Oh yeah, someone had.

To add to his misery, he hadn't heard from Nikki since she'd fled his house two days ago. To be fair, he hadn't tried to track her down, either. He'd laid his cards on the table; the rest was up to her. He'd heard from Bo that she picked up her car yesterday. That in and of itself told him a lot. He expected she'd already be long gone if what she owed Mike wasn't hanging over her.

At least Nikki was out and about in town, showing her face. That was more than he could say for himself. He'd cowered in his home, moping around, waiting by the phone—totally pathetic. Finally, not able to stand being with himself another moment, he'd gotten himself dressed and out of the house. That's how he found himself at Dirty Dick's, the next town's local dive. The place looked as if the health department hadn't paid a visit in a while. That, or the owners had paid them off last time around. Jett respected people who wanted to live on the edge, but eating here pushed his limits. Nonetheless, the beers were served in bottles, and he expected that was safe enough.

It was only two o'clock in the afternoon, but the place was packed. Did anyone work a full day anymore? Like he could throw a stone. Still, the clientele looked as if most of their business was done at night and on the other side of legal. Jett fiddled with the bottle cap; the clientele wasn't his concern. He'd taken on way too many of other people's problems. Time he took his own damn advice and looked the other way. He should just sit here and nurse his black eye and broken heart with his warm beer.

Jett saw the reflection of a couple staring at him in the mirror behind the bar. He ignored them. He wasn't exactly sure what they were saying, but even he wasn't that much of an idiot that he couldn't guess the gist. Apparently, all a person had to do to rise to notoriety around here was handcuff a naked woman to his bed and, um, leave her there.

He was sure he'd be hearing from his father soon. *Treat every year like it's an election year, son. The family reputation is on the line.*

He groaned out loud just thinking about it. He couldn't blame this one on Nikki—this screw-up was all his own. There seemed to be a direct correlation between his IQ and the proximity of Nikki—the more involved with her he was, the dumber he got. Maybe it was better she didn't stay, it would keep him from ending up watching re-runs of *Wheel of Fortune* and drooling down his wife-beater shirt.

Jett caught the eye of the bartender and indicated another round of overpriced beer. If he was really goal oriented he should be downing tequila shots, but he had no stomach for the taste—it reminded him of Nikki. Better to stick with beer and his self-delusion that he didn't care whatsoever about a foul-mouthed, pouty lipped, combat-boot-wearing, pain-in-the-ass girl.

He dropped his head into his hand and tried hard to concentrate on peeling the label off his bottle of Bud.

"Avery, you son of a—"

He didn't need to hear the rest of the greeting to know it was Cole. And like a poor relation on payday, it was just like Cole to show up when he was the last person on earth Jett wanted to see.

This time Jett didn't even bother with a groan, just spun around on his bar stool, distinctly aware of the hushed murmurs and blatant stares throughout the bar. It didn't take a course in body language to see Cole was pissed, and Jett would bet another black eye Cole had heard about Nikki.

"How could you do that to me . . . to my family?" Cole towered over him, his face a shade of red that did nothing for his complexion. "I told you to stay away from her. Don't you think she has enough on her plate without you disrespecting her in front of the entire town?"

Jett took in the other patrons, down-on-their-luck cowboys, and worn-around-the-edges women all hanging on every word. Jett had no desire to be this afternoon's entertainment. "Cole, let's go somewhere else, and I can explain—"

"Why? Is there anyone in this town who doesn't know that you handcuffed my sister and left her in your house?"

Not anymore.

"Don't forget the naked part, Cole. Handcuffed naked!" said one of the cowboys standing in the quickly forming circle around Cole and Jett.

"Thank you!" Cole gestured with his hand to give the cowboy his due. "Let's not forget the naked part. Lord knows, no one else will."

There was a snicker from the peanut gallery. *Great.* So this was where it was going down. *Damn Logans.* Jett set his bottle down and stood, suddenly regretting ever leaving his house.

Cole must've come straight from the ranch. His shirt had rings of sweat under each arm, his hat was covered in dust. His eyes were strained and red-rimmed, probably from lack of sleep, but underneath there was something besides anger and stress. They were best friends, had been through years of crap together, stood by each other's side. He'd performed the ceremony for Cole's wedding.

And Jett felt sick because there was real hurt in Cole's eyes. The knot in his stomach doubled, and he started to regret not doing the tequila shots. "I'm sorry. Really. I was an idiot."

"You're sorry? *Sorry?* That was my sister. What were you thinking?"

"I was . . . I—" *Damn it.* "I didn't want her to leave."

Okay, even he admitted that sounded horrible, and he would've been surprised if the crowd didn't laugh at that one. They didn't disappoint.

"There are other ways of keeping a woman in your bed," someone yelled out. "And ways where the gal would be a bit more willing."

More laughter. *Hell.* And the humiliation just kept coming. Nope, beer wasn't going to be enough. He'd heard Jäger had a nice kick to it.

"She was willing, okay?" Jett needed to clarify or else it sounded like he was some kinda sick rapist.

Apparently, that's what Cole thought because he took a swing. Jett ducked just in time and backed up. The last thing he wanted was to get in another fight over Nikki. He needed to get Cole to see reason, he needed to explain. "It's not what you think, Cole. Nothing happened."

"If I had a hottie like Nikki Logan tied up my bed, you'd better believe something would've happened," yelled a man from somewhere in the back. Was that Billy Moore? Who did he think he was? A bloody stand-up comedian, here for the two o'clock show?

"Yeah!" This time from a woman. "Maybe Avery needs some lessons. I'll be more than willing to give him a few pointers."

A few catcalls and whistles followed another shout, and Jett was starting to feel like he'd just dropped in on the set of a reality television show.

"You've spread your advice around to anyone, regardless if they wanted it or not," joked Billy.

"Shut your trap, Billy!"

The volume in the bar rose as everyone threw out their one-liners and comebacks. The whole scene was turning into a full-out soap opera. All that was missing was a man announcing . . . and like the sands through the hourglass . . .

"Now you're lying to me?" Cole yelled. "You expect me to believe that nothing happened? I know exactly what happened."

Cole lunged and tackled him around the waist. Jett went down and sensed rather than saw the crowd back up. Nice of them to get out of his way.

Violent pain shot through his side. Jett jerked into a roll to get Cole off of him. And yet, the same tenacity that had enabled Cole to build a successful ranch, pull his family through both his parents' deaths and a crushing amount of debt, and pursue the woman he loved despite every disadvantage, made him a bear in a fight.

Simply put, Cole never gave up.

They ended up rolling around in saw chips, and Jett didn't want to think what else. In a series of moves Jett swore defied the laws of physics, Cole got Jett into a headlock. Or maybe physics had nothing to do with it. Maybe righteous indignation had its own power. "You think she's nothing? Just some easy lay that you can take advantage of?"

Jett couldn't answer. He was too busy trying to see past the black swirling spots in his vision. His survival instinct broke loose a desperate piece of information, and Jett grabbed hold of it. Cole had a bad foot, which had been stepped on by a horse a little over a week ago. Jett took the knowledge and used it to mark his aim. There was a small crunch as Jett's boot slammed down on Cole's foot.

Cole screamed some choice phrases, but he let Jett go. Jett rolled to one side and coughed air back into his lungs. The spots were gone, but the room hadn't stopped spinning.

"I can't believe you stepped on my foot," Cole yelled from the floor while holding one knee to his chest. "You know it's broken."

Jett grunted in dismay as he got to his feet. Leave it to the Logans to think fighting dirty was okay as long as they were the only ones doing it.

"I'm sorry, Cole," Jett said, bracing himself on his knees. "If I hadn't already been in two fights in the last two weeks, I'd let you go at it."

"Fine." Cole stood and gingerly put some weight on his foot. "I'm getting too old for this crap. I think I've got arthritis in my arm," he said rolling his shoulder. He hobbled over to the nearest bar stool and plopped down. "So tell me, what it was like then? I know Nikki is a pain in the ass, but she didn't deserve that."

Jett held his side, breathing hard. He glanced around at the riveted crowd. *Christ.* He sighed—in for a penny in for a pound. "I love her." There. He'd said it. His humiliation was complete.

"Yeah." Cole shrugged. "The whole town knows that. So?"

"Great, so basically you're saying, I've been making a fool of myself over her for years?" Jett looked around the room for an answer. From the number of nodding heads and murmurs of "Yeah," he got it. *So this was rock bottom.*

"Yeah. So?" Cole asked.

"Yeah, so what happened?" asked the bartender as he handed Cole an O'Doul's.

Jett walked back over to where Cole was sitting, took a sip of beer, then addressed the crowd. "I told her I loved her. And nothing. She didn't say anything."

"Well, there's where you went wrong," Cole said.

"Thanks for the critique." Jett held up a hand to cut Cole off. "But I wasn't done. I told her I wanted to spend the rest of my life with her. I asked her to marry me."

There were a few "Ahh"s from the women in the crowd. Jett raised his beer in response. In a certain light, some might consider him the victim in all this.

"My God, have you learned nothing in all the time you've known Nikki?" Cole said.

Apparently, Cole would not be one of those people.

"You never ask a Logan anything, especially when that type of commitment is on the line. You *tell* them."

And with that, Cole's fist found its way into his face. There was a black moment, and Jett came to with Cole standing above him. "And just so we're clear, that wasn't for the handcuffs. That's because you're an idiot."

Well, hell, Jett didn't need another black eye to know that.

Nikki put the last of her bags into the trunk of her hatchback. She'd cleaned out the refrigerator, vacuumed, dusted, and washed the sheets. Cole would be shocked. He would've teased her that it was such an adult thing to do. Maybe he was right. The drama was starting to get old. Maybe it was time to change, to stop being such an embarrassment. The last wave of rumors that had run through the town couldn't have been easy for Cole to bear. She could leave, was planning on it after she talked to Mike, but Cole had to build a life and raise a family here.

Nikki closed the trunk and got in her car. The whine of the AC hit her as she started the engine. She smiled. Bo had assured her that the Toyota was running as good as new. When she'd asked for the bill, Bo just shrugged and said she was family.

"Bo, I'm not family."

"Jett is. We're cousins on my mother's side."

Nikki shook her head. "I still don't get the connection."

Bo just smiled. "Well, if the rumors are true, you'll be family soon enough."

"That's not the rumor, Bo."

"Well, the one I heard was Jett told the mayor that you two were engaged. Was there another one?"

For once, Nikki didn't make a smart-mouthed comeback. It took all her composure not to run out of the garage. Instead, she thanked Bo and drove away.

Would it be so bad to be married to a sexy man, who loves you, treats you well, and is damn sexy to boot? Nikki put a quick stop to that line of reasoning because, really, it had never been about Jett. Jett was a good man, would be a good father, would love her even in her old age. The real reason was her. She didn't deserve him. She knew it, his family knew it. The only person who didn't was Jett.

Nikki tried to ignore the tightness in her chest that hadn't gone away for two days. The feelings would lessen as the miles between here and there increased. They had to.

She'd decided on Phoenix. An old roommate lived there and was looking for someone to share the rent. Nikki figured she could bartend anywhere. Tonight was dinner with Cole and Katie, and Mr. Harris. The morning was soon enough to be on the road.

Just one more errand to do. She needed to talk to Mike. Pull him screaming and kicking into the twenty-first century. She wanted to help him put his ledgers on the computer. She figured she could help keep on top of the accounts, but still keep enough distance that Cole could keep from ranting at her. She knew Mike would agree; she just had to wear him down until he did. Still, to get on his good side, it wouldn't hurt to bring a peace offering. She pulled into the

Sac & Save. The parking lot was pretty much deserted this Thursday afternoon. Most of the moms would be picking up the kids from school, and everyone else would be trying to finish the last few hours of the workday.

The cool air was a relief even after just the few feet from the parking lot to the front door. Sac & Save was a small family-owned grocery store that stocked the basics and not much else. If a person wanted capers or mushrooms stuffed with ricotta, they'd have to travel fifteen miles to the nearest gourmet grocery. Nikki had made that trip more than once when she'd had a craving for chocolate, and Jett had one for jalapeño-stuffed kalamata olives.

The Sac & Save was clean, didn't gouge the town with exorbitant prices, and most importantly, had what Nikki was looking for. Mike had a special nightly ritual of drinking a specific brand of chamomile tea, and the Sac & Save always had it in stock.

She'd give the gift to Mike, along with the check for thirty grand. That would be her way of saying sorry, thank you, and goodbye all rolled into one. Nikki had taken Katie's talk to heart, but she knew herself. There was no way she could stay in the same town as Jett and still remain strong. He'd always been too much of a temptation for her.

She turned to go and ran smack into a little girl. It took a moment to untangle herself from the mess of long arms and legs.

"Oh, so sorry," Nikki said as she steadied the girl by grabbing on to her twig of an arm. She recognized the uneven bangs, nondescript hair, and the strange-looking eyes that stood out against her pale face. "Frankie, right?" She'd seen the girl hanging around The Pitt often enough.

"Yes ma'am. Sorry about that. I wasn't looking where I was going."

Even though the words were apologetic, Frankie's own personal blend of sassy Texas twang had her sounding anything but. Nikki resisted the urge to check and see if her wallet was still in her purse.

The habit of assessing with a quick up and down was left over from her hustling days. It didn't take her long to sense something seemed off. She just needed a moment to put her finger on it. "What are you doing here? Shouldn't you be in school?"

Frankie flashed a hundred-watt smile that for some reason had

Nikki thinking of Jett, and tossed her hair out of her face. "Parent-teacher conferences. Half day. So I thought I'd pick up some groceries for my mom."

Nikki looked down at the two items Frankie was carrying—a can of baked beans and a package of freeze-dried noodles. She tilted her head and narrowed her gaze at Frankie, refusing to be distracted by the girl's spooky-looking eyes. "I've been lied to by much more creative people than you and haven't been fooled yet. So why don't you try again?"

Frankie scratched the side of her face and squished her mouth to one side. Still, Nikki had to give her credit. She held eye contact, not once looking down at her dirty feet in her two-sizes-too-big flip-flops.

Nikki took Frankie's hand and examined the girl's fingers. A line of green was embedded under her white nails, and the smell of pool chalk gave her away. "You've been spending quite a bit of time down at the pool hall, haven't you?"

Nikki could tell when Frankie gave up on her story and decided it was time to switch her hustle. The hundred-watt smile was back, but this time her eyes widened into big aqua pools of admiration. "You're a legend down there, Ms. Logan. They all say that you got your start at the hall where you spent hours practicing your famous trick shot. They say you got the best nine-ball game in the county."

"Flattery will get you places, kid, just not with me." But Nikki couldn't help a small turn of her lips. Something was way too familiar to her. If Nikki had had someone to help her out, give her direction, would she have spent all that time learning how to shoot pool for money? Or, as she looked down at Frankie's basket, learning how to pay for dinner? Nikki doubted it would've made much difference to her, but to Frankie . . . "I can't in good conscience let you eat that for dinner. Go find a cart and let's get some groceries."

Nikki expected some protests, but she'd forgotten an important rule—never underestimate hunger—and Frankie was hungry in more ways than one.

A cart full of food later, the two were unloading the groceries onto the conveyor belt. Mrs. Sanchez, who owned the store, was behind the cash register. The years seemed to have to been afraid to make their mark on her. Or maybe they just felt bad because she'd always been old. Old and very opinionated. Nikki had been subjected more than once to the wrinkled purse of her mouth, and the steel glare of her eyes.

Nikki rolled her shoulders and took a deep breath for courage as Mrs. Sanchez put down her newspaper crossword and studied them both as they unloaded the cart. Back and forth her gaze traveled from Nikki to Frankie, trying to make some kind of connection, all the while clicking and unclicking her ballpoint pen. Nikki could've told her not to waste her time. There was nothing here except a streak of luck on Frankie's part and a feeling of sympathy on Nikki's.

The total was rung up, and Nikki handed Mrs. Sanchez a small stack of bills.

Mrs. Sanchez looked up from the money, her gray eyes peering down her nose at Nikki like a steel-bladed knife.

Nikki could already hear the questions—what was a no-good Logan doing helping out another white-trash little girl? And how did a Logan like her get the money to pay for someone else's groceries? Ms. Sanchez didn't have to voice them, they were as loud as the chomping of Frankie's gum.

"This is too much," Mrs. Sanchez said, her voice one octave above comfortable. "And I don't have enough change in the drawer to cover it."

Nikki swallowed. "I want to open up a line of credit. What I gave you should hold Frankie for a couple of months. Keep track of whatever she spends over that. I'll pay you when I come back to town."

Both Frankie and Mrs. Sanchez looked as if Nikki had just told them that this was a holdup and to hand over all their money. On second thought, they'd probably be less surprised if it were a holdup.

Frankie stood silent as her mouth worked to find words that weren't coming.

Nikki wasn't as fortunate with Mrs. Sanchez.

"I don't know if I ever told you this, but I knew your mamma," she said with a click of her pen. "She did me a real good turn after my divorce from that ass—." Pen click. "I mean my ex. She was a good soul, kind, soft-spoken. And I know that she'd be real proud of you. She'd be real proud of you regardless, but especially now. I know you've had a few bad turns from some of the folks around here, but that's not everyone. Not everyone thinks that way."

Nikki seemed to have forgotten how to breathe; her boots felt cemented to the floor.

"And, well, I want to tell you that the whole town is rooting for you and Jett." Click, click. "There's been some hot and furious rumors going around about an engagement and some kinky, fifty-shades stuff with handcuffs. Not that I agree with any of that." Click, click, click. "But I do know that love can make you seven ways to crazy and everyone can see that boy is a total fool over you."

Nikki dropped off Frankie and drove the rest of the way to The Pitt with Mrs. Sanchez's words echoing in her brain. The comment about the whole town knowing that Jett was head over heels in love bothered her. It wasn't as if she didn't know herself. Jett had told her at least twice, but she realized now she'd never really believed him. No one had loved her and stayed with her. To Nikki, those two things couldn't coexist.

But if they could . . . If Jett could love her and really wanted to be with her, what did that make her for wanting to run?

A coward, Nikki girl.

And wasn't that just like her mother to make herself heard when Nikki wanted to hear her the least. Nikki tried to shake off the familiar feeling of panic and drowning with the consolation that she'd be leaving soon, but for some reason the thought only made her heart pound harder.

She pulled up to The Pitt and parked her car around back. She still had the key to the back door, another thing Mike was sure to want back. She grabbed the grocery bag and made her way to the door. She turned the lock and pushed. It was stuck. The back door was at the end of a small hallway Mike also used for deliveries. Sometimes, when things got busy, boxes were left stacked up, blocking the entryway. A fire hazard for sure, but keeping to code didn't seem to be Mike's biggest concern. So instead of walking around to the front, Nikki pushed harder, sure that a case of Wild Goose was blocking her way.

The rubber weathering on the bottom of the door smeared something reddish brown across the laminate floor.

Had she broken something? Damn, might as well just sign over her whole next year's wage the way she was going.

Someone groaned behind the door. "Mike?"

She squeezed through the space between the wall and the door. Inside, it was dark, and she had to blink a few times for her eyes to adjust. Then she saw him. Mike, lying in a pool of red. Leg at an odd angle, face lined and gray.

In the second it took her to inhale, to suck in the air she needed to scream, she realized where the blood was coming from. His leg—a gaping hole that looked exactly like a bullet wound. Gunshot? She closed her mouth and forced her scream back down her throat. Her gaze swept her surroundings, the dark hall, the back view of the bar. She took in the high-pitched screech of a drill bit against metal. The sounds of men arguing from Mike's office.

His safe?

Like the rapid cue shot of a fast break, adrenaline rushed into her blood. She grew nauseous at the taste of it.

Back out slowly. No one has to know.

She could go straight to the police station. Let Harry know. This wasn't her problem. She wasn't equipped to handle standing in a pool of red, watching a man die as his life slowly seeped out of him.

Mike groaned again. The plastic bag fell by her feet and with it all her illusions.

The plan would never happen. She had no phone and even if she drove straight to the station, it would take twenty minutes there and twenty back. Too long. By then all of this . . . would be over.

Her knees buckled. She dropped into the growing pool of blood as fear closed in like a noose around her throat. Her hands shook as she took the emptied plastic bag and tried to tie it around Mike's leg. Every crackle of plastic, every shift of clothing was loud against the background of the whining drill.

"Mike." She leaned over him, talking into his ear. "Mike, get up."

She spoke so low she wasn't sure he'd even hear her, but fear had constricted her voice to a whisper.

"Mike, please, get up now." He was two hundred pounds solid and wedged behind a door—there was no way she could get him out of here by herself.

He didn't respond.

He's dead. Leave him. Leave him.

"Mike," she sobbed. Her body shook so bad she had to grab hold of his shirt to keep herself close to his ear. "Please get up."

Some knowledge comes easy, some is hard won. She'd learned fear had different levels. And she would've sworn, right now, she'd found bottom. But then the bottom dropped out and there was a whole other level, because just then the drill stopped.

And silence had never been so audible.

Chapter 28

Nikki watched Mike slowly open his eyes. It took a moment for awareness to register, and then by the look on his face, pain was quick to follow.

Her throat was too paralyzed to speak, so she gestured with her head for him to move. She underlined her nod by grabbing his shirt and pulling him toward the door.

Mike shook his head, stilling her movements. His lips moved. She bent down to hear him as panic screamed at her to run.

"Go," he whispered. "Go."

Her heart responded, leaping at the chance to escape, before her mind did. Here was her permission, her chance to flee to safety. No one would blame her, not even Mike. There really was nothing she could do anyway. He was shot, couldn't move. The best chance for both of them was for her to escape.

Definitely the best chance for her.

"Here, I'll help you," she said, surprised at the calmness in her voice. "Put your arm around me. There, that's it. Now push with your good leg."

A voice from Mike's office broke across their stealth. "Dammit, I can't get this open." The man swore again as something crashed against the wall.

"You. You said this would be easy. You . . . you said he was old and wouldn't be a problem," said another man. His speech was thick and slow as if his tongue was too big for his mouth.

"Well, I wasn't the idiot who shot him, was I?" barked the first. "Go get the old man. If he doesn't tell you the combination this time, then shoot him in the other leg. But keep him alive. Dead, he's useless to us."

A gun cocked and footsteps sounded down the hall.

Nikki crawled, slid, knees sticky with blood, but she didn't care. She needed to hide. Her shoe slipped as she scurried behind a stack of boxes. Her heart had never pounded so loud, and she put a hand over her mouth to stop her panting.

Footsteps drew closer in a shuffle-shuffle-drag cadence. The man had no reason to be quiet.

Still, so still. Quiet, so quiet. Nikki pushed herself into the smallest of balls. From her vantage point she could see Mike's upper body and the whitewashed look on his face.

"Wake up, old man."

The thug was close, a mere five feet away. One step and a look around and he'd see her.

There was a thump, and Mike's body jostled with a groan.

"Wake up or I'll kick you again."

Nikki pressed harder over her mouth and nose, too afraid to even breathe. Black scuffed boots came into view, a pair of thick-fingered hands, then a sway of long stringy hair that covered his face as the man bent over Mike.

Wake up, Mike. Open your eyes.

Just a slight turn of the man's head, a minor shift of his gaze, and Nikki would be seen.

Meaty fingers dug into Mike's shirt and pulled up. Mike's head hung listless like wet towels on a clothesline.

Quiet, small, no sound.

Maybe there'd been a movement, a sound, or maybe it was just mere chance. Something had drawn the attention of black eyes, cold and hard, slanted with evil, dulled with drugs, staring right at her.

The air thickened, time slowed as if all movements were made through water. Mike was dropped; his head bounced with a sickening thud on the floor. Her leg muscles contracted as she sprang for the door. Her fingers clawed at the door ledge, letting in the bright light of the afternoon sun . . . inch by inch.

A man yelled behind her, but the words were muffled as if they were spoken through thick cotton. Fingers raked through her hair and pulled with excruciating force. She was pulled back, feet thrown out from under her.

Space and time snapped forward, colliding with reality. With his fingers tangled in her hair, she was dragged back toward the office. But she was more than willing to lose a little hair to save her life. And there was no doubt that it was her life at stake.

She fought. Twisted. Flapped like a marlin on a line. Her booted feet hooked on a pallet of bottles. It crashed over in an amber pool of foam. And still she was dragged forward. With one hand she grabbed a corner, and for one desperate moment of hope, his hold slipped.

But he was strong, and her fingers were slick with blood, leaving four long streaks of red against a grimy wall.

She must have been screaming. Her throat hurt, felt raw, but no sound got past the pounding in her ears. She was dragged into the office. Pulled forward on her knees. His grip on her hair eased.

"Stop the screaming," the man said, and backhanded her to add emphasis to the threat. Nikki didn't bother to pick herself up off the floor, but the roaring inside her head finally stopped.

Breathe Nikki. Stay calm.

She took in the room. The same desk and worn office chair. A power tool plugged into the wall and a large dent in the door of the safe. The safe was large, black, and old-fashioned. Heavier by far than anything else in the bar and constructed with metal as thick as her arm. Yeah, that two-bit power drill wasn't going to make a dent anytime soon.

Damn you, Mike, what idiot still put all his deposits in a safe? He'd told her he was too far from town to make getting to a bank convenient, and besides, he didn't trust the banks much. He'd said he was way too cheap to pay banking fees and believed interest was just a way to sucker people in so that the government could sock it to the little man by hiking up his taxes. Now, she just hoped they both lived long enough to pay their taxes.

Nikki looked from the safe to the other man in the room. He was thinner than the one who'd hit her. His gray hair, still showing blond at the tips, was slicked back from a hook-like face. A sharp, angular nose sat on top of a weak chin. Where the first man was all brute strength, this man was wiry and tall, like the stretched-out image in the house of mirrors.

Both were armed with handguns. It was a disgrace to her Texas upbringing that she couldn't tell what make and model. But she knew they were deadly, and that's all she cared about.

"Where did you find her?" the wiry man asked.

"By the old man. I think she was trying to get him out the back. She must've come in with a key. She's probably one of the strung-out dancers he picks up off the street."

The thin one slapped the slow one upside his head. "You're an idiot to bring her back here. Now she's seen both our faces."

The big one brushed off the slap as one would an annoying fly. "Won't be a problem. But maybe she could help. Maybe the old man told her the combination. He's no use to us. As good as dead."

Skinny man rolled his eyes. "Why would he tell some two-bit stripper the combo to his safe? He wasn't that stupid."

The big one arched a bushy eyebrow. "Was stupid enough to get involved with us."

Skinny man turned his attention to her. His red-rimmed eyes reminded Nikki of a lizard.

"You don't look like a strung-out junky." He smiled and showed a row of yellow teeth with one Chiclet-white front tooth, courtesy of some very bad dentist. He squatted down and brushed the hair out of her face. Nikki forced herself to stay perfectly still.

"I'm sorry he hurt you. I won't let that happen again."

Nikki, for once, had no problem keeping her mouth shut. As long as he was talking, he wasn't killing her.

His reptilian eyes traveled the length of her. "You are a pretty thing. Is it true? Do you work here?"

He already knew she had a key. Lying now would only make him angry. She nodded.

"Here, why don't you sit up? Hey," he gestured to the big guy with his long spidery fingers, "get that chair. There, now, that's better. A little ice on that cheek and you'll be right as rain."

He smiled and the white tooth flashed. He was close, and Nikki noticed the inside of his lips were abnormally red. Bile tickled the back of her throat as the fat one bent over Mike's desk and sniffed something up his nose.

"You wouldn't happen to know the combination to the safe, would you?"

Nikki had never been trusted with the combo. Mike never trusted anyone. But telling these men that would only shorten her life span . . . considerably. And she planned on living, well, forever.

"Maybe you need some motivation?" His backhand came out of nowhere and hit her across her cheek.

Nikki's head snapped back, and she barely kept her seat. Nope, no need for that type of motivation. She couldn't have care less if the Hope diamond was in that safe. She'd give it all up in a heartbeat for her life.

"You tell us the combination, and we'll let you walk out of here."

Nikki's check throbbed, and the iron taste of blood coated her tongue. If she got to crawl out of here, she'd consider herself lucky.

She shrugged. "Have you tried his birthdate?"

Mike never would've been that stupid, but she counted on these two men who'd shot their only source of information and were overly concerned with the coke they were sniffing up their noses not to know that.

"Which is?" Skinny's eyes shifted to the fat man as he did another hit. "Hey, only your share."

Nikki had no idea, but neither did they. She swallowed and rattled off her mother's birthdate, knowing Mike and she were close in age.

"Try that one and any combination of those numbers."

The two men turned their backs on her and hovered over the safe.

How long could she keep this up before they knew she was lying? She'd have some hope if she knew help was on the way, but no one knew where she was, and it would be hours before anyone went looking for her.

Her brain flipped through the different options. Make a run for it. Grab the gun behind the bar. Get to the phone.

What had Jett told her when he'd made her practice shooting the sawed-off shotgun? Aim small. Get even footing. Breathe out when squeezing the trigger. She looked around the office and then back where the bar was. The distance was only a few feet, but might as well have been a football field.

She closed her eyes to settle her heart. What else? *Think, Nikki.* He'd told her it was hard to hit a moving target and harder still to make a fatal shot.

"That's not it," one whined.

"Try them backwards."

Make up your mind, Texas. It's now or never.

Her heart pounded. The right side of her face pulsed as she estimated the distance between here and the front door. The door was no more than two hundred feet away. She'd trained her whole life for this.

You were born to run, Texas. Born for this.

A string of curses erupted from the fat one, and then he pulled out his gun and fired repeatedly. Bullets ricocheted, and Nikki threw herself to the floor.

You get one chance. Get ready.

Her throat constricted, but she pushed deep inhales through. She might doubt everything else about her, but one thing she knew: she could run.

"What's the matter with you? Are you an idiot?" screamed the skinny one.

Keep your focus. Get set.

"I'm gonna put a bullet in your head if you call me stupid one more time."

Go!

Nikki didn't wait for Skinny's response. Motion shot through her like a drug, flooding every cell. Everything grayed out. Noise tuned to a low hum.

Eyes focused. Eyes focused.

Her skirt rose high on her thighs. Legs ate up the ground as if meters were inches. A bar stool was overturned and in her way—she leapt it like it was a crack in the sidewalk.

Faster. Almost there.

Turned the knob. Opened the door. Bright light rushed at her. The sun hurt her eyes, but she ran through the blinding shadows.

To the car.

She turned the corner to where she'd parked her car. Except it wasn't there.

All the time she'd been running, her breath had never left her, but now, as she watched her red hatchback haul ass down the dirt road, it left in one shattering swoop. There was nowhere else to go—no more places to run.

Her legs buckled even before she heard the gunshot.

A fire fist of pain burned through her thigh. She was falling, but her gaze never wavered. Never wavered from her one chance of staying alive as it disappeared into the sunset.

"There's no way you're going to get elected for sheriff if you keep this up," Jett's father said.

It was Jett's worst nightmare. He felt like he was sixteen again, and his father had just picked him up from the principal's office. Except, in the past it was usually Cole's hot head that had gotten him in trouble. This time he had no one to blame but himself.

Someone had called, asking his dad to pick Jett up. Apparently the *concerned citizen* had told his father that Jett was in no condition to drive. So now, instead of enjoying another shot of Jägermeister (after the second one his tongue had gone numb), he was being lectured by his father, who'd fallen back into the habit a little too easily.

"Who says I'm even running for sheriff?" The throbbing in his face was starting to be constant, and he couldn't sort out where one ache left off and another began.

"Just about everyone in this town, that's who."

Jett did not want to have this conversation. They'd had this conversation a hundred times. Having it a hundred and one would not change his father's mind, or his. His father wanted him to run for public office—any public office. And Jett—well, Jett just regretted he'd ever opened his mouth in the first place.

"I've been getting calls from people in town. Your mother and I are getting worried about you." His father gave him a long look. "Seriously, should I be worried?"

Jett flexed his jaw, then immediately stopped when the throb in his eye doubled in time. Just thinking about his mother turned his stomach. Even though it was too late, he had to clear Nikki's name.

She might not care what people said about her around town, but he sure did. "Nikki didn't take that money. Well, not for herself, she didn't."

His father nodded his head, cutting Jett off. "I know. When I heard about the donation to the Track and Field Club I put two and two together. For what it's worth, your mother feels terrible. She's held on too tight after, well, after Sarah. But your mother really does have your best interests at heart, even if her methods aren't kind."

It took everything Jett had not to pound his fist into the passenger-side window. He was known for his cool headedness; it was time he started living up to his reputation. "Kind? Dad! She ruined any chance I had of marrying the woman I love."

His dad nodded, but tempered his gaze with wisdom that had voter after voter putting him back in the senate seat. "I know you're hurt, son. I know, but if she was really the one, if she really loved you . . . Well, all I know is that real love, true love, could withstand a disgruntled mother-in-law and much more. Love is not dew on the morning grass. Love is not a dandelion wish. Love is an oak, strong with roots deep in the earth. Love is faith like the rising of the sun. If this woman can't see beyond the past, can't see you, then is she really a woman worth fighting for?"

That stung. The suture that held his faith and hope in Nikki was severed, and his heart fell with the heavy certainty that his father was right. He'd always thought he'd had what Nikki needed to make her whole and happy. Lord knows, she did for him. But that was the cruelty of life; sometimes it didn't matter.

Jett leaned his seat all the way back to help with the nausea and to make sure he didn't bawl like a baby in front of his dad.

His father placed a hand on his knee and squeezed—the Avery version of a hug. They drove in silence for a while, and then his dad pulled into the police station. "I have to drop off a package for Harry. I'll only be a moment."

Which was more than fine with Jett; he needed the time to adjust his head and his heart to a reality with no Nikki in it. He'd done it once, he could do it again. Too restless to sit any longer, he got out and paced the parking lot.

The sun was low in the sky and throwing gold shadows over the expense of emerald green. A row of power lines was silhouetted against the warm backdrop, like soldiers at attention.

Some idiot was in the parking lot leaning full blast on the horn. The noise was like a drill bit into the side of Jett's skull. There was a group of officers crowded around the parked car outside. Jett started to go the other way. Then an officer stepped to the side, and Jett caught a glimpse of a red Toyota.

Nikki's car.

His gut clenched, throat tight, but he made himself walk, not run, to the car. Because really, it couldn't be Nikki's car.

Deputy Smith was standing in the open driver's-side door talking into his phone.

It had to be someone else's Toyota hatchback. Had to be. He'd just assumed it was Nikki's because, well, because he always had Nikki on the brain.

That was until Jett saw Smith's face. Saw fear as plain as the sun quickly slipping into the horizon.

Jett didn't remember. Must've pushed Smith out of the way. It took a moment, but he registered that the person slumped over the steering wheel and covered in blood wasn't Nikki. It was Mike.

Mike's skin tone matched the color of his hair—pasty gray. His eyes were closed, mouth slack.

Jett had no sympathy. He took a handful of hair and raised Mike's head. "Where's Nikki?"

Mike opened his eyes, but Jett had to repeat the question three times, each louder than the last, before Mike's eyes cleared.

"She's there. At The Pitt."

And just like that, Jett couldn't find any air.

"Hurry . . . they're gonna kill her."

Jett found his breath again, but as oxygen funneled to his lungs, it brought fear. Fear just like the fear he'd had when Nikki left the first time two years ago. Then he'd hated her for being scared. Hated her for wearing her emotional baggage and scarred heart like a bloody badge.

Most of all he'd hated her for running.

Now all he could think about was that he hoped she lived to run again.

Jett couldn't care less about police procedure or any other crap as he started hauling butt toward his dad's truck. All he knew was he had to get to Nikki as fast as he could, and if that meant he had to use his dad's truck and the shotgun behind the seat, then so be it.

The way Jett saw things, he had a concealed gun permit just like any other proud, NRA card-toting Texan. And if he happened to get there first, well, then they'd just have to arrest him, because he planned on killing whoever was hurting Nikki.

Chapter 29

The color behind Nikki's eyes turned from black to deep blood-red. She knew she was still alive because a hot poker of pain had engulfed her leg. The fire in her leg went on and on, matching the heavy pulse of her heart.

They'd dragged her inside and left her sprawled in the middle of the bar. Apparently, they didn't think she was any threat. She could've told them that.

She'd heard that dying didn't hurt. She just hoped it would come already, wasn't sure how much longer she could keep from squealing in pain.

"Shut up out there!"

Too late. She'd die with no dignity.

Nikki opened her eyes to the sight of the stage and stripper pole.

Oh my, how low the mighty fall. Of course, she hadn't fallen as far as most. She would've moved her head so her last view wouldn't be of her bigger failures, but it hurt too much. What did it matter, anyway? For sure, no one expected more than this kind of ending for her. No one except Cole, Mr. Harris, Mrs. Sanchez, Mike, her father, Jett, her mom.

The problem had never been what others expected of her, she realized, but what she expected of herself.

What had she been so afraid of? Being hurt? Being left? Giving her heart away? Nothing like hurting in a pile of her own blood to align some priorities. Or make her look at some hard truths. Really, could she have been any more stupid?

Don't answer that, Nikki.

She could hear the two men in the back office. They'd gotten into the vodka after they'd realized that Mike had ripped out the spark plug lead wires from their car's engine. There'd been a phone call and a conversation about a ride. Now they were just waiting it out. At least they'd kept her alive. Skinny man said if things went really bad, she could be used as a hostage.

A hostage or a bullet shield. At this point, she'd take it. Had to be better than slowly dying on the dirty floor of The Pitt.

The men came back into the main room—the fat one to get more booze, and the skinny one to check out the front door. The fat one's eyes were dull, his movements slow. She could predict his actions three moves before he made them. It was Mr. Skinny that made her nervous. He twitched more than he moved, sporadic and way too jumpy. There was nothing predictable about him and that made him dangerous.

Really, Nikki? What was your first clue? When he shot you?

No, it was time to face reality. She'd no doubt how this was going to end. Some things she just knew—like when her mother was going to take her last breath. When her pool career was over. When it was time to leave and never come back. Images sped through her head like someone flipping through a stack of cards. Each card a picture of her life. Her mother's face, pale but with eyes shining with happiness as she smiled at Nikki. Cole with his dimple that flashed quite a bit recently. And Jett. Many of Jett. The star-shaped scar, white on his tanned face. The way he kissed her, smiled at her, joked with her. Then there were some of her children. Her children—the ones she'd never have—with blond Avery hair and blue Logan eyes.

A deep sense of loss swept her like a wave. She was no stranger to that emotion. Grief had its own ability to color everything black, to wipe away any previous joy, to block any happiness from finding its way inside. She'd lived with grief and shame for so long, they felt like siblings. Like another arm or a fifth chamber to her heart.

But this time the loss wasn't a rip or an amputation like when her dad died, or the crushing weight of ending her mother's life. This time the loss was more bitter because she'd been the who'd thrown it away. Thrown away the possibility of her and Jett on the porch swing, holding hands, growing old. And all of a sudden she couldn't remember what she was running from. Wasn't everything she wanted here, in this town, with her whole family around her?

Get up.

She was so tired.

The Logans don't quit.

No, they didn't. It might kill them, but the Logans never quit. Damn Logan pride had its advantages. She set her jaw. No one would take her dreams, and her life, and live to tell about it. She could die. Or she could die fighting.

Nikki put her knuckle in her mouth and bit down hard. Blood slicked across her tongue, but it kept the scream behind her lips as she pulled herself across the floor. One hand, nails into the floor, pull, then the other hand, pull. Cold sweat ran down her nose and dripped on the floor. She swallowed hard. Her heart pounded as she dragged her body through years of tracked-in dirt, spilled beer, and tobacco spit.

It didn't matter. Nothing did as long as she kept moving. She never looked up, didn't have to. She would either make it or not. No one was ever gonna fault her for not fighting. For not standing her ground. She should've fought for Jett when his mother had come around waving a thick white envelope in her face. She should've looked the queen in the eye and laughed. She never should've judged Jett by his mother. She never should've doubted what was in her own heart. Or in his. Not again. Not anymore.

One hand in front of the other. Only when her fingers brushed the wood of the bar did she take the time to look behind her at the trail of blood, smeared brown.

Hurry now—no turning back.

Yeah, there was a time to run and there also was a time to turn and make your stand.

She reached up and grabbed the edge of the counter. She licked her lips and took a deep breath—*courage, Nik*—and pulled herself up. Starbursts of black exploded behind her eyes. And for a moment she thought the darkness would win. The contents of her stomach rebelled. How could she throw up if she couldn't even see?

With superhuman effort, she steadied herself, and the world spun back into focus.

She used her wounded leg to step. A groan escaped from behind her closed lips. Fire engulfed her in a blast of pain. *Too much.*

No, Nik. For once in your life, commit. Don't turn back.

Not risking another groan, she hopped on one leg to get up the bar step.

Almost there, one step up.

"Hey, what the hell are you thinking?"

She ducked, more like collapsed, behind the bar.

Her fingers brushed the shotgun. Adrenaline slammed through her body. She shook with the surge, body numb with the power. They said endorphins were the best painkiller, but even they couldn't touch the inferno that was her leg as she braced the gun against her shoulder and prepared to stand.

Please God, let Mike hold true.

One shell already in the chamber. A fully loaded firearm.

A scream ravaged her throat as she sprang up, gun butted up against her shoulder, finger on the trigger.

Wait for it.

The fat one's face widened in surprise, but even as he raised his gun, she knew he was too late. His barrel didn't get past waist level. A round of buckshot got him square in the chest. The impact lifted him off his feet and threw him into the wall behind.

Nikki caught a movement out of the corner of her eye. She could see Skinny's mouth move, he might've shouted something, but she couldn't hear above the roar in her head. He raised his gun. She shot and missed. He shot back. And she ran out from behind the bar straight toward him. The click of his gun loud even to her. With one hand she pumped her shotgun.

If she was going out in a blaze of glory, so help her God, he was coming with her. The dark eye of his gun didn't scare her at all. "Let's go, you mother—"

She saw his gun fire, but there was no pain. He'd missed, and now . . . now, she had all the time in the world as she raised her gun. Then with a coldness of heart and a smile on her lips, she squeezed the trigger.

One in the shoulder. She pumped the gun. *One in the chest.* Pump. His body jerked as each shell emptied into him, and yet, she still came. Pump, squeeze. Pump, squeeze until there were no more cartridges. She stood above him, his head torqued, one leg folded underneath. A metallic and ammonia scent hit her nose as pools of both fluids spread underneath his body.

The front door banged open from behind her. Bright light exploded through the dingy bar. She spun and raised the shotgun.

All she could make out was a shadowed man with a gun pointed at her. "Freeze!" he yelled.

She was out of ammunition and out of the adrenaline that had kept her on her feet.

So close. She'd been so close. *I'm sorry, Momma. So sorry. I tried.*

"Please, Nik, put the gun down so you don't accidentally shoot me as I try to rescue you."

Jett? Oh God, Jett.

She lowered her arms, the shotgun slipping from her numb fingers. "You came . . ."

She went to take a step toward him, but something was wrong with her legs. She couldn't feel her body. "He shot at me. I can't believe he missed. He was so close, but he missed. I'm so glad to see you. I have to tell you something."

Jett stepped closer, but didn't take her in his arms. Why not? She focused on his face though the edges were a bit blurry. She'd never seen his skin so gray or his eyes so wide. When his gaze flickered off her face to her stomach, she followed his path.

A dark brownish-red stain flowered on her grimy T-shirt.

"Oh," she stared up at Jett and gave him a half smile, "guess he didn't miss."

And the floor rushed up to meet her.

Jett caught her before she collapsed to the floor. Her head rolled listlessly over his arm as he lowered himself to his knees. Only the shallow movements of her chest told him she was still breathing. He'd been trained in simple first aid when he'd volunteered at the Boys and Girls Club, but for a panicked moment he couldn't remember any of it.

"Don't you die on me, Nik. You've been stubborn and bull-headed every day of your life. Don't you dare give up now!"

The stain on her shirt widened and deepened in color. He put his hand over it in an attempt to stop the bleeding. Then he just started to ramble on, more for himself than Nikki. "It's okay, Texas. I'm here now. It's all gonna be okay."

He could already hear the sirens in the distance. He just prayed they would come fast enough.

Nikki's chest hitched as her breathing grew shaky. He held tighter, put his face close to her mouth, relishing the feel of her faint breath on his cheek. "Just a bit longer. Help is here. Just hold on a little longer, love."

She was motionless. Her face colorless, lips already tingeing with blue. With two fingers he felt for a pulse, but all he could feel was cold where there used to be heat, and stillness where there used to be life.

Come on, Texas. You can't leave me now.

Chapter 30

Awareness came in a trickle. Slow notes of consciousness threaded through Nikki's mind. Pain was first, but nothing like before. Now the pain had dimmed to a low ache that seemed to radiate from her entire body, not just her leg. She dug around for the strength to open her eyes. A small line of light on the border of the darkness, and then finally she could see.

The hospital room was overly bright. A tad cold. But even the thought of pulling the thin blanket over her shoulders exhausted her.

With effort, she turned her head and took in the sleeping man in the chair next to her bed. His hat was off, hair a mess, face dusted with blond whiskers. She smiled. He never could grow a beard. Then her smile faded as she took in the dark circles under the fan of his lashes, the rumpled look of his clothes. How long had he been camped out by her bedside? She hated the thought of him spending the night in the chair. She smiled again; he probably did, too. When they were younger and went camping, he was always the one with the blow-up air mattress.

On the bedside table was a plastic cup with a bendy straw. She reached for it, but the tube in her hand knocked it over instead.

Jett was awake in a flash, his brown eyes dark with worry.

"You're awake." He looked down at the spilled cup. "You thirsty?"

She nodded. Her mouth seemed stuck together and beyond the ability to talk.

Jett quickly cleaned up the water and refilled her cup. After a few sips she lay back down, exhausted. Jett sat on the bed, careful not to bump her IV. With a finger she gently traced the faded bruise under his eye.

"The bump is gone," she said, tracing the ridge of his nose.

Jett smiled briefly. "The newest black eye was compliments of your brother. Seemed the first time he broke my nose wasn't enough for him."

"Why?"

Jett took her hand and stroked his thumb over her fingers. "You kidding me? When else does Cole become unreasonable? When it comes to his girls, the man has no sense."

The thought that Cole cared enough to throw a punch at his best friend over her caused a strange thickness in her throat.

"Has he been here?"

Jett smiled for real this time. "The better question is who hasn't been here? The wall of flowers to your right is from just about every person in this town. But, yeah, Cole's been here. I finally sent him home to sleep. Since there's only one chair by your bedside, and that one's mine, he didn't have a choice."

"How long have I been here?"

"Five days. You had us worried for a bit, but I've been worrying about you for a long time now."

Her eyes burned, and when she blinked, she was as surprised as anyone to see a tear fall on her hospital gown. What was it with her? She seemed to want to cry at every word that came out of Jett's mouth.

Jett's finger wiped her cheek. "You're crying, Nik." His voice was thicker than usual.

She blinked to clear her vision, determined not to break down. "I need to tell you something."

He shook his head. "No need, it can wait. You're tired."

But she'd waited long enough, and if she didn't say how she felt now, she might lose her courage, her strength. But how do you tell a man that you're sorry for everything? Sorry for making a mess out of your life and then running out on it altogether. She was sorry for not saying what she should have to his mother—like, go to hell. How could she tell him that she wanted to grow old with him and raise a family even though she'd never given an indication of either? How could she tell him that what she really was afraid of was that one day he'd wake up and realize that what everyone had said was true, that she was worthless? How did she tell him that he was way too good for her? And if he were smart, he'd run and never look back because, really, she came with baggage and had a tendency to acquire more.

She couldn't. There were just too many words, and she was too tired. So she conjured up the strength to say the three little words that scared her more than any other in the English language. The three little words that she'd never said to anyone.

The tears were flowing freely. She only had the strength to either control her emotions or finally tell him the truth. "I—I love you."

Jett grabbed some tissues and made an attempt to dry her cheeks. "Well, that was the sorriest 'I love you' I have ever heard."

To her shame, her quick inhale turned into one of those awful shuddering breaths.

He smiled. "Whenever I imagined you saying the words, I pictured you at least looking happy about it. Instead, you look as if you're telling me you just ran over my dog."

"No." She shook her head. "I didn't cry then."

His eyes widened. "That's right. You *did* run over my dog."

She held her side. She didn't want to laugh, it hurt too much. "He was old. I think it was suicide since you were too soft to go put him down."

The star-shaped scar crinkled as his smile reached his eyes. "My point exactly. I thought at least your declaration of love would trump you killing my dog. So I tell you what. Why don't you practice until you get it down perfect?"

She nodded, barely able to keep the sob behind her clenched teeth.

Jett grabbed her hand and brought it up to his lips. "The way I figure, the Logans are slow learners, so it might take a bit of repetition. So maybe you should practice, let's say for, what? The rest of your life?"

That was enough to push her over the edge, turning her tears into sobs. And Jett held true to his promise all those years ago the night her mother had died—he just held her tight and never left her side.

Three months later

Nikki did one last check in the mirror, decided on another coat of lip gloss, surprised at her attention to detail. Why it mattered that she looked perfect, she wasn't sure. Except something didn't feel right. Jett and she had been friends since forever. There'd always been an easiness between them, but ever since that day in the hospital when she'd confessed the worst "I love you," things between them had been on edge.

She brushed her dark chestnut hair back with her fingers. Gone were the harsh black and copper highlights. Cole had never been happier. Jett had just smiled and said he liked her hair any color. The changes hadn't stopped there. Even her clothing preferences had changed. She turned to check her backside and the flowy skirt of her blue dress twirled around her thighs. Cowboy boots replaced combat boots, and the haunted look in her eyes was replaced by something infinitely warmer. Maybe it had been her brush with death, the fight she had to regain her strength, or just the fact that she appreciated life more. Yes, life was fragile, but it was also enduring. She'd survived a gut wound and a bullet in the thigh, and Mike had survived a shot to the leg. Yes, there were no guarantees, but she wanted to try living like she was happy for the future, not afraid of it.

She checked the clock at her bedside table, then placed a palm over the flutter in her stomach. Jett had said he'd be here at four, and he was never late. She grabbed her purse and walked toward the front room. She had the house to herself, a rarity these days. Another thing that had changed since the shooting.

She'd been in the hospital for over two weeks, and when she was released, Katie had a room at their house all ready for her. There'd been no discussion, at least on her brother and sister-in-law's part. There'd been tons on her side, but at the time she could barely make it to the bathroom by herself. Really, she didn't have a leg to stand on. Or she did, but only one.

Jett, of course, visited often. He was such a regular that Cole threatened to charge him rent. It was strange. She thought she would've hated living with her brother and Katie, but even after she'd completed physical therapy, she never had the desire to move back to their childhood home. Here, at Cole and Katie's, it was noisy, the washer was always going, someone was always cooking, and Jimmy was loud enough to be heard two counties away, but Nikki loved the chaos. It was like finding a piece of a puzzle, one she never knew she was missing. Katie told her this was her home now, but Cole didn't bother with words to let her know that she wasn't leaving. He had their childhood home leveled.

She hadn't been there when the bulldozer came. Instead, she went afterward when all the debris was carried off and everything was clean and open again. There were plans to rebuild, but as of now, it was just nice to see the wide stretch of land. Jett, as he had every day since the shooting, was by her side when she visited the site. He helped walk her over, held her as she stood on the edge of where the porch used to be. She cried that day. Seemed to cry a lot after coming home from the hospital. But Jett hadn't minded. Told her some psychobabble about needing to grieve for all her losses, grieve for her mother, and that the tears helped wash the hurt away so that happier things could shine through.

She'd barely contained an eye roll on that one, but maybe Jett had been right, since she'd smiled more in these last few weeks than at any other time she could remember.

Nikki heard tires pull onto the dirt drive and opened the door to greet him. Jett's long-legged frame started to unfold from his truck. Boot by boot, leg by leg, he appeared, and the sun seemed to shine more freely on him than on other people. He stood there, sexy, confident, white Stetson on his head, button-down shirt, designer jeans, and it took everything Nikki had not to run headlong into his arms.

She tempered her reaction, and instead, slow-walked like she hadn't just been waiting by the window for his arrival. Because even though declarations of love had passed between them, Nikki couldn't help but be cautious. Jett had been nervous since the hospital, still was. And when easygoing Jett was unsure, Nikki got scared.

Even after all they'd been through, there was a hesitation between them. Something just below the surface. Anxiety? Cautiousness? She wasn't sure, but there'd been no move by Jett to take whatever they had between them to the next level.

Nikki walked over to him and did her best to relax her features into a warm smile.

"Hi, Texas." His grin was more of a smirk.

She remembered hating that nickname. Now, not so much. "Hi, Jett."

"You ready?"

She nodded. He helped her into the truck and soon an awkward silence settled between them as they drove down the road. She watched Jett turn on the radio, flip it off, adjust the AC vent, then turn it right back. He wiped some non-existent dust from his dashboard, once, twice. His nervousness was contagious, and Nikki couldn't take the suspense any longer. "So, where are we going?"

"Can't tell you." He threw her a smile, but she wasn't appeased. Something was going on. Every one of her spidey-senses was going off.

"Why?"

He didn't answer her.

"You're making me nervous, Jett."

"Don't be. It's all gonna work out for the best."

What the hell did that mean? Whenever she heard that, it meant something had worked out better for someone else. Never for her.

Maybe he was going to break up with her? She wished that thought had no basis in reality, but in truth, doubts had been lingering for a couple of months. What if she was the straw that had finally broken Jett's back? Not that she'd blame him; she just wished he'd told her over the phone or at her front door. That way she wouldn't have had to pretend her heart wasn't shattering for longer than it would take to hang up the phone or close the door.

All of a sudden she was cold and wished she'd brought a sweater. She wanted to pull her sleeves down, cover her palms.

"Is that new?" She pointed to his hat, not knowing why she'd brought up a sore subject, other than to lighten the mood.

Jett glanced over at her. "Yeah, thought I should get a new one."

It spoke to how nervous she was that she couldn't even laugh. She was in uncharted territory. She'd never really been in love before, much less gone through a break-up. They pulled into his driveway, and her heart sank. Was this where he wanted to break up with her? It seemed unnecessarily cruel.

Jett got out of the truck and walked around to open her door. Her legs were a tad wobbly, her heart racing as she looked up into his warm brown gaze. This was the gaze she'd basked under as a child, drawn strength from as a woman, found comfort in during her darkest days. But today she found no comfort there. There in his eyes, was stone. Set and determined.

Nikki swallowed, and with nothing left to do, followed him up the steps into his home.

Once inside, Jett left her to sit on the couch while he fixed himself a drink in the kitchen. As she watched him walk back toward her, his movements stiff, his usual easy manner absent, it took everything Nikki had to calm her rising panic when she realized that Jett, a southern gentleman to the core, hadn't offered her a drink.

She watched as he sat down next to her, elbows on knees, head in his hands. "I wanna ask you something, Nik. And I want you to tell me the truth. Okay?"

She nodded. After everything, he deserved that. They'd begun this relationship on truth. It should end there as well.

"Are you all better? Do you think you've gotten your strength back?"

Physically she was healed, emotionally was another thing, but she'd keep that detail to herself. Jett would never do what he had to until he was sure she could handle it. She'd never tie him to her. She'd seen her mother do that with her father, and everyone knew how that ended.

So she put on her hustling face, let her eyes go soft and a smile play along the corners of her lips. "I've never been better."

Jett straightened, and for the first time really looked at her since picking her up. "Good, because I don't want you to say later I took advantage of you."

She swallowed. "Advantage?"

He leaned in close, and for a second she thought he'd kiss her. "I want to finish our game."

"Game?"

She wasn't following. Was that what their relationship was? A game?

"I believe I was up one when we had to end our run at The Smoke House. The original bet was the first run to seven. Six more till game. You ready to finish this, once and for all?"

Her mind told her she had this, while her gut screamed to get the hell out of here. Totally at war with herself, she followed Jett down the hall toward the poolroom.

Jett unbuttoned his shirtsleeves and rolled them up to his elbows. He picked up his stick and chalked the tip. She watched as he racked the balls with quick, decisive steps as if he'd made the same move in his sleep.

"You remember what our bet was?" His break was good. Two balls pocketed, as if called home. Three others went into corner pockets before she could answer.

"Yes." The loser had to say yes to whatever favor the winner asked. When they'd first agreed to the terms, she had liked the idea of Jett indebted to her. That was when she'd been confident she could beat him. But now . . .

Jett cleared the table, ball by ball, then racked them for a second time.

The twisting in her gut increased. There was no way she could've been hustled. No way had Jett suckered her in. And yet . . .

"That's some good pool," she whispered, watching Jett accomplish a break, a run, and then a clear, which successfully put the second rack to bed.

"You know, I hate pool," he said, making his way around the table to set up the third rack. At his break, the solid one and two balls were pocketed, and he followed up with one perfectly set-up shot after another.

"You do?" She almost choked on the words as she braced herself on a nearby stool, suddenly dizzy.

Rack three was cleared before he continued. "I couldn't stand it. Too much math and angles. Way too much patience. Did you know, I flew to Vegas every weekend for the last two years to get lessons from The Scorpion, the two-time WPA nine-ball champion?"

"No." Her answer more of a gasp than a response.

"He didn't want to teach me. Teaching nine-ball to an amateur was way below him, but the three-hundred-dollar-an-hour fee changed his mind. He thought I was crazy, thought he'd gotten a great deal. What he didn't realize was, I'd have paid double."

"No." She shook her head, not wanting to take in the implications of what he was saying.

His brown gaze swept up to hers, then quickly focused back on the table. "You know, you say that word a lot. You're the first girl, well, only girl who's ever said 'No' to me."

Rack four.

"I couldn't believe it. The first woman I've ever said 'I love you' to not only turns me down flat, but leaves without a word."

Rack four came and went in a blur. It wasn't until rack five that Jett broke with no shot at the one ball, so he played defense and placed the cue ball up against the rail where Nikki couldn't get a shot off. Since it was the first time she'd been able to take a shot since they started, Nikki took her time and studied her options. There weren't many, but she could at least not make the rack easy for him. She kissed the one with a bit of right-english sending it to the opposite rail in defense, leaving Jett no shot.

Jett barely paused. He'd gotten to that place where aiming balls had become automatic. Playing pool was easy for him, and as soon as he lowered his hand on the table the calculations were already done. He popped the cue over her blocking ball and potted the one , at an almost right angle, into the side pocket.

That's when she lost all composure and leaned herself against the barstool. "Holy . . . Oh God, that was beautiful."

Jett ran the table, and cleared his balls, leaving only the nine at a straight angle to the side pocket. Then he sank the nine quicker than a paper boat in a rainstorm.

The warning in her gut grew hot, her mind foggy. Sweat pooled under her arms. She crossed them to keep from shaking.

"So how do I keep a girl who is programed to run, and run you will, because something will piss you off, my mother, your brother, hell, it might even be me. How do I keep a Logan, I wondered? Then I knew. When the Logans give their word, they keep it. However stubborn and pig-headed they are, once they say 'I do,' they stay for life." Jett placed the nine at the dead center of the diamond formation as he prepared for the break. He looked up at her from across the royal blue felt. "Last game. Anything you want to say before I seal your fate?"

Game six? What happened to game five? "You hustled me. This whole time, you were hustling me."

The smirk across his face sent chills down her spine and the heat in his eyes did something else altogether. "You bet your sweet ass I did. I hustled the best. I hustled Texas."

Chapter 31

The yolk colored nine dribbled off into the corner pocket, the small click of the balls soft even in the silence.

Nikki's light summer dress was clinging to her. A rush of hot and then cold caused her to have chills under a light sheen of sweat.

Jett looked up at her over his pool stick and smiled. That was the seventh game. Seven in a row. He'd won when she would've believed he'd never had a chance.

He leaned the stick up against the wall and started toward her.

She swallowed hard at the raw heat that fired his gaze and rode the devilish corners of his mouth. He stood before her. His chest rose and fell as his breath quickened. "Take off your dress."

Nikki almost suppressed her sigh of relief. Almost. That she could do. That she was more than willing to do. She unbuttoned the top button. Each one a small push through the cloth without her taking her gaze from him. "So is this your favor?"

Something wicked and very secretive played across his face. "Really? You think I dropped that kind of money, spent that amount of time, and studied that many strategies of pool just so I could get you naked and in my bed?" He shook his head. "I could've gotten that for free."

She glared at him, but got her revenge when she dropped her

dress into a puddle by her feet. She stood before him in her best black lace bra and panties. She'd always guessed he liked naughty; by the loss of composure on his face, she now knew she was right.

"Get up on the table." He didn't wait for a response, just lifted her and placed her on the edge, her legs level with his waist.

"Is that your favor?" She fell back, letting her elbows support her weight behind her. She arched her back for good measure.

"No," he answered. "Now spread your legs."

She did.

"Wider."

She did.

"Was that the favor?" Her voice was breathless and soft. She bit her lip to keep herself from falling into the heated fog of her mind.

"No." His voice was a low growl as he stepped between her parted thighs.

He was still fully clothed, the denim of his jeans rough against the inside of her legs. She felt vulnerable and exposed and for some reason completely turned on.

He took her hips and pulled her flush against him. She could feel his erection through the constraints of his pants. Her mouth grew dry, and her breath came quick. She reached for the button on his shirt, desperate to feel his skin against hers.

He caught her wrists and slowly pushed her down, her hands restrained by one of his.

He kissed her, but her sigh of disappointment was quick to follow. A soft brush, and mere whisper of his tongue against hers and then he was gone.

She moaned, but quickly pressed her lips together to silence her neediness. His mouth found her ear, the soft spot of her jawline, the flatness of her breastbone. With one hand he reached behind her. She arched her back in response. With expertness she didn't want to consider, he unsnapped her bra. He released her hands only to strip off the small barrier.

He grabbed her wrists and pushed them high up over her head. Her back bowed, and she panted at how her body was forced into contact with him. Jett dominated her. His mouth was a whisper above her nipples. Her skin was a riot of chills at his implied touch.

And yet, he still didn't touch her. Just loomed over her. Forced her to lie there. Him on top. Her beneath.

Desire coursed through her. The thin fabric of her panties grew wet. Her breath came in small sips of air. She bucked her hips, desperate for friction. Desperate for him to be seated deep inside her.

His hands found the soft skin of her inner thighs and traced a path higher to the wet dampness at her center. But just before he reached paradise, he stopped.

"Do you want to know what my demand is?"

She nodded yes or maybe she groaned it. Either way she couldn't imagine saying no.

His thumb rested on the thin strip of satin that separated her from heaven. One light brush and her body jolted as if a current rushed through her.

Over and over his thumb played her like a string instrument. Never enough to make her sing, but just enough to keep her strung tight like a bow.

"I want you to be my wife."

His words were heard through a haze of passion and need. It took more than a few breaths for the meaning to sink in. Cold water on a flame, and she was sitting up, pushing his hand away from its skillful distracting.

"What?" She shook her head. There was no need to hear that demand again. She saw the seriousness in his eyes. "No."

There was no way she was ready to be his wife. To be anyone's wife. Wasn't it enough she'd confessed her love?

He laughed, a sound anything but joyous. With the devil's gleam in his eye, he pushed her hand away and pushed himself over her. His weight bending her to his will. Bending her back flush to the felt of the pool table.

His mouth was by her ear. His breath a kiss down her spine. "No. This is not the way this is going to happen. There's no way I'm letting you overthink this one. Everyone has got to trust at some point. And this is yours."

Her heart pumped double-time and not just from his proximity. There was a gasping for air and a closing in around her throat. She fisted her hands in his shirt, not sure if she wanted to push him away or draw him in closer. "You don't understand, Jett. What you're asking of me. What you want. It will kill me. I'm drowning."

Was that her voice? She sounded so small. Little. And why the hell did she sound so scared?

If it was sympathy she wanted, she got none. "That's what falling in love feels like. Like going under, jumping off, letting go."

Was that true? Was there some point at which she just had to trust? But everyone she loved ended up dying, or worse . . . left her.

Jett had suddenly had enough. He kissed her. His mouth hot on her skin. Somehow his shirt was gone and the skin on skin contact almost threw her over the edge.

"Do you feel it too? The drowning part?"

"Texas, I've been drowning since the day I met you."

He took one nipple in his mouth and sucked, then traveled to the other. Her fingers fisted in his hair and held him as she arched her back to bring her breasts closer to his mouth.

"Go under with me." He whispered between kisses. His tongue circled the hollow of her navel.

"Let go."

He went down lower.

"Come under with me," he whispered against the quivering flesh of her inner thigh.

"Hold your breath and let go."

She trembled in his hold, hot with fiery need and cold with the thought that if she really made a grab for what she wanted, she wouldn't survive the "after Jett."

Jett growled. He removed her panties with a snap, and his jeans went the same way. He grabbed her by the hips and seated himself between her legs. She felt his desire thick and proud as it teased at the entrance of where she wanted him most.

"Damn it, Nikki, marry me or else this is it. I can't keep chasing you. I've done everything I can, cheated, lied, mastered the most boring game on the planet. You love me, I know it. And lord knows, I've never loved anyone else. But if you don't give us a chance, you'll regret this your whole life."

He slammed into her. Entered her to the hilt with the full thrust of his desire behind him.

She screamed as her arched body hurried to accommodate him.

The rhythm he picked was slow and controlled, but that wasn't at all what she wanted. She wrapped her legs around his hips and pushed for harder, faster. More.

But there was no way Jett was going to let her get the upper hand. "Tell me you will. Let me put a ring on your finger so ostentatious it'll be an embarrassment. Tell me you will, and I'll give you what you want."

Fear pumped along with desire in her blood. His caresses were making her crazy, but it was his words that were making her question everything. Making her heart soar. Making her want to slip under the water and lose herself in the ocean of his love.

"Just stay. Say you will. Just stay."

How could she not?

"I don't want a wedding. And if we have to have a wedding, then a very small one. And I don't want to plan it. Just the thought of making all the arrangements has me breaking out into hives. And I won't wear white. White always makes me look pale and washed out."

"Nik, is that a yes?"

Nikki took a deep breath. "Yes, that was a yes." Tears were in her eyes, but she held his gaze unashamed. "Don't leave me, Jett. You can never leave me."

There was a huge sigh of relief, and then he thrust deep into her, bringing them both to the cusp of a climax. "I never have."

Her world exploded and for one terrifying moment she did go under, but only to find herself all over again in the arms of her future husband.

In the end, Nikki did have a wedding, a big one—the town wouldn't have it any other way. The way the townspeople saw it—two local heroes were finally tying the knot. It was the stuff of legends that even the diehards deemed romantic.

And Nikki did wear white. It was funny, without the black hair, white looked better than any other color. And everyone agreed that there hadn't been a prettier bride since Nikki's mother.

There'd been less resistance from her new in-laws than she expected. Maybe all the fight had gone out of the queen. Or maybe Nikki's letting Mrs. Avery take over all the plans for the wedding went a long way to smoothing any ruffled feathers.

Of course, what no one knew was that underneath the tulle and satin was Nikki's confidence—her black combat boots. But in the end, she found out she didn't need them after all. All the wedding nerves and performance panic faded away when she saw her husband-to-be at the end of the aisle. Jett was her confidence now. He was her rock, and she'd never felt happier.

* * *

"My God, I thought that would never end," Jett said, once they were safely in his truck—decorated with the words "Newly Married" and empty beer cans.

Nikki did an exaggerated eye roll. "Oh please, you were the belle of the ball."

How many toasts had been raised in his honor? The whole town had showed up for their favorite bachelor's wedding. Jett was one of their own. What she hadn't expected was to find that she was one of their own also. The town had rallied around her. Surrounded her with love and kindness. The nice gifts, the genuine hugs, the teasing advice. People seemed genuinely happy that Nikki was home to stay.

She let her gaze linger over her new husband. She'd never seen him more handsome—dressed in black pants, white shirt, and a black vest with one pop of color—a red rose in the lapel, and, of course, his black Stetson. "So, are you going to take the mayor's offer?"

Jett gave her a sly smile. "You mean, the one about running for sheriff? I may. Would you mind? It's getting involved in politics. I'm not sure you'd want such a public life."

Nikki laughed. "My life has been more public than anyone else I know. It'll be interesting to be the subject of gossip over something good for a change."

Jett pulled into his—their—dirt drive. He'd offered to have them spend their wedding night in a luxury resort up in Austin, but Nikki begged to spend their first night as husband and wife in the place where they'd spend the rest of their lives.

Just as he had in getting them married, Jett wasted no time. He carried her over the threshold and straight to their bedroom. Nikki couldn't help but laugh. Her heart was so light. The heaviness that habitually rode her shoulders seemed to have slipped off.

He started on the buttons of his shirt, untucking it as he went. He stopped undressing and her heart skipped as she looked at the wide expanse of his chest, strong arms, warm eyes.

"So, was I worth the chase?" Nikki was a bit breathless. She swallowed hard as Jett closed the distance between them. He cupped her face with his palms. "More than worth the chase, but damn if you didn't give me a run for my money."

Nikki sighed against his lips, her whole body melting in his arms. There was a flutter of clothes and a bark of laughter when Jett saw her boots.

"Those damn boots."

Nikki couldn't agree more. "Get over it. Get them off of me, and get me into bed, cowboy."

His warm brown eyes shimmered and Jett did as he was told. Nikki thought he'd be a very compliant husband.

Soon they were skin to skin, and Nikki ceased thinking at all. All the rumors about Jett and his conquests were false. He must be far more experienced than anyone knew. True to his promise, Jett took his time. This was no ride on the express train. He worshiped each part of her body, her ear, behind her knee, the arch of her foot, the tender flesh on the inside of her thigh.

It was the thigh kiss that did it. Nikki had nowhere near the patience that Jett had. "Okay, okay, now please."

She felt the vibration of his chuckle even more than she heard it. "I wasn't done yet."

She tugged on his arms, desperate to get him into position. "If I promise to give you another chance, will you get up here?"

Jett lowered himself on top of her. "I have the smartest wife," he whispered in her ear.

And then all talking stopped because Jett was inside her, filling her, and nothing else mattered.

Jett felt his smile spread across his face even before he opened his eyes. Did life get any better than this? Making love all night with the prettiest wife in all of Texas, waking up on his own with the prospect of doing it all over again? They didn't need to leave for their honeymoon until late that evening. So to his way of thinking he had time to enjoy the better things in life. He turned his head and buried his lips in Nikki's hair. He'd never met anyone whose hair smelled like summer rain and fire all at once. He'd planned to wake up, make coffee and bring her breakfast in bed, but she was lying so peacefully next to him as he spooned her, he didn't want to wake her. Her behind wiggled against him, which had him thinking of an altogether different type of breakfast.

He moved to wrap his arms around her and pull her closer. That was until he heard the clink of metal against wood and felt the movement of his arm halt abruptly.

And he knew, before he even looked up, that he was handcuffed to the bed. He looked down at his wife cuddled against him. "Nik?"

"Hmm, good morning," she mumbled as she buried her face back into the pillow.

"It was a good morning. Until just a second ago."

She rolled over and smiled at him. Her hair had grown out. The deep chestnut color looked like honey spilled across his pillow, and his breath caught for a whole other reason.

Damn, his wife was hot. He loved saying that—his wife. *His wife.* He'd never get tired of those words. Or the way her cat-like eyes were all lazy from sleep or the way her full lips could pout and smile at the same time.

But if he was going to start off this marriage on the right foot, he would have to be focused. She'd have to learn that this kind of behavior was in no way acceptable. He was soon to be an officer of the law, soon to be sheriff, and there was no way he was going to let her get away with this. So he inhaled deeply and tried again. "You seem to have miscalculated what I find amusing, and what I don't."

She stretched, arching her back and pushing her behind closer to him. He had no doubt that the move was intentional. "Um, no miscalculation," she almost purred. "This was definitely planned."

He made a move to grab her, but she was quicker. She rolled out of bed and was on her feet in a heartbeat.

Jett was cool. He didn't get mad, so he unclenched his jaw and spoke in his most even tone. "So what exactly are you thinking of doing?"

Nikki got her phone from the dresser and raised it as if she were going to take a picture.

"Nik, I am not kidding around. Whatever you're thinking about doing, we need to talk about this first." All of a sudden he wasn't having as much fun as a minute ago.

She tilted her head and tapped her lips with her finger. "Hmm. Though this is a mighty fine view, I have to remember that there are children in this town."

"Nik!" he growled.

"Here, use this." She threw him the new black hat he'd worn during the wedding.

He caught it one-handed. "What am I supposed to do with this?"

My God, how long was she planning to leave him here? The thought of what she'd used his last hat for set his heart racing.

"To cover yourself, of course." She raised her phone. "Now smile."

"I'm not smiling, Nik. This is not funny. Don't you dare— Nikki!" But he got his hat in place just before the click.

Four months later

Found in the community section of the *Grove Oaks Tattler:*

"Come out and support our town at the new community center. Our very own celebrity 'Sexy Sheriff' and his wife, Nikki Avery, will be out signing his calendar. Photo opportunities also available. All proceeds will be donated to our sheriff's favorite charity, the Track and Field Club."

KC Klein has lived most of her life with her head in the clouds and her nose buried in a book. She did stop reading long enough to make a home with a real life hero, her husband, for over seventeen years. A mother of two children, she spends her time slaying dragons, saving princesses, and championing the belief in the happily-ever-after. As the author of *Texas Wide Open*, the first in the Texas Fever series, *Dark Future,* and the award-winning *Hotter on the Edge,* a sci-fi romance anthology, KC loves to hear from readers and can be found desperately pounding away on her laptop in yoga pants and leopard slippers, or more conveniently at kckleinbooks. com.

CPSIA information can be obtained at www.ICGtesting.com
Printed in the USA
BVOW04s0231250614

357284BV00001B/13/P